the coincidence engine

sam leith

BLOOMSBURY

LONDON · BERLIN · NEW YORK · SYDNEY

First published in Great Britain 2011

Bloomsbury Publishing Plc
36 Soho Square
London W1D 3QY

www.bloomsbury.com

Bloomsbury Publishing, London, Berlin, New York and Sydney

A CIP catalogue record for this book is available from the British Library

ISBN 978 1 4088 0234 2

10 9 8 7 6 5 4 3 2 1

Typeset by Hewer Text UK Ltd, Edinburgh
Printed in Great Britain by Clays Ltd, St Ives plc

Mixed Sources
Product group from well-managed
forests and other controlled sources
www.fsc.org Cert no. SGS-COC-2061
© 1996 Forest Stewardship Council
FSC

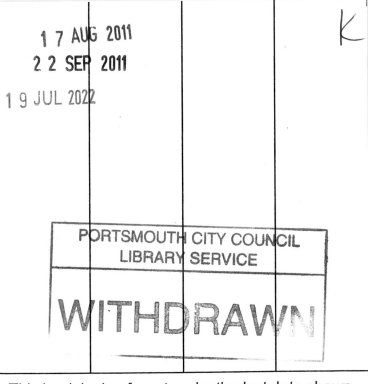

For Alice, who makes me feel lucky

AUTHOR'S NOTE

It is customary to announce on this page that all resemblances to characters living or dead are entirely coincidental. It seems only courteous to acknowledge, though, that in preparing the character of Nicolas Banacharski I was inspired by the true-life story of the eminent mathematician Alexandre Grothendieck. 'What is a metre?' is Grothendieck's line. But *The Coincidence Engine* is a work of fiction: I don't know any maths, and Banacharski is no more Grothendieck than Robinson Crusoe was Alexander Selkirk.

People may also complain that I have taken liberties with both the laws of physics and the geography of the United States of America. I can only respond that reality, in this book, does not exactly get off scot-free.

SL, London, September 2010

'They've found the pilot.'

Twelve hundred miles away in New York, Red Queen breathed out.

'What do we know?'

'More or less nothing. Hospital sweep sent up flags. Field agents in Atlanta called it in. He's in Mobile. Name of Arno Fisk. I'm headed over there now to talk to him.'

'Condition?'

'Cuts and bruises. Some – well. They're saying some cognitive issues.'

In the background, Red Queen could hear wind across the mouthpiece of the phone. Behind that, the sound of heavy traffic moving fast: trucks pounding south on the interstate.

'It's not clear. He was dressed as a pilot, but he's not a pilot. There's nothing on him in the FAA database. He was unconscious for some time. What I hear –'

The wind picked up and the next few words were inaudible.

'– consciousness. I need to go.'

'OK, go,' said Red Queen.

The phone went down in its cradle.

Red Queen's desk was broad and made of dark wood. The top was covered in red leather. It was out of place. It belonged among other antiques – not in this oblong box with its ozonic air conditioning and its twenty-four-hour fake sunlight. There were no books in the room. An uncomfortable two-seat sofa, against the wall, faced the desk. On the other wall there was a locked cabinet. There were no windows.

A corner of the leather surface of the desk looked like it had been chewed by mice. Red Queen picked at the leather with a fingernail for a moment, staring at nothing.

Then Red Queen turned to the computer, waggled the mouse to bring the screen alive, and brought up the Intercept to read it again.

Bree, on the highway, hung up the phone on the timber wall of the Snacky Shack and walked round to the door. It was late morning and the sun, already hot, bounced off the dusty glass and winked at her. She'd been driving for three hours already. Red Queen could wait half an hour while Bree got waffles.

Bree was the only person in the place – an awkward L-shape that had once been a barn, or an auto-shop or something. Formica tables, pairs and fours. Booths lined the window onto the highway and Bree sat in the furthest one of those, with her back to the corner wall. She sat a while, watched the traffic tick past, waited while the waitress finished scratching in her hair with her pencil.

The waitress leaned down by the chef – a good-looking Latino wearing a greasy checkered dishcloth as a bandana – and produced a laminated menu the size of an occasional table. She dropped it wordlessly in front of Bree, left, returned with a clear plastic beaker of iced water, set that wordlessly down, fished a pad from her pouch and pointed at it, expectantly, with her head-scratcher.

'Morning,' said Bree.

'Mornin'' said the waitress.

'Belgian waffles,' she said. 'Three eggs over medium, Canadian bacon, chicken sausage and sourdough toast; two rounds.'

The waitress wrote it down.

'You want a side of fries with that?'

Bree's eyes flicked up from the menu.

'No fries,' she said. 'And no grits.'

The waitress looked at her. Bree looked back.

'Thank you,' said Bree, and smiled sweetly.

Thirty minutes later Bree was back heading south in the brown Chrysler with the windows up and the air conditioning on, and by mid-afternoon, she was rolling into Mobile. She left the inter-state and took Airport Boulevard.

Providence Hospital was a white building west of the centre of town. Bree drove in under a quaint old archway, swung the front of the car round and parked up under a shade tree, just out of the sightline from the main entrance.

She got out and the weather hit her. It was as if the humidity had tugged the leash on her breath. She'd worked up just enough of a sweat for it to chill on her, unpleasantly, when she stepped into the air-conditioned lobby. She ignored the potted palms and crossed to the desk.

'Visiting Fisk, room 325,' she said. 'Helen Fisk. I called earlier.'

She showed the woman her ID. The woman didn't seem interested. Bree wrote 'Helen Fisk' in the register, went to the elevator and went up.

It was a nice hospital. Someone cleaned it. Her flats didn't stick. She'd been in hospitals where only people in heels – and Bree hadn't worn heels since she could remember – were really qualified to make it down the corridors.

The room that the man who seemed to be called Fisk was supposed to be occupying was down a long corridor and through some doors. Bree had a pretty good sense of direction. West, it should be facing, over scrubland and away from the parking lot and the main part of the hospital. She listened at the door a little, then when she was satisfied nobody was in Fisk's room, knocked softly.

She didn't wait for an answer, but opened the door, slipped in, closed it behind her.

The room did face west. The blind was half lowered, and afternoon light came through the bottom half of the window and slanted across the foot of Arno Fisk's bed.

3

Fisk was awake but he looked a little glassy. He had dark hair, spilling from a bandage wrapped round the top of his head, and a purple, very shiny bruise bulbing out the right side of his forehead and casing the orbit of his eye. Underneath his right eye the skin was wasp-striped black and yellow.

There was something dark – looked like dried blood – in his nostrils, and a single butterfly stitch on his lip. He was a mess. Bree couldn't see what was going on under the blanket, but both the arms above it – resting side by side on the tray table over his waist and looking uncomfortable – were in casts to the elbow.

She'd been in the room for a couple of seconds before his eyes rolled towards her, as if in surprise, and focused a foot or two behind her left shoulder. They were shiny, and such a dark brown that the pupils and the irises, at this distance, were hard to tell one from the other. Even smashed up, he was a handsome man, though more tanned than Bree thought was ideal.

'Come in,' he said. It came out: 'Cerrm urh?' Then he looked surprised again.

Bree walked up to the bed. She didn't bother affecting hesitation. According to the medical notes the agents in Atlanta had skimmed, there had been no permanent brain damage or intracranial bleeding. Just a prize-winning compendium of fractures, breaks and abrasions – consistent, one of Bree's colleagues had said, with the rough prognosis for an eight-year-old child with rickets spending a half-hour in an industrial tumble dryer.

This spaciness was probably just drugs. If they had him self-administering he'd be no use to Bree, or anyone.

'Mr Fisk,' Bree said.

His eyes said, 'Who wants to know?' and his mouth said, 'Urr?'

'Mr Fisk, my name is Dana Hamilton. I'm from the Federal Aviation Authority.'

She reached into her top pocket and showed him Dana Hamilton's business card. He frowned at her wrist. Closer up, she could see where his pupils ended and where his irises began. His irises were fingernail-thin, chocolate-coloured haloes. He looked like a badly mangled bushbaby.

'Federr avuh urrdurr?'

'Yes, Mr Fisk. And may I say what a pleasure it is to meet you today?' Dana extended her hand. There were four fingers extending from the cast on his right arm. Dana shook two of them.

There was a chair by the bed. She pulled it round and sat on it.

'I've come to talk to you about your accident. I work as an insurance assessor for our pilot outreach branch, unexpected eventuality division.'

'Whur durr?' said Arno Fisk.

'There are certain anomalies in our records regarding the events of August 11th. We need to straighten out our files. Mr Fisk, I'm going to level with you. We have no record, precisely – and this is very probably our fault; the full-spectrum security audit ongoing since 2001 has, to be honest, caused as much confusion as it has cleared up – of your pilot's licence. You were admitted to the emergency room without ID, and the FAA – under the WelfAir insurance scheme – covered your bills during the time you were unconscious. We're now reaching a stage where we need to action an alternative funding stream for your medical care.'

Something stirred in Fisk's face. Somewhere at the murky bottom of his consciousness, what Bree was saying had snagged. That was the idea. If he wasn't too stoned to know he was in the hospital, maybe he wasn't too stoned to realise that whoever was paying for him to be there could stop paying for him to be there.

'Mr Fisk, we need to establish your eligibility for continued treatment. We need to find some way of reconnecting you to the FAA's database.'

This was not strictly true. Bree didn't give too much of a damn about the FAA's database, though she was curious as to who the hell this guy was. No ID, no known next of kin. They'd found his name through teeth while he was still out – busted crown done eight years previously back home in Illinois.

Arno Fisk, thirty-five years old. Born in St Charles. Moved away when he graduated high school. Moved back, apparently, for long enough to go to the dentist. Moved away again. He'd ended up in Mobile somehow, though he didn't seem to have driven there. There were three Arno Fisks holding driving licences in Illinois and two in Alabama, and none of the five of them was this guy.

'I'm nurr a pilurr. I tole the pleezmann.' He looked tired. 'Anno whurr huppen.'

'But you were found near the wreckage of a 737,' Bree said. 'You were found *in* the wreckage of a 737. Strapped into what was left of the pilot's seat.'

'Anno whurr.'

'You know what happened?'

'AnnNO.'

'You don't know what happened?'

Fisk subsided slightly, and his eyes refocused dead ahead.

'Mr Fisk, you were dressed as an airline pilot.' She reached a little. What the hell. 'As I'm sure you know, there are federal penalties attached to the improper impersonation of an officer of the Federal Aviation Authority, or an accredited pilot of that same body.' She softened her voice. 'We're sure you meant no harm, but it's very important that you tell us everything you remember about the events leading up to your being found.'

She looked at him, her eyes moving over his unbruised cheek. The skin was olive-coloured. It looked like it would smell nice. He kept staring ahead.

'Look, I'm honest? We just want to know where the plane came from. There were no identifying markings on the fuselage – at least none recognisably attributable to any known airline. No passengers were found. No planes were missing. We checked all the schedules in the continental United States for the two weeks

6

surrounding the time you were found. We checked private flights – and there aren't a large number of 737s in private hands; we checked scheduled flights; we checked extraordinary rendition flights. There weren't any scheduled flights across the South in any case, because of the hurricanes.'

This was mostly but not entirely true. They had recovered some identifying markings. One section that seemed to belong to the tailplane, according to the file, was made of tin-plated steel and stamped with a date of no readily decipherable significance in the summer of 2009. It seemed overwhelmingly likely it belonged to a can of beans.

'As far as anyone knows, this 737 airplane appeared out of nowhere. It didn't crash, it didn't fall out of the sky – there was no sort of impact evidence. OK? Planes don't come out of nowhere. They are big things. Then it broke up – without burning or exploding – at or near ground level. And it scattered itty-bitty little bits of metal debris over three square miles of Alabama backcountry, and left a guy with half his bones broken, strapped to a chair, hanging in a tree.'

Arno Fisk, to whom some of this was getting through, attempted to look as baffled as Bree. It was a very creditable attempt.

'That was you,' she added.

Bree tensed as she heard the handle of the door twist. A nurse came in, sideways, turned and looked startled to see a visitor. She was carrying a clear plastic jug of water. She frowned, then smiled politely, and was opening her mouth to speak when Bree interrupted her.

'Oh, thank you. Arno's mouth was getting so dry, wasn't it, hon? Just there, sweetie, thanks. No, a bit to the right. Perfect. I'll take care of his glass.' She put a little urgency into her tone, stopped just short of steering the nurse back out of the room by her hip. She could see the nurse making a snap decision; to go with the flow rather than submit to the awkwardness of challenging Bree's ownership of the space. One more firm 'thank you' was enough to see her off.

Bree had all sorts of outs, but unnoticed was best – unnoticed was always best. She knew the name on the register was different from the name she'd used to Fisk, and figured there'd be no trouble with it in a routine hospital visit to a badly if bizarrely injured man. She'd leave confusion, rather than suspicion, behind her if she left anything at all. But she'd rather leave it behind her than have it turn up while she was still there. As far as the nurse was concerned, if she checked, this was the cute Fisk guy's fat older sister. And if Fisk wondered why this lady was calling him 'hon', well . . .

He made a noise. She turned back to him. Fisk was looking a little more focused, as if he'd made a decision to pull himself, as far as he could, together.

'Uh durr rumberr much. I' was Sadderday. Uh wuzz a li'l drunk.'

The words came out slowly, and clearly with effort. 'Uh hadd a beer. Bit. Nommuch. Cuz uh wuz goin'a work. Uh member geddin dress. Geddin in car. Id was winndy.'

'You were going to work. What time was this?'

'Uh dunnuh. Evennuntime. Late. Iz dark. Winndy.'

He pushed his lips together and out, like a chimp puckering up for a kiss, and exhaled through them almost soundlessly: hwhhh-hhhhhhooooo. His eyelids drooped and his cheeks tightened in a secret smile. Some sort of morphine surge. Hwhhhhhhh . . .

'Winnndy . . .' Hwhhh . . .

'Yes, it would have been windy. There were hurricane warn-ings. A lot of people had left town. And you were going to work?'

'Ssssss.'

'Why? Nothing was leaving the ground that night.'

'Gudda work. Goo money.'

'Where do you work? You work as a pilot?'

'Nuh! Nudd a piludd.' He was trying to pull himself together again.

8

'You were dressed as a pilot. Could someone have done that to you while you were unconscious?'

If someone had done that to him, Bree could have added, they had a sense of humour. According to the admittedly sketchy paperwork she'd been able to obtain through the Atlanta relay, he was dressed in the uniform of a TWA pilot from the mid-1980s. A defunct airline. An emergency-room orderly's sniggering email to his college buddy had added the even more peculiar detail that, underneath his pilot's uniform, he had been wearing satin thong underpants with a tiger-stripe print. These had been soiled.

'Nuh. Uh dress muhself. Took muh uhn cloze inna bag.'

'Where do you work?'

He shook his head floppily and frowned. 'Anywhur. Uzz jus' anyone books. Wuzz jub up by – ahhh – Gumbuh Lake.'

Gumbo Lake was an enormous swamp ten or fifteen miles to the north of where Fisk had been found. Fisk's tree had been a couple of miles west of Axis, off the 13, which went up to Mount Vernon.

'What sort of job were you doing?' As she asked, Bree realised she knew the answer.

'Ubba darnzer.'

'A dancer. You're a stripper.'

'Ubba *darnzer*,' he insisted, but his face, even through the drug haze, looked bashful and a little bit pleased with itself. He attempted what would have been a well-practised, flirtatious, long-lashed look. The effect was not as he would have intended, but the attempt was enough that Bree could feel herself colouring at the base of her throat. She felt cross.

'Uh wuz onna urrway,' he continued, not noticing or minding much. 'Saw uh member. Uz drivin'. Larss thing uh member. Driving.' The casts bumped on the table as he attempted a shrug, then winced as he remembered what trying to shrug with two broken arms and a fractured collarbone felt like. 'Then uhz year.'

9

'You don't remember anything else? You didn't stop, didn't get out of the car, didn't meet anyone?' Like, anyone carrying a commercial passenger plane? Bree thought but did not say.

'Ur gur. *Nuh.*' He struggled a little in the mist. 'Yerrr. Uh gud ou'. Uh member. Or nuh. Uh think. Gudda pee.'

Oh shit, thought Bree, not knowing if or how she was supposed to help him do that – and it seeming likely it would bring another nurse.

'Pee. Beer. Heh. Uh gudda.'

Bree realised, with relief, he was still remembering. He looked confused again. 'Uh gud urr. Iss winnndy.' He made the whoosh-ing noise again.

And then his face shone and his lids sagged. 'Uzz inna plane . . . Inna . . . Hadda mos' amazin' dream . . .'

Bree got up. She didn't know what she knew, and she couldn't think of anything else to ask because she didn't know what she didn't know. That was normal. That was her job.

'Saw rrainbow,' said Fisk. 'Byooofu'. 'Mazin' dreammm . . .'

'Thank you, Mr Fisk,' she said, but he wasn't really noticing. She left.

As she crossed the parking lot to the Chrysler, she ran over the conversation in her memory. She didn't speculate. There was never any value in speculating. But something nuggeted in her mind.

'I'm not a pilot,' he had said. 'I told the policeman.'

Bree, who had seen the records, thought: What policeman?

An amazing dream.

Fisk, subsiding back into morphine sleep. Going down through the layers. There was a humming of bees. The air all around him was wet and it smelled of tin and electricity. The trees were dark, dark green and the sky was grey in all directions.

He was driving a car. Not his own car. He knew in the dream that it wasn't his own car, but it somehow belonged to him. The car was a vintage Plymouth as big as a whale. Fisk wallowed in a wide front seat upholstered in blood-covered leather. Fat drops of rain were splatting and dragging across the windshield, hauled sideways by the wind.

Rain was wetting his cheek. Fisk had the windows open. He knew he had a passenger, on the front seat with him – he could see them from the corner of his eye – but he couldn't bring himself to look round. He wasn't scared of his passenger – *sharer*, he thought; my passenger is my sharer – but something prevented him from turning his head to look. His eyes were on the road.

He cruised on the speed limit. Fifty-five miles per hour, but the scenery changed only very slowly. He felt unease as he looked ahead, at the road pulling towards him lickety-split, and the scenery making its way sluggishly past like a moving staircase with the handrail out of sync.

A bit away from the highway, before the treeline, he could see the gator fence. There were gators lined up behind it. They were moving their limbs slowly, purposefully. One, then another huffed and lolled and then, with lazy weight, started to haul themselves up the fence vertically, link by link. He noticed the passenger (*sharer*, he thought again) was gone. Nobody was there.

The wind picked up, flapping erratically into the driver-side window. It was sheety and gusty and it tasted like batteries on his tongue. Fisk suddenly realised that the car wasn't moving at all. The road continued to spool towards him, but it was a special effect, like in an old movie. He realised he needed to pee.

He was outside the car, standing by the highway. Fisk was experiencing something halfway between memory and hallucination.

He didn't remember getting out of the car, but he could see it. There was somebody, he couldn't see who, driving it, and somebody on the passenger side. The wheels were turning – whitewalls blurred – but it was keeping level with him.

Here in the wind he felt scared. The wind caught his cuffs and belled his sleeves out with a great sad sound like a foghorn. The navy fabric of his uniform trousers, wet from the rain, clung to his legs like Saran wrap. His captain's cap flipped up and vanished horizontally, end over end, out of his sight before he could turn to see it. He turned his back to the wind. The sky ahead, back down the highway where he had come from, over the delta, was black as stone.

He moved his hand to his zipper, and POOM! He was nowhere.

2

'The coincidence engine is starting to work. I saw it with my own eyes.'

The Intercept was from nobody. It had been more or less sieved from static. Shortwave frequencies, an echo of an echo. The original signal was, they thought, perhaps, a fax; it still retained some formatting features. But its origin and its destination were unknown, and the very fact that they found it continued to be a source of bafflement. It was a one in a million shot: the equivalent of getting a crossed line and hearing your best friend's voice from the other side of the world.

It wasn't even a term the Directorate's officers had been specifically searching for. But 'coincidence engine' was close enough to send up a flag: they'd been combing for 'probability', 'paradox' (since that had been the inaccurate but hard-to-shake term that had briefly attached to the project), 'singularity', 'Heisenberg' (in variant spellings) and a half-dozen other key terms and areas. Red Queen, who made no secret of not being a scientist, explained to the Directorate's staff that they were looking for 'weird stuff and people who seem to know about miracles'.

But then that was more or less a description of what they'd been doing ever since those wackos around the second Gulf War revived the Directorate of the Extremely Improbable. Red Queen would have preferred to work in the State Department, and Red Queen had made this noisily clear – which was almost certainly why Red Queen had the job. In this department, producer capture was not a good idea.

But the arrival of the Intercept, coming so soon after the hurricanes and the satellite photograph, had seemed too much of a . . . well, there it was.

Someone had flagged it, and now it was here.

The hurricane blew through the junkyard and it made a plane. I saw it. First the gathering wind, and then the sky was filled with metal clashing and screaming and spinning. Rivets swarmed. Currents of air dashed and twirled plates, chairs, tin cans, girders and joists, pinging and banging off rocks. Noise like you never heard. Unholy howl. Rushing and screaming.

Knock, knock, knock and the metal clashing and curving and denting and sticking with great screams. Beyond conception. Beyond seeing. The panel of a trailer. The corrugated sides of a container cracking and flattening. A flash in the middle of it, right in the middle, of a tiny man suspended in air, pedalling his legs like he's treading water and his tiny mouth open and his eyes little dots of terror. Something forming around him.

And finally the wind calmed and the thing was made, the metal miracle. Water running in beads down its flanks under the heavy sky. To the west, the cloud broke and in the distance the sky was bright, like through a tunnel. There was a double rainbow. And on the other side, the sky was a sheet of black. A terrible promise.

The rotors of the engines were idling in the last of the wind. And sitting high in the air, strapped safely in the cockpit, was the pilot – mouth opening and closing, eyes wide, staring into the enormous sky. It works. I saw it.

Its author, Red Queen reflected, sounded about as well adjusted as that guy who eats flies in the Dracula movie. But the thing about the plane had caught their attention.

And there had been a hurricane. This they knew. Hurricane Jody had moved through the Gulf of Mexico for three days in the first week of August, feeding on the warm air rolling off the coast in the unending heatwave. It refused to blow itself out and refused to come ashore.

Occasionally, like a big dog twitching its tail, it brushed against the land. In the early morning of the 24th, a kiss-curl of the fatal weather system – it looked like a wisp of cloud on the satellite image – had flattened four miles of the Florida Keys.

The contents of two recently evacuated trailer parks had been lifted sideways, chewed to splinters in the hurricane's mouth, and sprayed seaward like refuse from an industrial woodchipper. A film crew from Fox News went with them.

The hurricane's retreat had taken a near-perfect hemispherical bite out of the coastline. Thousands of tons of yellow sand were pulled into the sea. Small boats sailed inland through the air and anchored among defoliated palm trees.

The hurricane had retreated, circled at sea, ambled south and west.

It came ashore again sixty-one hours later, on a stretch of coastline where the civic contingency planners had not expected it. The centre of the storm had started moving north-west at twenty knots. Its leading edge sucked a renowned Louisiana gambler bodily through the window of a riverboat casino, never to be seen again, and a steel roulette ball punched four inches into the tree stump to which the boat was moored. The storm's left flank had sideswiped a single loop of the coastal highway, gridlocked with late-departing refugees, killing forty-eight motorists and 122 pedestrians.

Then, abruptly, it changed direction again and headed back out to sea, brooded.

And then, on the night of August 10th, it had headed inland again, and it did not stop at the coast. It had made landfall east of Mobile and headed up and over the delta with savage speed.

3

It was still just light in Glisson Road when Mary Hollis arrived home.

The bag in her hand, from the Marks & Spencer at the station, contained a fish pie, a small bag of prepared carrot batons and a half-bottle of red wine with a pink twist-off cap. Summer was on the way out. She felt a faint winter chill through her blouse.

She put the bag down and fished in her handbag for her keys. As she did so, a movement – barely more than a disturbance of the air – registered in her peripheral vision. She glanced briefly up the street towards the road that led to the station. Nothing there.

Silly woman, she said to herself aloud. Silly old bag. Only since she retired last year, though, had she started to notice herself looking over her shoulder when she turned the corner from Hills Road, or feeling nervous if she had to pass a man on the same side of the street. During all the years she worked up at the college, she had regarded the undergraduates as overgrown teenagers – unruly nephews and slatternly nieces, as exasperating and unthreatening as badly trained Labradors.

'All right, Mrs H?' bellowed in a cockney accent by a public schoolboy. 'Where's your gentleman caller, eh?'

'Mind your own business.'

Now, already, they had started looking bigger and more strange. If she was out at night and she heard young men walking behind her, she'd dawdle at a bus stop, or pause on the main road under a street light, to let them pass before she turned off.

Sometimes, when they looked drunk, she'd make an excuse to drop into a shop.

She was sixty-five, and she realised that she had started thinking of herself as an old woman. She had started thinking about what she looked like to others. Not the little vanities of make-up or hair – but the way her profile was changing. She felt as if she was growing smaller, taking shorter steps – as if she was gradually feeding herself to her fear.

She found her keys in the bottom of her bag, turned the heavy deadlock and rattled the sticky little brass one into the Yale. The hall was dark and smelled of polish. She picked up her supper, and turned on the light.

She tasted copper in her mouth, and felt her face go cold.

The drawer had been pulled out of the hall table and her letters were spilled over the floor. The rug had been pulled up and was rucked up at the other end by the foot of the stairs. Every one of her framed photographs had been knocked from the walls and there were big jagged pieces of broken glass across the floorboards, a different colour where the rug had been.

She felt her skin prickle. She made herself breathe, took a step and reached for the telephone on the hall table. It was an old brown plastic push-button BT model. She'd never owned a mobile phone.

It was when she fumbled the receiver that she realised her hand was shaking. It clattered heavily onto the table. She picked it up and brought it to her ear. There was no dialling tone.

Ahead of her, the darkness leading through to the kitchen seemed to breathe. She wanted to ask whether there was someone still there, but she didn't want to know the answer and her mouth was too dry to speak.

The door behind her was still open, and the street outside felt suddenly more cold and strange. She took a step away, not wanting to turn her back on the other end of the hall, and pushed her spine against the door jamb. She turned her head to look out. In the dusk just across the street there was an elderly man. He was dishevelled. Above his grey beard there was a kindly, perplexed face. He was standing still, watching her. Then something seemed to startle him. He turned his head sharply, as if looking over his shoulder.

She stepped back out of the house and called to him, or tried to. As she raised her hand, though, he turned and dipped his head, walking back up towards the main road.

'Sir!' she yelped. 'Sir! Excuse me!'

His pace seemed to quicken and then, just as he was coming up to a street light, something she could not account for happened. He seemed, simply, to vanish. There was a shimmer, and where a second ago she had been watching him there was now no more than a heat haze – a smear in the air.

A man's shadow on the pavement shortened as it approached the street light, then lengthened on the far side, at the pace you might walk on a brisk spring evening, and then disappeared.

By the time the police arrived, it was full dark and Mary was two doors down with Mrs Smart at number 62.

Angela Smart had left an open pan of pasta boiling in the kitchen and opened the door to a tremulous knock. She found the old woman standing there. She wore a shapeless greatcoat and hat, and was clutching a plastic bag from Marks & Spencer up against her chest. She seemed agitated.

'Mary?' she had said. She knew Mrs Hollis from the occasional Neighbourhood Watch meeting, and to say hello to in the Co-op, sort of thing. She had long had her pegged as a meddlesome ratbag of the first water. 'Is everything OK?'

'I'm terribly sorry to trouble you. I think I've – I've been burgled. May I use your telephone to call the police?'

There was a moment where it just hung there, and neither woman knew what to say.

'But come in, of course. Come in. My goodness, were you there? Are you hurt – you poor thing . . .'

She reached a hand to the other woman's arm, and saw her shoulder shrink back and her eyes drop. Her hand tightened round the thin green bag.

'I'm very well, thank you. I'm sorry. I mean, I'm fine. I think they've gone – but my telephone isn't working at the moment.'

Mrs Hollis's tight politeness was as brittle as porcelain. If she touched her, she felt sure that she'd start to tremble and cry. She didn't know quite how to cope with that, so she said: 'Of course. Yes. I'll put the kettle on.'

She made Mrs Hollis a cup of tea. Mary Hollis, who had not since she was a young woman and been told it was common taken sugar in her tea, had two lumps. Installed on the sofa, she sipped, and scalded her lips, looking around the living room with a bland show of curiosity.

The police showed up a little later. A man and a woman. She, a trim blonde in her early twenties; he, a thyroidal beanpole of a lad who looked barely out of his teens, and whose Adam's apple bobbed up and down his neck like a fisherman's float after a motorboat has passed.

The WPC called Mrs Hollis 'dear', which would have annoyed her had she been more composed. Her silent companion looked ahead, gulped and bobbed.

They went back into her house a little later. The interior of the house matched the wreckage in the hallway. Her single mattress had been heaved over and there were knife slashes through the fabric of the bed frame.

The little room she used for her study had received the most thorough going-over – books pulled from shelves and scattered open-faced on the floor; slicks of paper spilling from the disembowelled desk. She gasped, little fluttery gasps, as the woman officer asked her, patiently: what's gone?

She didn't know. The feeling wasn't so much loss as violation. And there had not been that much to go, as she would reflect later sitting alone in her ruined room – she declined with a politeness she regretted Mrs Smart's offer of a bed for the night. No. She couldn't possibly.

Not that much. They'd left her radio, the old television set. They probably wouldn't have recognised as valuable the fine old edition of *Peter Pan* that had been her mother's, the one with the Rackham illustrations. It, too, had been flung to the ground. She replaced it on the shelf.

The jewellery box on her dressing table had been upturned, its contents scattered onto table and floor below. She fished the big turquoise-and-silver brooch from the carpet when the police left, put it carefully back into the box. She started tidying. Gathering these little precious things back together, amid the destruction of the room, felt like combing the hair on a corpse.

The knife slash through the fabric of the bed frame was especially horrible – a casual, instrumental violence. She imagined herself on the bed, on her back, the knife descending. The man with the knife looking not at her, but through her, towards something else.

'You must have surprised them,' the policewoman had said before she left, making a note in her pad.

Mary didn't think she'd surprised them, still less scared them. Nobody had rushed past her or clattered in the bowels of the house as she opened the door. Nobody had hoofed it over the garden fence. They'd been here, and they'd not wanted her jewellery or her nice books or her television. They'd not cared what they broke.

She fingered the piece of paper the woman had given her – a form, something to do with being a victim of crime – and looked over again at the slash on the bed. Where the knife had hit the frame, the wood had splintered.

Mary had said nothing to the police about the man she thought she saw vanish. She wondered if she'd been hallucinating. She didn't want them thinking her dotty. Downstairs, she picked up the cushions and replaced them on the sofa. She slept on there that night, still in her clothes.

Mary was right about that much. They had not been interested in her jewellery, the men who had turned over her house, and they would not have been scared of her. They had not, in fact, been interested in her house, her nice books, her jewellery, her television or anything else. They went by the names Davidoff and Sherman, and they had been intending, in fact, to burgle another house altogether.

But the small flat Mike Hollis lived in on the other side of Cambridge from his aunt was a sublet, and the address and phone number appeared in the book under his landlord's name. So when discreet enquiries were made of Google by the accident-prone employees of MIC Industrial Futures, those enquiries yielded an M. Hollis in Glisson Road. And when those enquiries were cross-checked by the same accident-prone employees with the payroll system of Emmanuel College, Cambridge – a comically easy hack, they had thought – they confirmed 'M. Hollis' at that address, and in receipt of the sort of miserly monthly cheque that corresponded to their understanding of what research fellows in mathematics could be expected to earn. They were right about only one thing – research fellows in mathematics do earn about the same as a long-standing college administrator would expect to draw as a pension. But they are paid by the faculty of mathematics, and not by the college.

So, twenty-four hours after ruining Mary Hollis's home and her peace of mind for no good reason, the two men were standing in a room that smelled of dry-cleaning and swivel chairs and paper plates of stale biscuits covered in cling film.

Davidoff stood with insolent blankness, big hands nested behind his back, chin up. His hair was sandy and his cheeks permanently windburned so he always looked as if he had just shaved with a blunt blade. Sherman was smaller – wire-haired, sallow, all muscle and nerve. He was like a longdog constructed from twisted rubber bands. They were making their report.

Their report was that they had nothing to report. In search of their employer's fugitive piece of hardware, they had burgled a blameless old woman. On the evidence of her house she, also, knew no more about the device than you'd expect an elderly secretary to know. Then that old man had turned up. They'd no idea if he'd been a husband, a lodger, or what – he'd looked more like a tramp than anything else – but he had appeared as if from nowhere, and Sherman feared – though he did not tell Ellis this – that the guy had got a look at his face.

What had he been doing there? Everything had been quiet. No burglar alarm, no nothing. They'd watched the old woman leave earlier in the day, and lock the front door behind her.

It had given Sherman the fright of his life. The man had just appeared at the top of the stairs and started walking calmly down towards them. Sherman and Davidoff had bolted as soon as they'd seen him.

They had 'struck out – nil for one', as Davidoff, wearing his affected Americanism with an irritatingly complacent air, had put it on the way in. Davidoff seemed almost to relish failure; or perhaps he simply liked watching Ellis cross. What was being handed down to MIC's head of security was, it was reasonable to speculate, about three times as nasty as what he was capable of passing on to those below him.

'Gentlemen,' said Ellis, which was his customary overture to a bollocking. He thought it made him sound superior. 'Gentlemen, I don't need to remind you that a very great deal of this company's time and money is invested in the recovery of this device. And I don't need to remind you, either, that if it falls into the wrong hands – that is, any hands other than our own – my position is going to look very weak indeed.

'And that means that your position, gentlemen, is going to look even weaker still. This is incredibly *fucking* important, this thing,' he said, letting his profanity hang in the air for a bit.

There were people who knew how to swear, Sherman reflected, and people who thought they knew how to swear, and Ellis, with that stupid little vein throbbing self-importantly in his forehead, fell into the latter camp.

Ellis prided himself on his swearing, you could see. It was important for his self-esteem, as an ocean-going civilian sub-craphat, to be able to swear in front of ex-servicemen. Sherman worked really hard to see if he could bring himself to be even the faintest bit intimidated by Ellis. He could not. Davidoff, Sherman could respect. Davidoff was a squarehead, but he was quite a dangerous squarehead. Ellis was . . . His thoughts drifted off.

'This is the future of this company. We own this thing. We paid for it. And our proprietors are not going to sit back and give it away for free to any teenage geeks, Islamist loons, Marxist wackjobs, or any fucking fucking blue-hatted save-the-world fucking ponce-fucker.'

Ponce-fucker, eh?

'Fortunately, we have a lead. Our friend in the States has learned of a young man connected to the Banacharski Ring who has just unexpectedly upped and flown across the Atlantic. No warning. Just went. And there's no good reason we can see why he might have decided suddenly to go on holiday by himself.'

Ellis knitted his fingers together, and cracked his knuckles.

'His name is Alex Smart. Postgraduate student, close associate of this Hollis. While we were looking at the supervisor, this lad skipped out and there's very good reason to believe that he has the device. He was booked on a flight for San Francisco, but he wasn't flying direct. For no reason we can readily understand, unless he was trying to discourage pursuit, he flew via Atlanta. Two different airlines. Tickets booked at different times – the first through an agent. Only the second was on his own credit card. But the onward flight was grounded by the hurricane. He never got back on a plane, according to our intel.'

Intel? thought Sherman. He noticed that Ellis had a monogram on his shirt. He enjoyed hating him for a bit.

'We've lost track of him,' Ellis continued. 'But so have they. So enough messing about. Do not shoot anyone if you can help it, do not get shot yourself, and if and when you find it helpful to do something illegal, do not get caught doing it. I need scarcely remind you that we have no status either in the UK or in the States. You are private citizens. Whatever favours our proprietors are able to call in when from time to time we find ourselves in a legal grey area, you can be sure they will not call in for you. If you get in trouble, MIC will disavow you so fast your heads will spin.'

'Disavow' could mean lots of things. Which was, Sherman thought, probably why the two of them were being better paid than they would be if they'd been working for private hire even in Iraq.

Ellis looked at them both, one after the other, and then enunciated, slowly: 'Go to America, find him, and get our toy.'

'America's quite big,' said Davidoff. 'How do you suggest we go about that?'

Sherman was surprised when Ellis replied: 'There is one idea. Look – this device affects the way probability works, as we understand it. Like a magnet in iron filings. We think the effect is more powerful when it's closer by. But it's eccentric. For some reason one of the things it seemed to affect strongly, if the literature is to be believed, are these.'

Ellis, who had remained sitting throughout this conversation, reached into the drawer of his desk. He pulled out something attached to a tangle of white wires and put the tangle on the desk.

'There's one each,' he added.

'The literature,' said Sherman.

Davidoff's big hand went down first. He fished up a small square of plastic that brought some of the white wires with it. He looked at it.

'This is an iPod,' he said.

'An iPod Shuffle, yes,' said Ellis. 'It's preloaded.'

Sherman picked the other one up and looked at it.

'What are we supposed to do with these?'

'Listen to them,' said Ellis. 'Listen for patterns. Songs that seem to keep repeating; runs of the same artist; albums that come out in order.' He looked a little sheepish. 'Even things like . . . songs that begin with the same word, or something.'

'This is what we're supposed to use to hunt down this superweapon, or whatever it is. An iPod. Are you having a laugh?'

'I hate rock music,' said Sherman.

Three hours later he and Davidoff were on a plane.

4

'Does the name "Banacharski" mean anything to you?' Red Queen asked.

The man looked confused and disoriented, as he was entitled to. Four hours previously he had been teaching a class of students in MIT. Three hours and forty-five minutes previously, he had been on his way off campus when a couple of men in suits had started steering him by the elbows as if – he had thought with indignation – he were not a small, bald professor of mathematics but a small, bald bicycle.

Two hours previously he had been, for the first time, in a helicopter. An actual black helicopter, tilting over Boston and heading out into the country. During that short, fast journey, Professor Hands had become quite convinced that his voluntary work leafleting for a human rights organisation had made him a target for extraordinary rendition. His whole short body had been flushed, moment by moment, with the chemicals of terror and the lip-trembling self-righteousness of a liberal academic facing a non-fatal kicking from the forces of reaction.

America, he knew, was a totalitarian enemy of free speech – but it didn't actually kill middle-class white men. He expected to endure pain, speak eloquently, and become a cause célèbre. He imagined Chomsky talking about him on CNN; Glenn Beck denouncing him by name on Fox.

Now they were asking him about Banacharski.

'Of course it does,' the man said. 'He's a very distinguished mathematician. Or was, I suppose – depending on who you want to believe. But this has to do with Banacharski? I can't see why he'd be of any interest to the CIA.'

'We're not the CIA, Professor Hands,' said Red Queen. 'We do a different job than they do. Remember all those bits of paper you signed earlier?'

He nodded.

'They don't mean very much. They say that you're breaking various national security laws if you disclose the existence of this organisation, let alone disclose the contents of our conversation, but the nature of what we do means that we could never actually drag you through open court if you break the agreements.

'So we're adult about this. However, I do want to impress on you two things. One of them is that if you tell people about us, these people will think you are mad. Your first point of contact with us was, was it not, with two burly men in dark suits wearing wraparound sunglasses?'

Hands nodded.

'You were brought here in an unmarked black helicopter.'

Hands nodded again.

'And here you are, three floors below street level in New York in a secret –' Red Queen chuckled '– a secret underground hide-out. Talking to somebody with a name out of *Alice in Wonderland*.' Red Queen's palms turned upwards. 'It might be enough to earn you a sabbatical, but your accommodation would probably be chosen for you.'

Red Queen gave him a friendly smile. 'We are a serious organisation. What we do is extremely important. And we really do want your help. Contrary to the fantasies of all very highly educated and very poorly educated people, the government is truly not engaged in a conspiracy against the people. We do everything we can, in secret and in the open, to prevent them messing things up.

'So just listen to what we have to say, and to give us the benefit of what you know. Sit around here, talk, have a cup of coffee, come on board. And do us a favour: be an adult – and keep what we talk about to yourself. We need to be able to speak frankly with you.'

Hands followed the gesture and looked around the room. It was an odd room. Though it was windowless, on the wall behind Red Queen's desk there was something in the shape of a window that was giving off light, like a lightbox. The floor was pleasantly enough carpeted, and beside him there was a cardboard cup that said 'Starbucks' on it. Hands picked it up.

'Plus,' Red Queen added, fixing him with a harder stare, 'horrible things will happen to you if you speak about this. Really horrible.'

This was not true, in fact. Doing anything particularly horrible to a US citizen, particularly a member of a liberal institution of higher education, was almost always far more trouble than it was worth.

It was way, way outside the remit of the DEI – they didn't even have agents licensed to use lethal force – and even the FBI didn't do as much of that as people thought they did. If you want to keep a low profile, the two golden rules are: don't start leaving a trail of bodies, and don't, whatever you do, involve the FBI at any level. As for the CIA . . .

In any case, it was enough to focus the little professor's attention. Even if he suspected all of this, he didn't know it and he wouldn't be likely to want to test the thing out. He had been warned, flattered and warned. He was short, and Red Queen was tall. He was sitting on a low sofa without a table in front of him, and Red Queen was sitting upright behind a desk. He was as ready as he'd ever be.

'OK,' Red Queen continued. 'Banacharski. The organisation I work for has been very interested in Nicolas Banacharski for several years . . .'

Professor Hands, as Red Queen knew, was a number theorist with a very strong interest in Banacharski's work. And Red

Queen knew, too, most of the basic facts of Banacharski's life.

'Well, ehm, Banacharski was a prodigy. Born in Germany. Father was a Russian Jew, died in the camps. He won the Fields in the sixties – you know, the big mathematical medal?'

'I know.'

'Amazing work. Very, very high levels of abstraction. He more or less invented – well, completely reshaped – the field I work in. The Fermat solution wouldn't have been possible without his work. But he's barely been heard from since the early nineties. I don't know where he is. Nobody does.'

'Presumably he knows where he is,' said Red Queen.

'I wouldn't bet on it. He'd be in his eighties now, and he – you know – went *mad*.'

Hands scratched the back of his neck. He still looked a little uneasy.

'Banacharski had – well, they started as strong convictions. He was in Paris for '68 and he started to become more and more political. There'd been a chair created for him at the Sorbonne. He'd worked there for a decade or so, perfectly normally. Then he threw it up in 1972 on the grounds that his chair was partly funded by the military. He was a pacifist.'

'That's what was said.'

'It's the only explanation. He was still working at this stage, but he was getting crankier. Started claiming there was going to come some sort of scientific apocalypse by the end of the century if the physicists weren't kept in check. Then he upped and off.'

'Off?'

'Vanished.' The mathematician was starting to forget his surroundings and enjoy his story. 'He was living in communes, going Buddhist, vegan, some people said – stopped using beds for a bit. There were stories that he went round trying to sell buckets of his own faeces to farmers as fertiliser. He turned into a mad monk. He was notionally attached to the University of

Toulouse, but –' he blew air out between his lips and shrugged '– he was doing his own thing. Proofs, papers – he mostly just wrote thousands of pages of what he called "meditations". There'd be fragments of proofs in them, amazing proofs – some of them are in libraries. But he was cracked. That's how the story goes.

'One morning in the early nineties his girlfriend returned home to find he'd had a kind of manuscript bonfire in her garden. He was never seen again.'

'Literally never seen again?'

'More or less. These letters go out, though – of the long and rambling sort. People in the community, you know – they try to piece together what he's doing. He claims to have given up on math. He's living by himself and working something like twelve hours a day on mad material – some huge manuscript about the physics of free will.'

'That's where we come in,' said Red Queen. 'We know about the letters. We were keeping an eye on them. Does the name Isla Holderness mean anything to you?'

'Yes,' said Hands, and there was a moment before something dropped into place behind his eyes. Red Queen looked expressionlessly at him. 'Uh, yes. She's a mathematician in my field. She's one of the last people who saw Banacharski. She went to look for him in the Pyrenees.'

Red Queen exhaled. 'You know the story.'

' "What is a metre?" '

Red Queen nodded in recognition. 'What is a metre?' Banacharski's weird riddle: the last communication with Holderness before he disappeared for the final time.

'OK. We're on the same page. We know a bit more than you about some of it. But I'll lay it out. Our organisation is called the Directorate of the Extremely Improbable. It's a silly name, but it's always been called that, and the silliness acts as a sort of camouflage. We could just as easily have brought you here in a green helicopter, and had you picked up by men wearing clear eyeglasses and button-down shirts from Gap. As it is, we don't sound like what we are. That is the idea.

'Our job is to assess threats to national security that we don't know exist, using methods that we don't know work. This produces results that we generally can't recognise as results, and when we can recognise them as results, we don't know how to interpret them.'

Red Queen continued to look at him levelly.

'It's frustrating work. Here.'

Red Queen fished in a desk drawer, pulled something out, and lobbed it across the room to the little mathematician, who caught it. 'This is a souvenir from the days when we used to have our own memorabilia.'

He turned it over. It was a bronze medallion. Engraved on it was the pyramid-and-eye logo from the dollar bill. Above it, a scrollwork banner carried the initials 'DEI'. Curving below, a scroll carried the words 'Ignota ignoti'.

'Unknown unknowns,' Red Queen said. 'That's what we do. We deal with things we don't know we don't know about. Once we know we don't know about them we hand them over to the CIA, who –' Red Queen sighed '– generally continue not to know about them.

'Predecessors of the DEI have existed as long ago as the Salem witch trials. We had operatives in the Culper Ring during the Revolutionary War. This, at least, is how the story within the organisation goes – but there's no real evidence for any of it.

'We were shut down for reasons nobody within the organisation understands after the Kennedy assassination, but then, come the run-up to the second Gulf War, certain senior members of the administration became very interested indeed in the sort of paranoid *X-Files* material that was traditionally associated with the Directorate. Donald Rumsfeld, as Secretary of Defense, reinstated our work. Our off-books budget suddenly reappeared. It got big.

'Below where we're sitting this compound goes twelve storeys down. There are tea-leaf readers, distance seers, chaos magicians and tarot tellers. Dicemen. Catatonics. Psychokinetics, psychic healers, lunatics. Haruspices. Illuminati. Idiot savants. Hypnotists. Bearded ladies. Oracles. All drinking the same coffee, and all paid for by the American taxpayer.'

Red Queen didn't seem entirely sold on the tea-leaf readers, it occurred to Hands, but it didn't seem his place to point it out.

Instead, he said: 'So, ah, what *is* your interest in our mad genius?'

'Banacharski?' Red Queen said. 'We don't think Banacharski was mad. We think Banacharski was trying to build a weapon.'

5

Alex didn't know what made him stop in Atlanta.

He'd been rebooked onto an onward flight to San Francisco, after the hurricane, but he had never gone to the airport. He had sat on the bed in his motel looking at the clock, his suitcase packed on the bed beside him.

The time when he had planned to leave for the airport had passed. Then the time when he'd need to leave to have a hope of making the flight. Then the time that the gate would have closed. Had he looked out of his window he'd have been able to watch his flight lift into the air. He thought about the empty seat on the plane, carrying a ghost of him to San Francisco, another reality peeling off this one and heading its own way.

He imagined the ghost travelling into town, walking down Market Street, the khaki-coloured buildings and tramways and clean sunlight. It would be weary, T-shirted, happy. He imagined walking up over towards Chestnut, and surprising Carey at Muffin Tops while she was pouring coffee for a customer. Then – blank. Nothing. He wasn't imagining Muffin Tops. He was imagining Central Perk from *Friends*. And he wasn't imagining Carey. He was imagining Jennifer Aniston. And his images of the city were a mash-up of Carey's postcards and Google Street View.

He couldn't imagine Muffin Tops. He couldn't imagine Carey. That future was illegible. Instead he was in Atlanta, in a motel room with its brown curtains drawn against the daylight, while his more purposeful ghost flew across America to surprise his girlfriend.

He couldn't stay, and he couldn't go. He didn't feel sad, or scared, or anything at all. He'd flown here on an impulse, and now the impulse had left him and no other impulses had arrived to take its place. He examined the feeling, or lack of it. He felt like if he stabbed a knife into his leg it would make a dull thunk, and then stick out as if he'd driven it into a wooden table leg.

He took out the small cherrywood box and thumbed it open in his lap. The ring was inside, a half-moon of silver metal standing proud of its little velvet cushion. Where there might have been a solitaire diamond, there was instead a double loop in the metal: the lemniscate.

He shut the box with a snap, opened it again, shut it again. What a small thing it had been to decide to change his life. He tried to remember whether he had decided to ask Carey to marry him before he'd seen the ring in the antique shop, or whether the idea had come fully formed into his head when he'd seen its object expression in the world. He couldn't.

He remembered wanting the ring, and knowing he wanted the ring, and knowing what it was for. The ring had cost about half what he had in the bank. The infinity symbol. He'd thought it was cool. Now he thought it was tacky.

He didn't know if it would fit. He didn't know if Carey would say yes. He didn't know what he'd say if she did. He didn't feel hungry. Eventually, as the afternoon slid into the evening, he turned on the television.

'Isla Holderness,' Red Queen continued. Hands was more or less at his ease, now. And he was curious to know how this story would unfold. A weapon? That sounded wrong. Banacharski was a fierce pacifist.

He knew Holderness's story well. It had done the rounds in the mathematical world. She was the woman who had found Banacharski. She'd started as a disciple and they'd exchanged some letters. She wanted to see if she could talk him out, talk him back in. She'd schlepped through tiny villages in the Pyrenees armed with an old photograph of the mathematician. She'd found him, living in a shack in the hills, living like a monk.

Banacharski, to her surprise, had been friendly. The shack was a mess, by all accounts. Banacharski slept on a pallet on the floor, and – in one version Hands heard – lived on grass. Hands wasn't actually sure that was possible.

Somehow, though, he took to Holderness. He had even been flattered to hear that, since his disappearance, one or two of his conjectures had been proved, but he said he'd stopped doing mathematics. Then he'd started ranting about the devil and the physics of free will. He believed that an agency – he called it the devil, though Holderness hadn't been sure whether or not he meant it as a metaphor – was interfering in measurements, making precise knowledge impossible, minutely bending space time.

After she returned to England, they began to correspond. It went well at first. He indicated, so the story went, that he intended to make her the custodian of his legacy – that he'd pass her his findings. Then one day a letter arrived, apparently, demanding the answer to a question: 'What is a metre?'

Holderness had no idea how to answer it. A sheaf of further letters arrived before she had even finished composing her reply. The first was incoherently angry, filled with scrawled capitals and obscenities. It accused her of being in league with the Enemy. It arrived on the same day as another that appeared to threaten suicide. The third arrived a day after the other two. It was addressed to 'The Supposed Isla Holderness'. Every mention of her name in this letter was surrounded by bitterly sarcastic inverted commas. 'Since you are not who you say you are, you know that I cannot be who you say I am,' it opened. It was signed 'Fred Nieman'. Holderness had set off to find him. She had found the shack burned to the ground and Banacharski, again, gone.

'He thought Isla Holderness was a spy,' said Red Queen.

'Why would he have thought that?' said Hands.

'He was intensely paranoid,' said Red Queen. 'Also, he was quite right. She *was* a spy. She worked for us. We'd been monitoring all her correspondence with him. His letters dropped hints of what he was working on – I think he thought that was what was keeping her interested; after all these years of isolation, the human contact was welcome, and he was flattered by her interest. But you have to remember this was a deeply, deeply paranoid man. The hints were purposely fragmentary. We had to stay at arm's length, and she was deep cover.

'We thought we had the breakthrough, but "What is a metre?" completely threw us. It threw her too. But she waited to respond.

'That was when it became clear something was very wrong. Banacharski vanished. Then we thought Holderness had gone rogue. We knew enough about what this man was like to know that the longer she left her response, the more likely it was that he'd flip his wig. We'd sent the clearest possible instructions on receipt of the "What is a metre?" letter that she should go immediately, in person, to see him and find a way of talking him round. But instead she spent a week trying to work out the answer to his riddle.

'She was responding to none of our signals to come in. She didn't use the dead-letter drops, and the messages she was sending stopped making any sense: newspaper buying, for instance. There was a complex series of codes surrounding what paper she bought, at what time of day, and how much change she used.

'All of a sudden she seemed to be buying newspapers completely at random. It took us a while to cotton on to what had actually happened.'

'What *had* happened?'

'It turned out that – actually – Banacharski was wrong. Isla Holderness was just what she professed to be: an academic mathematician who was interested in his work.'

'I don't follow you.'

'He was right but he was wrong. Isla Holderness was a spy. But that was a different Isla Holderness. We made a huge mistake. This woman with Banacharski wasn't our Isla Holderness, and she wasn't spying on him. It was another woman with the same name. And she'd been buying newspapers completely at random all along.'

Red Queen looked a little bitter about this.

It was hard enough keeping track of all the DEI's agents, and the organisation's institutional reluctance to commit anything to paper for fear of being counter-surveilled made it more or less impossible.

Many DEI field agents didn't even know they were working for the DEI – and a good few of them actually thought they were spying on it for one of the several fictitious cover agencies that it ran. Red Queen occasionally pretended to be unsure whether the DEI was a real organisation or, itself, a red herring.

Hands looked mystified. 'So where was your Isla Holderness while the other Isla Holderness was with Banacharski?'

'Thousands of miles away in a cave network in northern Pakistan,' said Red Queen, gloomily. 'She had spent the previous three years infiltrating with unprecedented success – not that we knew about how she was getting on at the time, since we'd forgotten she was there – bin Laden's inner circle.'

'What?' said Hands. '*Osama* bin Laden? The terrorist?'

'No,' said Red Queen, brightening up a bit. 'As it turned out, not.'

The car was a box of smoke. It pulled into the parking lot of the International House of Pancakes where Bree had made the rendezvous and stopped in the rank of parking spaces across from where she was waiting in the shade of a tree.

Through the windshield, Bree could see nothing. It was like a white-out in there. The driver's-side door opened, and the car exhaled – a roll of what looked like dry ice furling out under the door and dissipating above the hard top. A hand, holding a cigarette, gripped the edge of the roof. A foot – a giant foot, like a beached canoe – appeared under the edge of the door, and a very tall man scissored out and stood upright, looking around, as the smoke cleared.

Bree reckoned he was about six foot three. He had a thin face, and short pale grey hair. She walked up with a hand in her pocket, and she could see his attention register her.

He put the cigarette in his hand into his mouth and pulled on it very heavily.

'Hello,' he said, without taking his sunglasses off. 'I'm Jones.'

'Bree.'

They didn't shake hands, though an awkward moment passed when they could have. They stood opposite each other in the hot parking lot, and even from this distance Bree could smell the smoke on him. There was a parchmenty greyness, close up, to his skin. It was like wasp paper under his eyes.

He indicated the car with a gesture of his arm. 'This is my . . . wheels.'

He looked oddly pleased with himself.

Bree had been told a little about Jones. She still didn't understand it, not exactly, but she was comfortable with that. Red Queen had said only that Jones's 'condition' was going to be an advantage in the hunt – and that Bree shouldn't be disconcerted if he seemed a little eccentric. Bree had, in her time, spent days staring earnestly into crystal balls alongside people who, in Brooklyn accents, assured her that they were 500-year-old Mittel-European Gypsies. She had a wide tolerance for the eccentric.

She guessed she'd find out about Jones as they went along; provided she didn't asphyxiate first.

'Jolly Rancher?' she said.

She held out her hand, and the thought came to her momentarily that she might have been pulling a dog biscuit from her pocket. Jones looked at it, and paused as if confused.

'Yes – please,' he said.

He took one of the little candies from her hand. Bree noticed with satisfaction that it was the peach flavour, which was the only one she hated. Jones unwrapped it fastidiously. He removed the cigarette from his mouth, popped the Jolly Rancher in, and replaced the cigarette.

'Thank you,' he said.

Bree took one of the green-apple flavour, and after a moment or two they climbed into Jones's rental car and they slammed the doors and Bree wound down her window and Jones pumped the air conditioning to full and lit another cigarette and then they drove out of the IHOP parking lot and into the world.

Alex's mental fug lasted most of that evening. He had watched pinky faces on CNN until he had got bored, then he'd turned over to the orange faces on Fox News, then – briefly – the BBC, where he didn't know whether it was the familiar rust-coloured graphics or the familiar green-yellow face of the correspondent standing by the railings in Downing Street that made him feel homesick.

Then he flipped again, to a show called *I Want a Million Dollars NOW!*. Some girls in bright swimsuits were screaming at each other.

He had noticed that the wall of his room, by the door to the bathroom, had a bottle opener fixed to it with screws. So you could lever the crown top off a bottle of beer, presumably, before you took it into the toilet to settle in for a shit.

Alex didn't have a bottle of beer. There was a little plasticky coffee-maker on the table by the television, though. He had plugged the two-pin plug in, filled the glass pot awkwardly from the shallow sink, filled the coffee-maker's reservoir from the pot, replaced the empty pot on the hotplate. Beside it there was a plastic basket designed, apparently, to fool the passer-by into thinking it was made out of bright blue wicker. He had picked up the heat-sealed plastic envelope that said 'Coffee', and torn it open. It contained, apparently, a giant tea bag full of coffee, some of which had spilled out of the torn tea bag onto the table.

He had picked up the other plastic envelope, a paler brown, which contained the decaf. He had liberated the giant tea bag intact this time, smoothed it into the round space for it in the top of the coffee-maker, flipped the hinged holder so it sat back over the pot. Then he had replaced the two-pin plug, which had fallen out of its slot. Then he had flipped the switch on the base of the coffee-maker so it glowed orange, and waited for the machine to cough and splutter to a natural death.

Then he had unsheathed one of the two white styrofoam cups from its plastic wrapper, poured the scalding caramel-coloured coffee into it, waited for it to go cold, then drunk it.

Now he had run out of things to do.

Alex had never been to America before. Having set out with a sense – now, he saw, entirely bogus – of purpose and adventure, he felt suddenly small and pathetic and alone.

In his imagination, it had been a vector transformation. Going to America would, necessarily, make him equal to the setting. America, far away, looked big: he would become big as he travelled towards it. America, close up, was enormous. And he, travelling towards it, had become even smaller. He imagined himself labelled 'Shown actual size'.

There was an entire country out there to be seen, and he couldn't bring himself to leave his motel room even to eat. How hard could it be to walk round the corner and get a pizza, or go to a bar? He knew he was exacerbating things by inactivity. He felt low enough to do nothing but not so tired that he could go to sleep. Now the numbness was fading, the pleasurably dismaying shock of simply not doing what he intended and expected to, he found it hard to put the wasted cost of the flight out of his mind.

And while he sat here his mind was moving, never quite settling, on a survey of his situation. He was twenty-four years old. The most important thing in his life, for three years, had been a PhD that his gut told him he wouldn't finish. Now it was a girl whom his gut had told him that he would marry, and in marrying whom, his gut told him, he would change his life. Now his gut had vanished. He was gutless. He looked down, miserably, at his gut, as if he imagined someone was watching whom he ought to impress with his wryness if not his resolution.

Nobody was watching. He zoned back in. A bikini girl on the television shouted, at a buff-bodied and gormless male competitor: 'Alix!'

He flicked the channel, and a British sports commentator said with lugubrious sonority: '. . . run . . .'

Flick.

'. . . run?'

Cricket, this time. Flick.

'. . . run away as far and as fast as you can . . .'

A cowboy film. Flick.

'. . . circumstances are conspiring there . . .'

Politics. Flick.

'Out!'

Tennis. Flick.

'To get you . . .'

An advertisement for an ambulance-chasing personal injury lawyer whose swiftly scrolling small print was just beginning to make its way up from the bottom of the screen.

Click. Alex turned the television off. Something nagged at him – a feeling right at the back of his mind, almost below the level of consciousness – that someone somewhere was trying to tell him something. He shrugged it off.

He decided, finally, to make himself go for a walk. He swung his legs off the bed, and himself up onto his feet. He pulled back the chain from the door, shrugged his jacket on, and with not the slightest enthusiasm left the room, crossed the broad balcony and took the single flight of stairs down to the car park.

The light was orange and the night hot and tarmacky and strange-smelling. It was about nine o'clock, he reckoned. The motel consisted of an L-shaped block of rooms two storeys high, up to the foot of which parked cars nosed shell by shell. The motel was about a third full. Looking behind him as he crossed the tarmac, he could see a guy with his face in shadow, drinking a can of something on the balcony, two rooms down from his room.

At the registration office, strip light blared from the Perspex window where the teenage night clerk sat watching television. The door adjacent was half lit, with a sign hanging on it saying 'Closed' and the brightest light source the Mountain Dew decal on the vending machine.

Alex walked past the office and onto the broad highway: three lanes in either direction. He turned right. There wasn't much traffic. To his left, a pickup and a family car waited for the overhead lights to turn green.

There were no pedestrians. On the opposite side of the road was a long car park on the other side of which was a Pet Superstore, a CVC chemist and a 7-Eleven. On his side of the road was nothing at all: a pavement, a broad grass verge, a low hedge. There was some sort of office building set back from the road behind a network of drives and flower beds.

It took him ten minutes to reach the end of what he presumed to be the block, and still there was nothing doing. He kept walking. He assumed that this was not downtown.

It took him another ten minutes to reach the end of the next block. There was a twenty-four-hour photo shop. It was closed. He kept walking. It took him twenty minutes more to reach a drive-through McDonald's on the other side of the road. Alex felt a shade ashamed to have travelled to America and to be eating at McDonald's, but he was now tired and he thought that

42

something comforting and familiar might see off his self-pity if it didn't exacerbate it.

He walked up towards the ordering window. There was one car – an SUV – pulled up by it, a meaty forearm and a measure of beard protruding from the driver's window. It rolled on with a jerk, and Alex walked up to the booth.

'Ah.' He tried to see past the kid behind the microphone to a menu somewhere, though he didn't need it. 'I'd like . . . two plain hamburgers please. Small fries.' This had been the food Alex had ordered while alone, and passing McDonald's, for years. 'And a –'

He was interrupted by the blare of a horn, close enough to cause him to jump with fright. Ice-white headlights washed past him, and the horn went again.

'Hell do you think you're doing? I could have killed you! Get in line, you little prick!' a woman with a frightened face shouted at him from the driver's window of her station wagon. He realised that behind the SUV had been a queue of two cars, one of which had not seen him walk past it in the pool of dark beside the cashier's window and had nearly broken his legs.

The cashier looked amused. 'Ma'am?' he said.

Alex, hot with shame, retreated and let the car jounce up to the window. The woman's attention left him. He walked down the curved grass verge. The car behind pulled up to the station wagon's bumper as if pointedly. Alex walked down further.

He stood by the offside back wheel of the car behind. Whoever was in it showed no sign of acknowledgement. Another car pulled in behind. The station wagon lurched off from the window. The car behind which Alex was queuing moved off to take its place – and the car behind Alex, as if he were invisible, moved up in turn behind its bumper.

'Hey!' Alex felt himself saying – or would have, had he not felt the ridiculousness of him saying it before it left his lips. 'Ahem!' would have been no more dignified or effective. He didn't think he had the courage to go and remonstrate with the driver. He was a pedestrian. He was nobody.

Alex stepped off the verge and stood behind the rear bumper of the car that had jumped the queue. He didn't look to see what if any expression the man in that car was making in his rear-view mirror.

It took about a minute for the car to move off. Another had pulled in behind him. He could see the shadow of his own legs across the bumper and boot of the car in front. Then it was gone, his shadow lengthened across the tarmac, and the car behind him honked its horn.

He held his ground, and moved forward deliberately. Finally, he reached the window.

'Two hamburgers. Medium fries. Regular fries. And a Sprite please.'

He ate his supper out of the paper bag on the verge. The burgers were not like they were at home. They were hotter, flimsier. The buns were different. More scrunched-up, somehow.

He felt, again, lonely. He walked back to the motel without meeting another pedestrian.

When he got up the stairs the man on the balcony was there again. He couldn't reach his door from the staircase without walking ten feet towards him, so he bobbed his head and said: 'Night.'

'Night,' said the man, in what sounded like a British accent.

6

Davidoff was lying on the bed nearest the window when Sherman came back in. He had his white earplugs in and was rapping his knuckles in the same annoying way on the wooden bed frame. That was what he had been doing to cause Sherman to go outside in the first place, Sherman remembered.

On the table was the wreckage of a service-station sandwich.

Still standing up, Sherman plugged his own iPod into his ears and pressed play.

There was a high squalling guitar noise and then what sounded like a teenage girl's voice even higher through a gale of feedback. Sherman winced: a teenage girl with serious emphysema, apparently.

'Waaansathoudahsawyou . . .' the girl's voice wailed, '. . . innacrowdiyazybaaaah . . .' A drumbeat started to thump insistently in the background, and another wave of guitarry fuzz came over the top. Sherman pulled out the headphones.

'This is pointless,' he said, just loudly enough to break Davidoff's reverie. The younger man picked his big head up a little and looked at him. He stepped over and pulled out one of Davidoff's earbuds, at which he frowned. Music leaked from the dangling earbud: '. . . bompTSSSSS, bompbompTSSSSS, bompTSSSSS, bompbompTSSSSS.'

'What?' said Davidoff.

'Are you receiving your directions from the cosmos all right there, mate?'

'No,' said Davidoff. 'I'm listening to REO Speedwagon.'

Sherman dropped Davidoff's earbud so it dangled by the bed, inhaled, and shuffled impatiently. It bugged him to be doing so little. It also bugged him that Davidoff pronounced REO 'reeyo', but that was just part of a wider discontent.

They had arrived late the previous night into an airport still clogged with backlogged passengers, and after picking up a car and driving around had finally hit on this unlovely motel. They had spent the day getting the lie of the land.

Davidoff had either bought the daft idea that this next-generation weapons system could be tracked down with the use of a last-but-one-generation MP3 player; or he had embraced the possibilities Ellis's plan offered for bunking off. He had spent most of the day with the earbuds in, nodding away to himself, now and again saying something moronic like: 'I've just had "Love in an Elevator", "The Only Way is Up" and "Stairway to Heaven". Do you think we're closing in on it?'

'Fuck. Do. I. Know, mate,' Sherman would respond with unfailing regularity.

His own iPod was clearly broken. Since they'd arrived in the motel it would play nothing but that Neil Young racket over and over again.

The money on this job was good – if Ellis was going to pay them to listen to music, on his own head be it – but the doing nothing was not. Sherman would have been happier back in the desert, slotting ragheads from a long way away. He wondered about slotting Davidoff from less far away.

He took another can of Mountain Dew from the small fridge, cracked it open, and went outside to drink it and wonder what to do next.

'So we got this.'

Red Queen showed Hands another photograph. It was the satellite image of the aeroplane.

'It's an airplane,' said Hands.

'Yes,' said Red Queen. 'This is a satellite image taken from space. When the weather is doing what the weather was doing over most of the Southern states last week, satellites can't see much of anything. There's cloud, rain, electrical interference. This is the only image we've got.'

The image, though distinctively the shape of a plane, was blurry and pixellated. It was more than half obscured by a wisp of grey-white that Hands assumed must be cloud.

He adjusted his glasses with his right hand and looked at it again.

'I still see a plane. I only just see a plane. As you say, it's not a very accurate picture. So what's special about it? What does it have to do with me?'

'What's special about it is –' Red Queen hesitated. 'There are two things special about it. First, this plane is sitting on the ground, nowhere near anything that looks like an airport. It's in the middle of a field. So how did it get there? And second is that this plane doesn't exist. Didn't exist.'

'What do you mean?'

'It's a 737. There aren't that many of them made. They register every one. We have access to those registers. All accounted for. This one not. This plane appeared from nowhere.'

A look passed across the professor's face that conveyed, with a pink wrinkling of the forehead from eyebrows to scalp, that he was still wondering, from time to time, whether he was the victim of a practical joke.

'Ri-i-ght.'

He decided to show willing.

'So how do you think the plane appeared from nowhere?'

'This image was taken not far from a large scrap-metal disposal facility in Alabama, in the immediate aftermath of Hurricane Jody. We think the hurricane assembled the plane.'

'That's completely absurd,' said Hands. 'Hurricanes don't build planes anywhere outside undergraduate philosophy lectures.'

'Who knows,' said Red Queen levelly. 'Perhaps the hurricane was showing off. But that's the only working explanation we have. And we got this.'

Red Queen showed Hands the Intercept. Hands frowned at it. Noting the spots of pink on his cheeks, Red Queen expected him to dismiss the Intercept one sentence in. He got to the end, though – and again, there was something indecipherable in his expression as he read.

'I don't know anything about engineering, or about satellites, or about – whatever *this* is supposed to be. But I'm afraid this is complete garbage,' he said. 'The whole thing. Impossible.'

'Improbable,' said Red Queen.

'Garbage. Impossible.'

'Improbable enough to be effectively impossible.'

'No, just impossible.'

'We think that what Banacharski was making was a machine that would make impossible things probable.'

Hands looked uneasy at this point. Red Queen watched him very closely.

'That sounds highly –'

'Yes. Improbable. Extremely improbable, in fact.'

'So where is this plane, then? Surely your . . . men in black helicopters –' Hands pronounced the last phrase with notable distaste – 'will already be halfway to Area 51 with it.'

Red Queen looked pained.

'Our men in black helicopters, if you want to be crude about it, didn't get anywhere near it. Professor Hands: do you remember what happened twelve hours after Hurricane Jody?'

Hands looked blank.

'Hurricane Kim.' The second storm had been even faster and more violent than the first, curving in from the north. 'By the time another human being was in a position to stand where the satellite image shows that plane, there was nothing but fragments of twisted scrap metal spread out over the surrounding area as far as the eye could see.'

'So who wrote this?'

'You tell me.'

Hands emitted a long sigh, and decided it was time to come clean.

'Me,' he said. He took a sip of the coffee from the paper cup. It was stone cold.

Red Queen's eyebrows climbed half an inch. 'Really?'

Alex woke up feeling better. He showered, trying not to let the discoloured nylon shower curtain touch his body. The curtain sucked onto the whole of his flank in a big wet kiss, held there by static electricity. But the towel was clean enough, and Alex stood on the scrunched, wet mat in front of the sink afterwards and in the yellow light shaved for the first time since he had left London.

He dressed in jeans and a clean white T-shirt, then put on his blue denim jacket, then opened the curtain onto the scrubland out behind the motel. The sun was dazzling white and the sky pale. He thought better of the jacket and took it off, rolling it up under two straps of his rucksack.

You are always nearer by not keeping still. That was a line from a poem Carey had quoted to him. It had made him think of centrifugal force – the way the earth falls constantly away from us.

He wondered, fleetingly, about calling Carey. But he didn't know yet what he was going to say to her – and he didn't want to spoil what was supposed to be a surprise. He realised, though, that he'd now been gone long enough that he'd be missed. It was – what?

His watch said 9:50.

He wondered if Saul would be at home. He grabbed his phone from the bedside table, thumbed two buttons to unlock it and prepared to dial. Before he was able to touch a button, though, the screen said 'Unknown' as if there were a call in progress.

He held it to his ear. There was silence at the other end, but an open silence, a breathing silence, like the sea in a shell.

Alex listened, then he said: 'Hello.'

As he did so, another voice said 'Hello' simultaneously. It was a girl's voice.

He said 'Hello' again, quicker this time, and her voice, once more at the same moment, like an echo so instantaneous as not to be an echo at all, said 'Hello'. Then he paused and heard the breathing sound.

He had had his own voice in his ear when the girl had been speaking, but he was pretty sure now that the girl's voice belonged to Carey.

He felt a chill. He must have speed-dialled her by accident. He pressed the red button and spiked the call.

He dialled his brother, listening to tiny, insect click–clacks and then the long distant ring of a transatlantic connection. Saul answered on the third ring.

'All right, bumface?'

'All right, Saul.'

'I would like you to know,' said Saul, in a voice of some seriousness, 'that I have now owned every last level in *Peggle*.'

'Saul, I have literally no idea what you're talking about. Is this one of your computer games?'

'Not just any computer game, my friend. I'm talking *Ultra Extreme Fever, Beethoven's "Ode to Joy", Magic Hats* . . . Compared to this, *Plants Versus Zombies* sucks balls.'

'*Plants Versus Zombies*? Was that the one with the –'

'. . . Plants and the . . . zombies? Yes. And the sucked balls. I knew that hoity-toity Oxbridge education wasn't lost on you. Now I'm insis—'

'Never mind that. Saul: I'm in America . . .'

There was a pause. The forward progress of Saul's onslaught had been impeded, momentarily, by this new piece of information. The phone was on the end of the breakfast bar in Saul's flat, and he imagined Saul's whole-body gesture of surprise and interest catching Tim's peripheral vision. Tim's *Evening Standard* would go down and he would make a silent question mark with his face.

'Alex. He's in America!' Saul would be mouthing to his boyfriend, his eyes wide. The image was so clear to him Alex felt homesickness lurch in his stomach.

Saul started to sing 'I wanna be in Ameh-ri-cah' but Alex cut him off with 'Saul –', and his voice changed, became more serious. 'Skidoop, what are you doing in America? Are you OK?'

'I'm fine, Saul. I just had a thing where – I wanted to get away. It's not a big deal . . .'

A thought occurred to Saul.

'Are you with the girl?'

Alex said nothing for a moment and Saul ran, in triumph, with the silence. 'My *God*! Tim! This is so exciting. This is more exciting than anything that's ever happened. Alex has eloped with the American girl! He's going to go live on a farm in Iowa and make sweet love to livestock and breed a*dor*able little one-eyed children in dungarees . . .'

'I haven't eloped,' Alex said. 'Saul, I'm not with Carey. Look, I haven't got long – I'm calling on my mobile phone. I didn't tell anyone I was going, and I'm fine, but I don't want people to worry about me or call the police or anything.'

'Where *are* you? Where in America?'

Alex looked out of the window.

'Atlanta,' he said.

'*Atlanta?*'

He ignored the question. 'Can you call Mum and tell her – I don't know what you tell her, actually. Don't tell her I'm here, though. Please. Tell her I'm staying with you if you have to. Make something up.'

'What happened, little brother? Are you *alone*?'

'Nobody's here. I'm fine,' Alex said. 'I'm going to go and see Carey, but I'm not sure what's going to happen.'

Saul seemed to digest this.

51

'You're not going to go all *Thelma and Louise* on us, are you?'

'No,' Alex said. 'I'm not going to go all *Thelma and Louise*. I promise.'

'Well, you have a fabulous holiday, then. And seriously: take care.'

'Thanks. See you soon, Saul.'

'Laters, bumface,' said Saul. And he rang off.

Alex put the phone in his hip bag. He had a plan in mind. On the road, he'd be able to think. He opened the door of the room and stepped onto the balcony. The man who had been there last night was nowhere. He walked down the stairs and across the car park to check out.

The clerk said the nearest Hertz office was back out by the airport. Alex crossed the highway and waited for the bus. The bus shelters here didn't have benches, like in the UK. This one didn't even have a shelter. Alex dropped his rucksack between his feet and leaned back on a concrete post. A tramp with a piled shopping cart was approaching from the direction Alex was watching for the bus. He was the only other person Alex could see, and wore a grey felt hat of shapeless design, filthy brown trousers hanging low on his waist, and some sort of twist of webbing slung round his bare chest. He was barking like a seal. 'Raup! Arrp!' he said. 'Aaarrp!'

Alex could hear it from some way away. With each exclamation, the shopping trolley, with its cargo of stuffed 7-Eleven bags, would take a jolting bunny-hop forward and its owner would whip his head round to the left. It looked like a nervous tic, or like he was anxious that something unwelcome was on the point of arriving unannounced on his left shoulder. Alex couldn't think of why exactly anything would want to go near the man's left shoulder.

'Aarrp! Raaup!' Alex looked at his feet. There was no sign of a bus.

The tramp made slow progress up the road. The barking sounds he emitted sounded more and more like dry heaves with each moment that passed. And from what Alex could see out of the corner of his eye, what he was expecting to arrive on his shoulder wasn't welcome. His eyes were rolling like those of a terrified horse.

When he got level with Alex, whose existence he had not appeared to notice, he suddenly whipped his head the other way, so his face was pointing straight into Alex's, and shouted: 'BOO!'

Alex's stomach flipped and he jumped back in fright. He stumbled over the rucksack at his feet and landed with a painful thump on his coccyx. He scrambled to get his feet under him.

Leaning against his shopping trolley, the tramp was wheezing with laughter.

'Faggin' aaaRRGH! Gotcha. Faggin' liberal!'

Alex's face flushed with blood but, fearing violence, he snatched up his rucksack and took a step back. The tramp scissored into another burst of mirth, then apparently took fright again, and his head jerked back round to look over his shoulder.

'Arrrp!' he exclaimed, then looked piercingly at Alex.

'Spare sssigarette?' he said, sending a hot gale of rotting pilchards in Alex's direction. There was a furze of white stubble on the bulb of his chin and his cheeks were sunken. His lips moved and ticced, flashing teeth the colour of toffee. His right hand probed under the webbing round his chest and scratched absently at his left nipple.

'Hnuh? Eh?'

Alex shook his head.

'Asshole,' said the tramp genially, and stood, left arm on the trolley, laughter passed, sizing Alex up. Alex coughed officiously and looked distractedly past the tramp down the road. There was still no sign of the bus.

'Sorry,' he said. The tramp shrugged, and barked again. Alex looked at his feet. It occurred to him to whistle a thin tune, but his mouth felt dry. And then, as they stood there with Alex looking at his feet, the tramp grabbed Alex by a twist of shirt and walked in until the hot physicality of him, sour stink of skin, dried sweat, rancid mouth smell, enveloped the younger man.

Alex's eyes flicked up. And the everyday madness in the man's face had been replaced by something different. He looked as if he was having a seizure. The muscles on his neck were standing up, and a coil of vein went across one.

'Nobody's here,' he hissed. You could hear the wet breath whistling against his wrecked teeth. 'Trust nobody. Nobody can help you. Bring them together. Bring them back. Forgive.'

The tramp was breathing very hard now, and he had Alex clenched to his chest. But whatever he was doing wasn't directed at Alex, apparently. His eyes were milky, absent, staring into Alex's face as if seeing someone else there, or as if seeing someone through him. He opened and closed his jaw wordlessly. A creamy crust of foam moved where his lips met.

Alex grabbed him by the shoulders – his skin was like dry rubber to the touch – and pushed him off. The tramp's hand released the hank of T-shirt, leaving a smudge of dark grime.

'Isla . . . Kara . . . Ana . . .'

'Are you – are you all right?' Alex tried. The man's voice had changed and his face looked – grief-stricken.

'Nameless,' the tramp said then. 'Nameless ones. All the nobodies . . .'

Then something passed – whatever neurological event had upset him, whatever mental weather had passed across his brain, blew itself out. The man swayed, blinked as if confused, and then his focus found Alex again. He stepped back as if a little embarrassed, and put a tetchy, proprietorial hand on the bar of his supermarket cart.

Out of the corner of his eye, Alex saw the bus arriving. It swung into the stop where they were standing and the door opposite the driver opened with a slap and hiss. Alex shouldered his pack and hopped quickly on, fumbling a rolled-up dollar bill into the feeder and wriggling down to the end of the bus, sitting on a hard plastic seat.

A couple of seconds later, he heard the tramp's voice. He had climbed onto the bus, and was now arguing with the bus driver. Alex saw him fishing in his horrible trousers and waving something at the driver.

'My money stink? My money stink? Zat it? Faggin' liberal.'

The bus driver said something Alex didn't catch.

'. . . take a piss right here, lady. Just ask.'

He started a second, more purposeful rummaging in the horrible trousers before the driver shot out an arm and snatched the note from his hand. The door slammed shut behind him.

'Heh,' he said, and ambled stinkily down the aisle of the bus. Ignoring several vacant pairs of seats, he hoisted himself into the one next door to Alex, sat down and looked straight ahead. He seemed to have stopped barking.

'Spare cigarette?' he asked, then answered his own question with a long sigh. 'Nahhh.'

Alex wanted to move, but he was sort of wedged in, and he didn't like to seem impolite.

'Ah, sir, your . . . things . . .' Alex pointed at the window.

The tramp shrugged.

'Ah, none of that stuff means . . . it's just stuff, you know?' He looked as if with the slightest curiosity out of the window at his shopping cart, orphaned on the sidewalk as the bus lurched away.

The tramp fished a single bent cigarette out of his trousers and put it in his mouth. He didn't light it.

'Don' need bags of stuff when I got . . . my freedom. I can do anything, go anywhere . . .' He delivered this in a tone of flat unenthusiasm. 'Yessir. Whee. Free will. The open road.'

He paused, apparently reflecting on all that the glorious exercise of his freedom had brought him.

'Where you from, kid?' he asked.

Alex became conscious of a certain stiffening in the neck of the Korean girl a few seats in front. A raisin-skinned old woman down at the driver end of the bus adjusted her bag on her lap and looked pointedly out of the window. Everyone was pretending not to be listening. Alex felt acutely self-conscious.

'Ah. Cambridge.'

'Mass?'

'What? Oh. No. England. Britain, England.'

The tramp's head bobbed thoughtfully.

'You –' Alex coughed – 'know it?'

'Yarp. Posted there. Inna war.'

Another long pause, as the tramp seemed to zone out. Whenever he stopped talking his marine funk seemed to cycle chromatically through a range of species: now tuna, now kipper, now lobster-on-the-turn.

'Fred,' the tramp said.

Alex felt himself colour.

'Alex.' He twisted awkwardly in his seat and shook Fred's hand. Always him, he thought. Always him. How much longer was it going to be before he asked for a –

'Dollar? Y'lemme a dollar, pal?' His voice now a confidential growl.

'I –'

'Gotta get inna shelter. I get inna shelter I can – look . . .'

Fred, surprisingly limber, ducked his head down, grabbed his own foot and levered it up on his knee. His shoe was like a Cornish pasty, split at the seams. The filling looked unappetising. He pulled it off, revealing a foot that had seen a lot of life. Its crowning glory was the nail on the big toe: a full inch long, with dry blood crusted at the base, it was the shape and colour of a tooth rather than a toenail.

'Horrible,' he said.

'Um,' said Alex.

'They got clippers inna shelter. Lend me thirty bucks.'

'Thirty?'

'All I ask.'

'I'm really terribly −'

'Forty. Pal. I'm mentally ill.'

The unlit cigarette bobbed and wagged as if it were glued to his lower lip. The back of the Korean girl's head looked fascinated by the exchange.

'I get fits. Pal. Alex. I can't work. There's a bullet in my brain. Right here, look.' He grabbed Alex's hand and guided it to a place at the top of his forehead near his hairline where there was a scar. He pushed Alex's fingers against it and there was a disconcerting boneless give under the skin.

'Wenn in. Docs could never get it out. I pick up radio signals. Get visions. I know what's going on. You better gimme forty dollars.'

'I don't − I'm really sorry. I haven't got that much money. I'd like to help, but −'

'Pal.'

'I've − will this . . . ?' Alex pulled a note from his pocket. Shit. It was a twenty. Fred snatched it.

'Humph,' said Fred. Then: 'Wait up.' He produced something from his horrible trousers. It was a very, very crumpled one-dollar bill and a stub of pencil. 'I got your change. Hah.' He unfurled the bill and held it in front of Alex's face. He twitched his finger and thumb, seigneurially. Alex found it very irritating.

'Thank you,' he said a moment later, snatching the bill from the air. Nineteen dollars down. And sitting next to a tramp on the bus. Alex put the bill in his pocket. It felt like their business was transacted, and they sat on in a tense silence, Alex looking out of the window and breathing, shallowly, through his mouth.

They pulled up to a stop, finally, within sight of the wire-fenced expanse of the airport car farm.

'Bye,' said Alex.

The tramp said something, but it was a little slurred. It sounded like 'I'll see you around'.

Alex wriggled past him and walked with relief down towards the front end of the bus to alight. Fred stayed where he was, and as the door shut behind him Alex heard from the inside of the bus what sounded like the bark of a seal.

What Hands told Red Queen about the Intercept was not what Red Queen had been expecting to hear. Not by a long chalk. What Red Queen took for signs of guilt or complicity had been, as it turned out, something entirely other. It had been embarrassment.

His first action when asked what he knew had been to protest, in a squawk whose sheer volume spoke of outraged innocence: 'Nothing! Nothing at all!'

Red Queen had known, from early on, that there had been something odd about the professor's response to the Intercept, something shifty. When put on the spot, he had gone crimson.

'I don't know what you mean,' he said, 'by trying to humiliate me this way. But if I hadn't been transported here in a style quite beyond the means of even my wealthiest students, I'd long since have thought this a sophomore prank.

'Where did you get this from?' he asked, in the too-shrill voice of a man who was now all bluster.

'Professor Hands,' said Red Queen, 'where we got it from is far less important than your having written an eyewitness account of the event that is at the centre of our investigation, and then lied about it. There is a man in the hospital in Mobile with severe injuries as a result of this event – an event that we have no choice but to treat as an act of war. You have professed not to know anything about this event, or its architect, but you are one of a handful of people on earth who works, at a high level, in Banacharski's field. At the moment you are looking very much indeed like a prime suspect. You are on the point of becoming

–' Red Queen finished with a hard stare – 'a known unknown. And that entitles me to hand you over to some people who will be a lot less nice to you.'

Hands had the face of a man in whom panic and bewilderment were wrestling like drunken teenagers at a pyjama party.

'But I don't know anything about this – event, as you call it. This document: I should have told you what it was but I was, I don't know, embarrassed. It's –'

'It's an exact description of the formation of an airplane out of a junkyard!'

'It's fiction!'

'Professor Hands, I put it to you that it is not. Look.' Red Queen's hand stabbed, again, at the blurry satellite photograph. 'That is an airplane. Right there. In Alabama backcountry. An airplane.'

'No, I mean this has nothing to do with anything. The passage you read, yes, I wrote it. But years ago.' The professor took his glasses off and started to clean them. The pink on his skin had intensified to the point where it was coming out in creamy spots of white at the cheeks and the angles of his forehead. 'I wrote that a decade ago or more. It's *fiction*. I was trying to write a science-fiction novel – I, I don't know. Call it a *jeu d'esprit*. It's silly. Pure nonsense. It was about someone who builds a sort of magic probability machine. That was the first page.'

'A novel. Like a what – like you'd buy in a bookstore?' said Red Queen, who knew perfectly well what a novel was, and didn't want to bother to pretend not to know what a *jeu d'esprit* was.

'Yes,' Hands, now a little piqued. 'With pages and writing. Just like you've probably seen on TV.' He regrouped, replaced his glasses. 'Mine never got as far as the bookstore stage. I considered self-publishing, but after I'd had rejection letters from a number of agents I decided that, probably, I was a mathematician not an artist.'

The panic was leaving him. What he said next was tinged with something almost wistful.

'I loved − as a child − loved reading science fiction. I was of that generation of children for who Einstein was a hero − and the lunar landings. I ended up in pure math − and that's a whole other story − but it was science fiction that got me on the path. I had the idea I could do it myself.' He pursed his lips a little. 'Evidently, I couldn't.' After leaving it for a little while, he said: 'So, where did you get this from?'

'Nowhere, more or less. It was highly corrupt when it came in. From general surveillance. We think it was originally a fax, but it was impossible to isolate where it was coming from or where it was going.'

'Well,' said Hands, 'I can tell you for sure that it's nothing to do with me that it's come to you. My only remaining copy of the manuscript has been in a cardboard box in my garage in Cambridge for years, and is likely to remain there.'

Red Queen put on a mulling-it-over face. It was possible Hands was lying, though it seemed unlikely, and trying to work out what truth he was lying to conceal was the high road to a migraine. If this was an eyewitness account, it would have had to have been from someone standing in the middle of a hurricane. And detail after detail didn't make sense. How could they have heard the noise above the wind?

Red Queen felt irritable; then, not.

'So this thing was written ten years ago?'

'At least. At least.'

'Yet it describes exactly what happened in Alabama.'

'No. It describes exactly what I invented ten years ago,' said Hands prissily. 'It's only you who says this thing has happened with the airplane − and only this satellite picture as evidence.'

'Let us say it describes what happened.'

'It had an unreliable narrator.'

'Zip it. It describes what happened. And less than a week after

60

what happened happened, someone transmitted it and it came to us. Doesn't it slightly stretch credibility to imagine that this is a coincidence?'

'Ah,' said Hands. 'I think I see what you're driving at.'

Red Queen let him run. It seemed worth giving him a little satisfaction, a moment of control.

'So you're saying,' said Hands, 'that a document describing an imaginary coincidence engine, arriving just after something that might be a real coincidence engine takes effect, is proof that the real coincidence engine actually exists?'

'We work with what we've got,' said Red Queen.

7

Jones and Bree had spent the morning doing what Bree thought of as old-fashioned detective work, not that she had ever been a detective. The Mobile line of enquiry having gone nowhere, Red Queen had now told her to find this kid from England who they knew 'the other side' was looking for. Bree didn't ask who 'the other side' was; in the DEI it could mean anything.

Red Queen had shuffled the DEI's ring of skeleton keys and pulled passenger manifests for commercial flights out of Atlanta. He had been supposed to be on a flight. They had staked out the airport. He hadn't showed up. Red Queen had also slipped into the Customs and Immigration database and found the photograph they'd taken at border control in Atlanta when he'd got off his plane from England. It showed a lean, long-jawed young man. Early twenties, tired-looking, perhaps from the flight. Tousled blond hair, a slightly off-centre nose. This was an improvement on the photograph on his Facebook profile, which was a picture of a duck.

There had also been a few frames grabbed from the CCTV in the luggage hall. In one of them he walked in – you could only see the back of his head because of the positioning of the camera – and crossed to the luggage carousel, where he stood unhelpfully behind a pillar. He had been carrying a briefcase – apparently his hand luggage from the plane – but what he fished off the carousel had been a backpack. It had seemed odd, to Bree – people who travel with backpacks don't usually have briefcases as their hand luggage. The camera had lost him as he went through customs.

There was one more of him getting into a taxi at the rank outside the airport. He still had the backpack on him, and a fanny pack round his waist. But no briefcase. Bree had pointed it out when the pictures came through.

'I know,' Red Queen had said. 'We're working on that end of it. You stay on Smart. Don't approach him for the moment. Just find him, and stay on him, and as soon as you do, tell me. If he's got this thing on him, he could be . . . unpredictable.'

Alex Smart's 'unpredictability' was the reason, according to Red Queen, that Bree had been teamed with Jones. The current thinking about this thing, if it existed at all, which Bree somewhat doubted, was that it was somehow affected by what people around it expected.

'Do you know about the observer's paradox?' Red Queen asked.

'Is that the one with the cat in a box?' Bree said.

'I've got people here who know all about it. Essentially, it says that you affect something by looking at it. Or you can't look at something without affecting it.'

'How's that?'

'I'm not the expert. It's something to do with physics.'

'If you stare into the abyss, the abyss also stares into you,' Bree said.

'You're joking,' Red Queen said.

'Yes,' Bree said. 'I am joking. Tell me about the observer's paradox.'

Bree felt annoyance in the quality of the pause. Bree didn't know, quite, why she felt the need to get on Red Queen's nerves, but she knew that her boss seemed to be unusually tolerant of it. It was, perhaps, the nature of the work they did: facetiousness was a way of expressing scepticism. Too much DEI stuff head-on and you started circling the plughole. The material you were dealing with started to seem plausible. You didn't want to end up in one of the deep levels, gibbering about impossible angles, elder gods and colours unknown to man.

Red Queen continued. 'We know that this thing does weird things to chance. Right out on the end of the bell-curve things. It's not like it weights the dice a bit. It's like it makes the dice land on one corner and stay there, or makes all the spots fall off spontaneously. Well, this plane.'

'If it did assemble this plane –'

'Which we're assuming for the moment it did. This plane is not purely random. It's a thing. It's an idea. It has to do with an expectation – whose, we don't yet know.'

'Why should it be?'

'That's what they think. That's what we're working on. In quantum mechanics you can't look at something without affecting it – that's for very, very tiny things, at least. But if they could . . . well, the working theory is that this has somehow turned that round – there's a professor we pulled in – MIT guy, came highly recommended – who says that it might be designed to "weaponise the observer's paradox". It will take what you're expecting, and then something else will happen. Or, if you're expecting it to do that, perhaps it will make the original thing that you were expecting happen after all. Before you stopped expecting it.'

'How does it know what you're expecting?'

'When you stare into the abyss . . .'

'Now you're being facetious.'

'Yes. We don't know. If we did, we'd have built it ourselves.'

'So it's affecting random events and making them not random?'

'Not quite. It's more as if it's doing things that are surprising.'

'Plane appears in Alabama,' conceded Bree. 'That's surprising.'

'Yes,' said Red Queen. 'It is.'

'So, Jones,' Bree said later. It was lunchtime and they were eating burritos. Bree hadn't wanted to broach what she'd been told about Jones with him until she'd had the chance to size him up. But now she'd spent more time with him, she'd got a better sense of the way in which Jones's condition might relate to the job in hand. Besides, she was curious. 'You're hard to surprise?'

Jones looked at her levelly. He had taken off his sunglasses and his eyes were a striking ceramic grey. He was, Bree thought, quite attractive. They had, earlier on, reached an accommodation on the smoking issue. Bree's asthma, aggravated by Jones's perpetual smoking – how many packets a day did he get through? – had reduced her to near-speechless wheezing.

She had wound down first her window, then – pointedly – his, then cranked the air con up to full blast. He hadn't so much as interrupted his stream of cigarettes, so much as asked her whether she minded if he smoked. Nothing of the sort.

Finally, she had said: 'Jones, I'm dying here.' He had looked at her with quizzical sharpness. 'Would you mind, please, not smoking while we're in the car together?'

'You want me to stop smoking cigarettes.'

'Yes. Please.'

'Certainly.'

And, with no signs of ill will, he had.

As soon as they'd got out at the Taco Bell, though, Jones had lit a cigarette. They were outside in the children's play area. Bree had ordered first: two beef combo burritos and a big Sprite. Jones had ordered the same thing. Now Bree was eating her second burrito. Jones was still on his first, because he was smoking in between mouthfuls.

'Hard to surprise,' he said. 'No. Impossible to surprise.'

He took a drag from his cigarette, and continued to chew. He showed – as he tended to – no real sign of continuing to speak. Bree pressed him.

'This special condition of yours,' she said. 'Tell me about it. Why are you not possible to surprise? See everything coming, do you? Got it all figured out?'

'No. I don't see anything coming. I don't expect things,' he said without inflection. 'I'm apsychotic.'

'You're what?'

'Apsychotic. Not "psychotic". It means no soul. My doctor told me to explain it this way: I don't have an imagination.'

Bree chewed her burrito and looked at him.

Jones waited a bit, then continued to speak. He sounded dutiful, as if what he was saying had been learned by rote. 'I say my doctor told me to use that phrase, but I do not know what it means. I cannot imagine an imagination. I do not know what you mean by "surprise". I can't talk about "future". Things take place. I do not expect them. I do not expect anything else. I have no expectations at all.'

'Whoa,' said Bree. 'Jones, how can it be possible for a person not to have an imagination?'

'There are areas of the brain that associate objects that are not the same together, that associate –' he hesitated, frowning – 'imaginary objects with real ones. Those areas in my brain are not the same. Imaginary objects don't exist for me. I can't understand how they exist for everybody else. I cannot use metaphors. I don't know what it would mean to do so. Dr Albert said it's "like explaining colour to a blind man".'

Bree continued to chew and continued to look.

'I don't understand that,' added Jones, 'either.'

'There exist more extreme forms of my condition. I can use language. I can read photographs and even some pictures. I know that –' he pointed to her burrito – 'this food is called a burrito and that both this food –' he pointed to his – 'and that food –' he pointed back to hers – 'is the same food, called burrito. Olga Thurmer, twelve, in Oslo, has severe apsychosis. She cannot – Dr Albert says this is a joke – "see the wood for the trees"? She went to a wood. The wood was not "tree and tree and tree and tree and tree and tree and tree": she gave all the trees proper names. She could not see what they had in common.

'James Hart, seventy-two, in Brisbane, Australia, has severe apsychosis. He has never spoken. Nelson Kogbara, thirty-four, in northern Nigeria, has severe apsychosis. He cannot perceive the borders of objects. When objects move in space he does not recognise them. Ava Howard, twelve, and her identical twin sister Ana, from Bushey in the United Kingdom, have severe apsychosis. They cannot tell themselves apart. Han Fa, ninety-nine, from –'

'OK,' said Bree. 'OK. Stop. So you can talk.'

'It means I can't think about anything that doesn't exist. I can't –' he seemed to reach for a phrase that did not come naturally – 'see things coming. I don't desire things in the future.'

'You seem to like cigarettes,' said Bree, who was already starting to wonder about the wisdom of letting Jones drive the car.

'That's a chemical craving. That's habit. I don't make mental pictures about cigarettes. It's hard to explain. I don't fear things in the future.'

'Apparently not,' said Bree. 'Do you know what those cigarettes are doing to your lungs?'

'Yes,' said Jones, and didn't say anything else.

'Ain't hearda your Mr Smart,' the guy in the hat said in the umpteenth motel Sherman and Davidoff tried. Best Western, Motel 6, Holiday Inn, Marriott, Days and Crown Plaza had, as Davidoff had predicted, come up blank. Now they were onto the small places, the ones without computerised directories you could get into; and, probably, the ones that might waive the need to show a passport or a driving licence.

These were the sorts of places he'd be staying. The chances, mind, that if he was bothering to stay in this sort of place he'd be doing so under his own name, were slimmer. But they'd nothing else to do, and Sherman had insisted on at least trying so that they could say they had tried. It beat listening to Neil Young over and over again, and as long as he hadn't been through the airport he was not likely to have got far from Atlanta. A picture of him might have been helpful, though.

The old man was running a thumb down a paper register on an old clipboard. 'You can leave a message. Maybe he shows up,' he said, evidently moved to compassion by Sherman's affecting story. 'I'd sure hate for him to miss his momma's funeral.'

They had briefly entertained the idea of leaving a message at the first place that had offered them the option. But it seemed more likely to do harm than good. If he was deliberately moving about, he'd be unlikely to return to somewhere he'd been. And if he'd been there, or was there, under a false name, he wouldn't like finding a message under his real name. And if he hadn't been there he'd like finding a message for him even less. Whichever way you looked at it, he seemed unlikely to call an unknown number and arrange to meet even a kindly-sounding stranger in a non-public place in order to be robbed.

But Davidoff – who was lazy and irritable – wasn't giving up. They stepped a little bit away from the clerk's window.

'How about: you've won the lottery, call this number?' the bigger man suggested, pulling the sweaty patch on the front of his T-shirt away from his skin.

'Davidoff, of all the bad ideas you've had in your long career of having bad ideas, that is the most idiotic.'

'Seriously,' he said. 'I'd call the number if I got that message.'

Sherman had let that hang in the air as its own reproach.

Davidoff thought for a bit longer. Then he said: 'No ticket.'

'No ticket,' said Sherman. 'No ticket. No American citizenship. No reason for the Georgia state lottery ever to have heard of him. Mind you, he does have a machine that wins lotteries.'

'No way,' said Davidoff.

'Don't pretend not to remember,' Sherman said. 'You were there when we were briefed. Didn't Ellis say that in the early days, when they'd sent two experienced people after this thing, both of them won the lottery within a week of each other and instantly quit the company? Real problem. They thought it was the machine doing it.'

68

Davidoff turned his palms upwards and smiled at the memory. 'Yeah. That's why winning the lottery was on my mind,' he admitted. Then, looking at his feet: 'I spent two hundred pounds on tickets.'

Sherman wasn't going to share with his partner that the same idea had occurred to him, at least briefly, before being dismissed. I mean, what if this thing really was that powerful? He'd conceived the suspicion that Ellis somehow wanted them to believe the story about the lottery winners, or at least know it. But if this magic device really did keep evading pursuit by making its pursuers so rich they gave up the chase, he didn't imagine that Ellis would have assigned them to the task of hunting it down with quite such obvious relish.

No. Ellis had probably not been telling them the whole truth. It seemed far more likely, he reflected, that this probability machine had decided to change tack and start putting its pursuers off by, for instance, having them be hit by a meteorite, eat a Snickers bar infested with MRSA, or suffer a plague of agonising boils. It might bend the very laws of probability around it . . . but that was no reason to think it would necessarily be nice. If you could choose carrot or stick, you'd choose stick, wouldn't you? Every time.

As he went over these speculations in his head, it occurred to Sherman that he'd started thinking oddly. He had used the word 'decided' of a piece of inanimate technology. He'd cast himself as its 'enemy', come to that. He'd started to think of this machine itself almost as a person: as if it, rather than the guy carrying it, was the one making the decisions. He had started to acquire the paranoid impression that this fugitive piece of property might not *want* to be recovered.

'Two hundred pounds?' he said. 'You muppet. Did you win?'

'Three numbers. A tenner.'

'Unlucky.'

'Yes. No note then?'

'No note, lad. Now. Have we gone through all the motels?'

Davidoff looked at the page they'd torn from the phone directory.

'Yup.'

Something nagged at Sherman. 'Davidoff?'

'Yup.'

'Did we try our own motel?'

Davidoff let his jaw hang open for a moment while he considered the proposition.

'No,' he said at length. 'We didn't.'

'Well, shall we go back and have a look, then?'

It took them thirty-five minutes to drive back to the Hazy Rest Motor Inn through rush-hour traffic.

The adenoidal kid in the faded Skynyrd T-shirt was back manning the office. Sherman noticed that the boy had painted his fingernails black. They offered, by now with more briskness than conviction, their line about why they were trying to find out whether there was an Alex Smart in the motel.

'Aren't you the guys in room 9?'

'Yes,' Sherman said.

'Here y'go. Yeah. Yeah. He was here. English dude, yeah? I thought you were like together or something. Two doors down in room 7.'

He shuffled the register round so Sherman could read it.

Alex Smart. Checked out late that morning. They'd probably passed each other on the balcony.

They thanked the clerk and went back to the car where Davidoff had parked it across two spaces at an angle. They sat back down and Sherman thought for a while.

'What are the chances of that happening?' Davidoff asked. He put his sunglasses on and looked out of the window. Sherman thought he was probably admiring himself in the reflection. Something occurred to Sherman.

'Car hire companies,' he said.

'Can't we check them online?' Davidoff grunted. 'And get some lunch while we're at it?'

'No,' said Sherman. 'Most of them are at the airport. He's only got a few hours on us at the moment, but by the time we finish buggering about on the Internet he'll be long gone and they'll all be shut. Let's go.'

Davidoff sighed, turned the key, and wheeled round the car park just over-fast enough, and stopped at the junction with the highway just over-abruptly enough, to signal his exasperation.

They made good time. Twenty minutes later the two men were at the Hertz office in a Portakabin in the airport rental car park. They joined the queue behind a tall kid wearing a rucksack, Davidoff tapping his feet impatiently, Sherman looking about him, sucking his teeth, wondering the best line to spin the clerk . . . Conversational was what was needed, he thought. A bit of finesse. Use the English accent. Something about a stag party that got separated . . . phone not working in America . . . groom in danger of not making it to the church on time. That might – well, that or something like . . .

'Smart,' said an English voice, and Sherman's awareness returned to the room. 'S-M-A-R-T. Yes. As in clever.'

Well, I'll be, Sherman thought. The boy in front of him in the queue pushed a British passport and driving licence across the counter. The woman smiled indulgently but professionally. Sherman risked a slight craning of the neck. Yes. Come to think of it, he did look vaguely familiar from the motel.

Davidoff wasn't paying any attention. Sherman gently put finger and thumb around the bones of his elbow and dug the tips in harder than was necessary.

Davidoff hissed something and his head whipped round. He looked at Sherman crossly. The kid in front didn't notice. Sherman made his face tense and looked at the boy's back. Davidoff cottoned on. He blinked and frowned.

'All right, Mr Smart, you need to sign here –' she circled something quickly with her biro – 'and here and here –' a couple of dashed crosses. The boy cocked his head, started scribbling.

'Here are your keys. The car's a silver Pontiac, mid-size. It's in space number 137, row 8. Remember to return it full.'

'Thanks.' The boy shouldered his rucksack and walked out of the building.

'Next,' she said, turning her empty smile on the two men waiting in the line. They looked at each other, then one of them mumbled about having forgotten something and they walked out of the office and round to the right, where young Mr Clever had gone. She looked at her nails and wondered what Chef Boyardee was going to prepare for her dinner tonight.

Outside, Sherman and Davidoff walked among the rows of cars keeping the kid in sight. They pretended to be looking for a car of their own – though Davidoff's nervousness meant that he had to be prevented from hard-targeting behind the nearest SUV whenever the boy glanced round. As soon as they'd made the boy's car and noted down the number plate, they returned to their own, parked up outside the fence within sight of the exit. Davidoff turned the engine on and let it idle.

He'd be nervous driving a new car. They had no way to know whether or not he'd driven in America before, but it was a safe bet he'd take a bit of time to familiarise himself with the controls. Sure enough, it was getting on for five minutes before the silver Pontiac rolled out of the car park and turned, hesitatingly, onto the road and rolled west.

The two men gave him six car-lengths or so of a start, and then pulled out behind him and began to follow.

He joined the 285 heading north towards the west side of the city. Davidoff was driving. Sherman opened the glove compartment and pulled out the little map of the area that they'd given him at the hire car place. Their own car, too, was a rental and they hadn't thought to buy an atlas. Sherman thought that if the kid headed out of town that was a decision they might regret.

The silver Pontiac pulled out ahead of them and was momentarily obscured by a white eighteen-wheeler. It had 'Xpress Global Systems' written on the side in blue block capitals, and underneath, in smaller letters: 'A division of MIC Industrial Futures'.

'Fancy that,' Sherman said whimsically. 'On our team.'

'What?'

'The truck.'

'Uh?'

Davidoff squinted.

'This haulage company or whatever it is. Works for the same people we do. We should flash our lights.'

Davidoff grunted again, plainly having not the faintest idea what Sherman was talking about. He pushed the pedal down and came up behind the truck, glanced in his wing mirror and pulled out round it. A corner of the silver car became visible again, back in the slow lane, a few cars ahead. As they got closer, though, Sherman frowned.

As their angle on the front of the truck narrowed, a second silver Pontiac came into view, on the tail of the other. At this range it was hard to make out the number plates. One of them was their boy, but the other one . . .

'Better get a bit closer. There's another silver bloody car up there. We don't want to lose –'

There was a bang.

Davidoff abruptly pumped the brake and Sherman was thrown forward. Something flew up from the road, very fast, and smacked the top half of the windscreen before bouncing up off and behind them. Sherman, startled, looked round and looked behind. Something black disappearing under the wheels of the car following.

'What was –?'

Davidoff, frowning a little but with the car under control. Up ahead Sherman could see the front tyre of the eighteen-wheeler

73

flapping in rags. The driver was slowing down, trying to get a slight fishtail under control. Davidoff let the car fall back, then powered forward past it. They'd lost a couple of hundred metres on the Pontiacs.

'Blowout,' he said. 'Step on it. We're losing them.'

Ahead, there was a cloverleaf junction and the traffic was slowing down as a column of cars joined the freeway from the right. The two Pontiacs, further on, went under the shadow of an overpass. A car joining the freeway shot across their bows without signalling. Davidoff muttered something and braked again.

It was a silver Pontiac. It lurched out wide into the left-hand lane, accelerated round an SUV, waggled back into the middle lane and shot off up under the overpass.

'It's – hang on . . .' Sherman could see, through the traffic ahead, the other two silver Pontiacs. The third caught them up. 'We've got to catch up with the –'

'I can see,' said Davidoff in a voice at once distracted and alive with irritation. 'I'm trying but these – SHIT!'

The people in this place were maniacs. They were carved up again, this time someone swinging in from behind, then undertaking and cutting back in front of them, before going wide and, with a honk of horns, screeching round that SUV.

Another – oh, for crying out loud.

As Davidoff concentrated on trying not to be crashed into, Sherman scanned the road ahead. He could now see four identical silver Pontiacs. At least four. One of them – one of them was taking the exit. It was marked Arthur Langford Parkway East. He couldn't make out the licence plate.

'Davidoff – he's leaving. He's taking the exit.' Davidoff wrenched the wheel. They were in the slip road. Just as they were about to be committed, Sherman had second thoughts.

'No! It's the other one! Don't take the exit! Stay on the road.'

Davidoff swore again, wrenched the wheel back and they crossed the stripy lines back onto the main road, narrowly missing the sand-filled oil drums protecting the junction. A dirty white Toyota behind them roared up the exit, missing their rear bumper by a smaller distance than Sherman was comfortable with, its horn emitting a wail of outrage.

He could see three Pontiacs several car-lengths ahead. Davidoff was making valiant efforts to catch up with them, weaving freely in and out of all four lanes of traffic. To their right, Sherman became aware of another line of traffic sloping down a ramp and waiting to join the freeway – the westbound traffic from the road they'd just passed under. Rush hour was approaching and these would be the first people making their way out from the centre of town into the western suburbs. The Pontiacs, where he could make them out, glimpsing the tops of their roofs, were just past where the traffic merged.

The traffic had slowed to twenty or thirty miles an hour. The sun winked off an angle of one of the cars waiting to join the freeway and Sherman glanced sideways. Just ahead and to the right of them, spilling into the traffic ahead, were three more silver Pontiacs, tailing a wood-panelled station wagon, which was itself tailgating another silver Pontiac.

Sherman had lost count. Seven, was it? Maybe eight. A rise in the road a little later on allowed him to see them all at once, spread out across four lanes and a couple of hundred metres of the road ahead.

Sherman had by this stage formed a hunch. The boy was leaving town, and he was most likely to head west. West was where the aeroplane thing had happened. West was where he was supposed to be flying, or had at least bought a ticket to. West was the best bet. Two Pontiacs whose numbers were impossible to see took off along the eastbound exit.

The main pack of Pontiacs carried on. Sherman leaned forward in his seat, his jaw working. The exit for the westbound carriage-way of the interstate came off the left, the fast lane. One of the silver cars, its indicator winking for a good forty seconds before it made its way into the faster traffic, pulled out. The indicator stayed on. It was travelling slightly too slowly – as if its driver wasn't confident about what he was doing.

He had slowed enough to give a glimpse of the first two digits of the number plate . . . B4 . . . 84 . . . B4? Was it?

'Got you,' said Sherman. 'Follow that one.'

Davidoff swung out across two lanes of traffic and entered the slip road only three cars behind the target. None of those cars was silver. 'Hope you're sure about this,' he said.

'I'm sure,' said Sherman. The slip road rose in a gentle left-hand curve from ground level up and over the southbound carriageway of the 285 before cresting and then sloping down to join the fat interstate heading west. The silver car disappeared round the curve ahead of them, and as they coasted over the top of the rise and faced down, they were momentarily dazzled by the sun.

The silver car must have already joined the main road. Cars were shuffling between lanes just off the slipway. The I-20 ribboned off towards the horizon, and as far as Sherman and Davidoff could see – three lanes of faded blacktop – the roofs of cars reflected the sun's coppery light like the scales of a snake. It was beautiful, all those cars crawling westwards together.

Every car for as far as the eye could make out was silver. Every one – Sherman knew at that moment in his guts – was a Pontiac.

'Let's go back to the motel,' he said. 'We may have to think again.'

Davidoff steered them off at the next exit and they looped back round towards Atlanta, Sherman dialling Ellis's number, letting his thumb hover over the green button to call, and then thinking better of it.

8

There did seem to be an awful lot of silver cars on the road, Alex thought as he drove out of the city. Odd. Perhaps there was a factory nearby.

Then he was back into his thoughts. Those thoughts. They seemed less pernicious, less circular, less – if he was honest about it – *thinky* than the thoughts he had been having beforehand. Always nearer by not keeping still. Now he was moving and his thoughts were calm to the point of being almost contentless.

He was even able to avoid thinking about some of the things he usually found himself thinking about. He had decided not to think about the effect on his credit card of hiring a car for two weeks, and lo and behold, here he was, not thinking about it. He had decided not to think about the likelihood that he'd fail to finish his PhD, lose his funding and have to move back in with his mum, and lo and behold, here he was not thinking about it. He had decided not to – well, he was really not thinking about that. He ran through a whole list of the things he wasn't think-ing about – some more quickly than others, and none of them bit him.

'I might take up not thinking for good,' he said aloud to himself – something he realised he had started to do over the last couple of days. Not thinking was working splendidly. He knew from the atlas on the passenger seat that he was headed for the west, and that it would take him a few days to get there. All he knew was that the next big town was Birmingham. That was fine.

He weaved past another of those silver cars. They seemed to be thinning out. This was much better, he decided, than driving in the UK. Once you got the hang of driving on the right, obviously. No roundabouts. No changing gear. As a teenager, Alex had driven into the back of a stationary Volvo as a consequence of a misunderstanding that had involved both roundabouts and changing gear.

Now, here, this was very satisfactory. No roundabouts, no gearstick – no corners, practically. The highway was dead straight, and cool air from the air con blew onto his arms.

The car had a docking station for his iPod. Letting his eyes leave the road in brief guilty bursts, he put on the Talking Heads. 'Things fall apart,' David Byrne announced to the car. 'It's scientific!'

Alex sang along with 'Road to Nowhere', and then 'Psycho Killer', and just as his own jollity started to sound forced to him, 'Once in a Lifetime' came on and his mood turned.

It was a song about a man waking up to find himself in and out of time. . . . Then a rushing chorus, something about water rushing over and under and everywhere. Was it a song about drowning? If so, it was a very exultant one. Alex felt uplifted and estranged. Nobody was with him. He realised he didn't know, again, whether he was happy or sad. The music decided for him.

When he'd been a child, sitting in the back of the car, the music on the radio had been the soundtrack to his life. He'd watched fence posts, pylons, stanchions tick past – slowly up ahead, then too fast to see when you looked at them right at the side of the car, then slowlier behind. He had sat, entirely absorbed in himself – or, rather, himself entirely absorbed in what was around him. Watching the English countryside roll by. On the long journeys from Cambridge down to their Cornish holidays in summer: red clay churned in fields to each side. This was where his mother was from. Eurythmics. His father taking him to boarding school. Springsteen. Coming back late at night, sleepy, from the airport when they'd taken their first holiday to Corsica. He must have been ten, then. Tom Waits singing about an 'old '55'.

Alex started experimenting with the cruise control button. If you pressed it, the car kept to its speed. You could put your feet on the floor – even dare yourself, just momentarily, to take your hands off the wheel until the car, very gently, started to slide towards the lane markers at the edge of the road and you grabbed the wheel again, just between finger and thumb.

He remembered hearing about 'cruise control' as a child, and imagining it at first to be something they had in America where the car drives itself. Someone later had told him a story of how someone had put on cruise control on a long desert highway and fallen asleep. A very slight bias on the steering – no more than a fraction of a degree – had caused the car to wander off the road and out into the flat scrub desert. The man had woken up maybe half an hour after the the car had coughed its last of petrol and rolled to a halt. There had been no sign of a road or a river or another human being in any direction: just level low scrub, and dry dirt, and behind his car a long and imperceptibly curved pair of tyre tracks in the dust, slowly being erased by the evening wind. Nobody had come to get him. He had died there.

This story had stayed with Alex. What looks like a straight line turns out to be a curve. A tiny fraction of error could scale; a trivial multiplier could propagate into a cascade. A fragment of a degree in the angle of approach was the difference between a stable orbit and slingshotting into deep space; a fraction of a second's lag in a clock could make a GPS system put an aeroplane into a mountain. The curvature of a miniscus could scatter light, or focus it to a point.

When Alex had been travelling in his gap year, he'd gone to Tibet. He'd left Lhasa on a local bus bound across the Himalayas for Kathmandu, him and his big brother – then on his summer holidays from university. It had taken a couple of days, rattling over the passes where the air was thin and the sky was blue-white. The high points in the passes were marked with cairns of stones, and bleached prayer flags, muddy snow in pockets of the ground.

When they stopped to get out at one place to take photographs, Alex remembered thinking how you could plot lines radiating out from his position there by the bus. At any moment, to move along one of those lines in one of those directions would be to die. He was entirely safe in the bus – but walk thirty feet to the left and you'd tumble down a steep bank of scree. Set off to the right, let the bus leave you behind, you'd be dead of exposure in forty-eight hours, maybe.

You could do that at any time, anywhere. You were almost never more than a strange decision or an accident, or a movement of a few feet, from extinction. Alex had started to imagine himself as the centre of a spiderweb of lines, constantly adjusting, on the map. At the end of each one a black X. As you walked beside a busy road, on the road side of you the lines would be compressed to no more than a couple of metres – to the other side they'd extend hundreds of metres, maybe. Stand on the edge of a cliff and the lines would fan out from your feet all along the clifftop – and the same would be true of every other human being. Everyone would carry their own invisible, unmonitored, 360-degree asterisk of harm.

If you credited the alternative universe idea, in every one of those universes there would be a you who had taken a different one of those decisions, suffered a different one of those accidents. There were versions of you who would have jumped or stumbled across every micrometre of that cliff face. And every moment spawned a new position of you in the world, a new 360-degree signpost to catastrophe, a new sheaf of alternative yous in alternative worlds around each of whom radiated another set of fresh positions, divergences, threats.

That idea had struck Alex most vividly when he was eighteen, but it had stayed with him. He became aware of it re-entering his thoughts: not threatening, but a source of wonderment. At any moment at all he was one sharp twist of the steering wheel away from the universe not existing. How on earth, with all that risk, had it survived so long?

A game he started to play with himself was to see how long he could keep cruise control on. He fixed it for the speed limit, and everyone was overtaking him. He dabbed the brake to override it, then tried to keep a steady distance behind the car in front and thumbed the button.

Over a few minutes, he found, his car was up towards the back bumper of the car in front. The trick then was to signal and move out without touching either brake or accelerator. You had to be lucky – if a big truck was passing you at the wrong time and you were boxed in, you'd have to brake . . . but you could cut it pretty fine.

It was absorbing. As the sun got lower and redder, and the mile markers told him Atlanta was further and further behind him, he felt settled again.

He'd never done anything like this before. He felt in and out of himself, lost and in charge. Nobody now knew where he was. Not his mum, not anybody. He was starring in a film that nobody was watching. He was unobserved.

It reminded him of his friend Rob's joke when they'd been undergraduates together.

'Erwin Schrödinger's bombing down the M4 in his Porsche.' He remembered Rob saying this, and just how he'd said it – Rob in his horrible velvet jacket and his black corduroy trousers, lolling on Alex's green beanbag. Rob's voice cracked and dry from weed.

'You've got it wrong, Rob. It's not Schrödinger.'

Rob, pink-eyed, thinking.

'No. Crap. Heisenberg, right. Sorry. Heisenberg is bombing along the road . . .'

Now Alex laughing very hard, helium-pitched giggles. Carey, then, who they were both trying to impress, simply looked perplexed, smiling her oval smile. The joke – Heisenberg is pulled over by the police, and when asked if he knew how fast he had been going retorts: 'No, but I can tell you exactly where I am' – had taken Rob hours to tell, and even longer to explain afterwards.

'It's – you know about Heisenberg's Uncertainty Principle, right?'

'I heard of it,' she said. Carey was doing English and American Studies on a two-year exchange scheme. She was a year older than either of them. Her hair was brown and curly, and she was better at smoking weed and holding it together than either of her suitors. She'd done it all through high school.

As Rob had lumbered through the contrived explanation of the contrived joke, she had smiled at Alex with a studied bashfulness he thought might, just, be coquettish. Then Rob, still on the edge of hysteria, had moved onto a joke whose punchline was 'Zorn's Lemon' – he remembered that, and Carey, not understanding the joke at all and finding it even funnier because of that, burst with laughter. She fell back on the scratchy old carpet and lay there with her knees up and her chest shaking with laughter. Her mouth was pink and her teeth were very white, and she snorted a little when she breathed in. Alex could have died with love, then, just looking at her.

Three days later, to Alex's astonishment, she kissed him after the college dance. He was drinking vodka and lemonade out of a plastic cup, and the room was very dark and very, very noisy. The lights were maybe ten minutes away from coming up. In the middle of the low-ceilinged common room drunken undergraduates were staggering and stamping in a big hairy many-legged alcohol-smelling tangle. Alex was looking into the middle of it, a little glassily, when Carey appeared beside him. She had taken the plastic cup out of his hand and put it on the floor, and then she leaned in decisively and kissed him on the mouth.

That had been — nice. And afterwards they had staggered out of the room like a three-legged race and into the midnight air smelling of grass from the lawns. Without the darkness and the thumping noise, Alex had felt drunkenness wearing off and self-consciousness intruding. But then, quite briskly, she had taken him to her girl-smelling single bed in her room across the quad and had taken charge of getting the sex out of the way, as if her soft belly and miraculous breasts and unexpected tattoo had been no more to her than the facts of her own body.

Then she'd gone to sleep on her back, snoring very softly, and Alex had lain awake not minding that her neck was cutting off the circulation to his arm. Her breath smelled slightly sweet from Coca-Cola and slightly alcoholic from rum. The duvet was askew, and one of her breasts was exposed, spilling down towards her armpit, where he could see a patch of sore skin and a bit of stubble. She had a mole on the soft skin just where her neck met the hinge of her jaw.

On Sunday morning, when he woke up, Alex had shyly and, as he thought, politely made an excuse about having to be in the library, kissed her awkwardly and said something non-committal and gone.

That was how their relationship had started. When Carey arrived in the college she was sexually confident, easily flirtatious, at home in her skin. Now, having quietly worshipped Carey for months, domesticating the relationship by making a friend of her, he'd actually gone to bed with her.

But the relationship between Carey and Alex had not, as he had expected, fizzled out in embarrassment and apology. At the cost of a certain showy huffiness from Rob, who felt excluded and maybe liked Carey more than he had let on, they had gone from friendship to established coupledom almost without passing through the in-between stage of tugging and scrabbling and kissing in public.

They were at ease, and that seemed to suit them both well enough. Alex found passion, or the expectation of passion, unsettling. Why make something private so public? And the courtship thing – he knew he had to do it but the self-exposure it involved and the risk and the game-playing and the humiliation . . . If you liked someone and you fancied them, why did you have to go through all that?

Carey had taken that out of his hands. They knew each other. Alex knew that she liked peanut butter on the cheapest white bread she could find, that they had the same Veruca Salt album, that she got on well enough with her foster-father, argued with her foster-mother, had no sisters and was liked better by boys than she was by girls. He put this down to jealousy; she was pretty, and neither worked it nor apologised for it. It was a fact about her.

Alex didn't know what attracted her to him, though. Men fancied Carey; women did not fancy Alex. Alex's place, ordinarily, was as the nerdy but unthreatening best friend of girls whom he chastely worshipped but who didn't think of him that way. Carey, on the other hand, had befriended Alex – and yet she also wanted to sleep with him. She did think of him that way. It was almost unprecedented, this state of affairs, and he intended to reward her with his loyalty. But it made him understand her less.

He wondered for a long time whether she was attracted to him by something she imagined he had that he didn't; or whether later, that illusion having vanished, the relationship was sustained by her affection for something else about him, such as his family, with the dull and affectionate stability that hers lacked; or whether there was something lacking in her – a simple failure of nerve or imagination that led her to idle in his shallows when with her looks and confidence she could have been with anyone else she wanted.

He studied his face in the mirror, sometimes, wondering what she saw there, and not liking what he did. Alex, when he looked at himself, saw a weak chin and watery features. He had eyes that flinched away from the camera. In the family photograph, blown up big and behind glass on the half landing of the old house, the two brothers stood in front of their parents: Saul already as tall as their mother, wearing his four-square smile; Alex's head minutely blurred with motion, eyes down and to one side, hooding his lids. The old wallpaper from that same room in the background, gold striping the green.

But it went on, nevertheless. Alex never asked Carey whether he had been a factor in her choosing to do her postgraduate work in Cambridge. And – at her request – they still hadn't moved in together. She said she was 'funny about sharing space'. But the fact that he loved her, after they had been going out for three years, was something he took for granted. It was another fact about her, like her beauty and the fact that he didn't understand her.

She wasn't delving, introspective, exhausting in that way some girls he'd known had been – even though, as he knew, she'd had it tougher than most of the thoroughgoing neurotics he'd been out with previously. She didn't talk endlessly about her emotions, or expect him to. Good.

Alex, there and here, had made some miles without even thinking about it. He'd noticed the state line going past about an hour back. The afternoon was mellowing, and he was in Alabama. He turned off the air con, wound down the window. Warm air came in, the smell of gasoline. He thought of singing Lynyrd Skynyrd to himself but the urge to sing had left him.

What Alex didn't know, as he was moving west, was that things were happening all around him.

Ahead of him, in Birmingham, a man stopped dead on the steps of the 16th Street Baptist church, in slanting sunlight, startled by the sound of birdsong. He shook his head. In the chattering of half a dozen birds on a telephone wire he could have sworn he had heard the first few bars of 'Amazing Grace'.

In the time it took Alex to pass through the Talladega National Forest, every shop in the state of Alabama sold out of Chicken & Broccoli Flavor Rice-A-Roni. In one shop in Gadsden, a fight broke out over the last packet on the shelf. A pregnant woman, overcome by her craving, pulled a gun on the teenage boy who had beaten her to it. She did not shoot.

In two small towns, equidistant to north and south of the I-40, the highway down which Alex was travelling, two men fell back in love with their wives for the first time in forty years. The names of both men were 'Herb', and both of them had woken up that morning and rubbed their stubble sleepily while looking in the mirror and thought about shaving but decided not to bother. One of them was to live happily ever after. The other one was to fall down a well on his next birthday.

All over the state, brothers and sisters bumped into each other by chance as one was leaving the dry-cleaner's, and the other was running in to try to pick up her laundry.

In Las Vegas, still many miles away, the odds tilted for the first time very slightly against the house in low-stakes blackjack. Red Queen would be told about this in due course – as soon as it became detectable.

Unknown to anyone but you, in the Gulf of Mexico a sailfish of prodigious size, aided by a freakish current off the coast, spent thirty minutes keeping pace exactly with Alex's car. Then a shark took it.

Other things were happening. Things unknown to you, but known to me.

And other things, I suspect, were happening that are unknown even to me.

9

You need to know, though, what happened when Isla Holderness met Banacharski. That's where this begins. It begins with a woman with short, dark blonde hair, and a handsome pointed nose, and windburned cheeks, walking up a cart track in the French Pyrenees. This is May 1998, and the hills are very beautiful. Buttercups nod in the cold wind.

Isla is carrying an old-fashioned backpack – it belonged to her father, and has a frame made of hollow aluminium poles. She has on thick hiking socks, made of grey wool, and jeans tucked into them. She is tired. She has been walking and – where possible – hitchhiking around this area for nearly two weeks now. In her pocket is a passport-sized photograph snipped from an academic journal. It has been creased and recreased.

It shows a thin man frowning with an expression of, she judges, concentration or toleration of having concentration broken. His hair is dark, and very close-cropped, nearly a skinhead – a reaction, perhaps, to a hairline already prematurely receded. It suits him. His cheekbones are sharp and he looks handsome. He's looking not at the camera, but downwards and slightly to one side. Something like amusement plays around his mouth. The photograph is ten years old.

She is excited, because she thinks she may have found him. She started from Carcassonne, and she has been walking from town to town, going deeper into the countryside. She told her colleagues, most of them at least, that she was going on a walking holiday. Nobody mentioned Banacharski, except Mike – Mike, she thought, liked her – who when he heard she was going to the eastern Pyrenees said: 'Off for a tryst with your boyfriend, I shouldn't wonder.'

She is on a walking holiday. She's thirty-two years old and she's happy. She has been camping most nights, not more than one night in three treating herself to an inn. It's warm in the days, but most mornings she wakes in her tent with dew on her feet. She hasn't got much money. She eats chunks of *saucisson sec* with a penknife, and tears bits of bread to go with it. She has, in a compartment of her backpack, a jar of cassoulet and a tin of pineapple pieces for an emergency.

But when she passes through each village, she shows the photograph. She enjoys doing what a tourist would do – sitting in the village square, if there is one; eating her lunch quietly. She asks, with her halting French. At first it was hard. Now easy.

'*Cet homme – un ami . . . vous savez ou il est?*' She'd show the photograph. Cheeks would be rubbed, grunts emitted, more grizzled friends summoned over sometimes.

'*Il s'appelle Nicolas. Nicolas Banacharski. Il est un . . . il fait le mathematique . . .*' Here, she'd find herself feebly miming something halfway between a scribble on an imaginary table and a scribble on an imaginary blackboard. Her mime for mathematics was no more necessary, nor more plausible, than her mime for telephoning, or typing – the former consisting of an imaginary Bakelite earpiece and the latter of a peculiar ragtime piano solo played at the level of her clavicles with her eyebrows around her hairline.

Still, all this seems to endear her to the gruff old Frenchmen. Most of them seem to have heard some stories of a crazy mathematician. She has been following, generally, whichever wave of an arm her last informant offered. She's tried to pick market towns when there were markets. But she isn't hunting. Her idea is simply to have a holiday – to give it shape by hoping she'd stumble across the great man, but that isn't the point of it, not at all.

Then, yesterday, she was buying her lunch in a *boulangerie* in Nalzen and waiting for the orange-haired old chimp to ring up her sandwich. She was wondering how long that display of Chupa Chups lollipops had been there, when she looked out of the window over a display of baroquely iced cakes and exquisitely lacquered strawberry tarts.

It was him. To the life. He was going past on a bicycle, lolling, with one hand on the handlebars and the bicycle describing lazy, open sweeps back and forth across the empty street.

The woman squawked as Isla barged out of the shop to give chase. She left her backpack in the shop, yanked open the door and hop-skipped after him in her ridiculous socks.

'*M'sieu! M'sieu!*'

Half of her had imagined that if she ever met him he'd run or yell at her. She wasn't quite prepared for him simply to stop. He braked, and turned round. He looked startled, but not yet annoyed.

'*Pardon . . . pardon . . .*'

'*Quoi?*'

'*Nicolas?*'

'*Quoi?*'

'*Je suis Isla.*'

His look was shifting from startled and sympathetic, to alarmed.

'Isla Holderness – *nous avons . . .*' She remembered he spoke English. They'd exchanged letters in English. 'It's me, Isla. We've – I mean, I've sent you letters. I'm Isla Holderness.'

'*Mam'selle . . .*'

The man on the bicycle was kindly. He stayed put for her stammering explanation, and was gentle in telling her that the words 'Isla Holderness' meant nothing to him in any order at all, and that he was certain they had never exchanged letters. He was a handyman, not a scholar – he had used the word 'scholar', clumsily, when she'd said 'mathematician'. He laughed when she showed him the photograph, though. He had to admit, it looked like him. No, no apology necessary. *Au contraire.* His name was Pascal. *Enchanté.*

But a mathematician? Lived alone? Pascal thought he might know him. Yes, bald. Not looking like this, though. He was an eccentric, sure enough – Pascal didn't remember his name but it might have been Nicolas. He looked at the photograph, blotting out the lower half of the face with his thumb and looking at the eyes. Isla could see they were different, now, Pascal and Banacharski, about the eyes.

They were still standing in the street. It was a small town and no cars had come. Pascal rolled his bicycle back and forth with his hips, turned the handlebars lazily with his free hand. He seemed to be smirking.

'*Peut-être.*' It was an old photograph. He couldn't tell. But there was this *type* living in a shack up above Tragine. Pascal had gone to fix his septic tank. Had a lot of paper. He was – Pascal made a waving gesture with his hand . . . Big beard, Pascal said. Like a *blaireau.* People talked about him. Jewish, he thought. Maybe an inventor?

He left her after a few minutes, scribbling his phone number, as an act of gallantry, with a blunt stub of pencil on a bit of cardboard torn from a packet of cigarette papers. She folded this once and tucked it into the coin pocket of her jeans. They had made friends, though as she watched him cycle away she noticed that the bicycle was wagging less than previously and his head was wagging more.

She went back into the *boulangerie* and endured a foul look. The baguette, which she ate sitting on a low wall in the sunshine, was delicious. She spent the night in a field outside Freychenet, more excited than she was prepared to acknowledge to herself.

Now Isla is walking up, leaving the last outbuildings of the farm she passed behind her. The cart track is dry, and the sun has baked worm-curls of mud on it. Her new walking boots bash satisfyingly and painlessly off them. As a contour slopes round she glimpses the roof of a wooden cabin. The quarter-acre of land in front of it has been raked out flat and hoed, and there are lines of bamboo poles with brilliant green-yellow bean shoots curling around them. Chickens scratch in the dirt.

She doesn't think that Banacharski knows she is coming to look for him. She underestimates how small these towns are, and how close together. Banacharski knows she's coming.

He didn't know, at first, whether he wanted to be found. But now he sees her starting up the path towards him, smiling, and he thinks that he has been too lonely for too long.

'So, Jones,' said Bree. 'This thing. This thing you have.'

It had been bugging Bree all afternoon, and she had been bugging Jones with it. It wasn't something Bree could quite make sense of. And – she being a naturally sceptical person – it wasn't something she completely believed, either. It was far from impossible that this was something Red Queen was doing just to mess her about. That Jones was a spy, or an actor, or some other damn thing. Indeed, that this whole thing might be some sort of fieldwork assessment exercise.

Jones didn't say anything.

They were in the car, and Jones was looking out of the wind-shield at the road. They were on the road west out of Atlanta heading for Birmingham. The sun was low in the sky ahead of them. They reckoned the kid was on the move, and that he was heading west.

Bree had asked how they knew that and Red Queen had said something about triangulation. They had tried the idea of using fluctuations in the ambient spread of probabilities to track the device. They conjectured that its effect on the world might leak out from it – little subtle ripples of unlikelihood, little freaks, unexpected variations from the mean could be discerned if you looked at large enough bodies of data. Their conjecture – unless what they were seeing was no more than the effects of chance itself – seemed to have been borne out.

They were monitoring regular big spreads: sports events, the patterns of roulette wheels and hands dealt in the major gambling centres of the North American mainland. Of course – and Bree would never have doubted it – they had access to those data in real time. Over the last several hours there had been spikes, outliers, runs of aces, improbable snake eyes, statistically signifi-cant fluctuations.

Red Queen didn't go into detail – just hints. Bree imagined low-level employees sitting in safe houses in all fifty states flip-ping quarters every ten seconds and noting down the results: 'Heads, tails, heads, heads, tails, heads, heads, heads, heads, coin landed on edge, heads, heads, heads . . .' Whatever was measur-able was measured.

Wispy though it was, all these variations, plotted together, seemed to signal some sort of gradient, something geographical, arranged around a moving focus. And the data was consistent with that focus heading westwards at approximately the speed of an automobile travelling down a highway. Crudely, as Red Queen explained it, the closer to this thing you got, the less likely it was that you'd roll a four one time in six. Dice were behaving themselves on the eastern seaboard, Red Queen said. Dice were becoming more unruly to the west.

That, then, was the weather report: that was the state of chance. Things were getting more unlikely in the south-western United States of America, with a front of downright implausible moving in from the east. Conditions in Atlanta and points east were calming, with nobody expected to beat the house for the foreseeable future.

★   ★   ★

'This thing,' Bree repeated. 'Does it make life fun?'

'I don't understand.' Jones said that to a lot of enquiries. Bree had learned to persevere. She stopped talking, and looked at the side of his face like he was a Sudoku.

'Knock knock,' said Bree.

Jones didn't say anything.

'I said: knock knock. You know about that, Jones. Don't pretend you don't. You grew up in some laboratory somewhere you never got told knock knock jokes?'

'I know knock knock jokes. I just don't know why they make you laugh.'

'So you know what you say?'

'I know.'

'So say it.'

'Who's there,' said Jones, but he said it without a question mark.

'Boo,' said Bree.

'I've heard that one,' said Jones.

'Say it for me, Jones,' said Bree with a wheedling intonation. If you'd been watching carefully you could have identified her coaxing manner as flirtatious, almost.

'Boo who.'

'Don't cry,' said Bree. 'It's only a joke.'

Jones continued to stare out of the windshield. Bree reached into the glove compartment and took out a Slim Jim and unwrapped it and began to chew. That hadn't been a success.

'Slim Jim, Jones?' she said.

'No thanks,' said Jones.

'OK,' said Bree, a mile or so later on. 'Not big on sense of humour. No GSOH, like they don't say in the lonely hearts listing. Jokes don't make you laugh.'

Jones didn't say anything.

'Jeezus, Jones. I'm trying to needle you here. Throw me a bone.'

Jones continued to look out of the windshield with bland attention to the road.

'OK. Needle means like . . . Bone means like . . . Means say something.'

'What would you like me to say?' said Jones.

'Make conversation.'

Jones left it a while. He seemed to be involved in some sort of mental effort. Bree could have sworn the hand with which he ordinarily smoked – the main hand with which he ordinarily smoked, given he seemed to be ambidextrous in this regard – twitched towards his pants pocket.

'Knock knock,' said Jones eventually.

'Who's there?' said Bree.

Jones didn't say anything for a bit.

'Who's there?' said Bree. 'Jones, you have to –'

'Mister,' said Jones.

'Mister who?' said Bree.

'Mister Jones,' said Jones. Bree laughed. Jones didn't.

'Hah, Jones,' said Bree. 'I like it. You were joking . . . Nice work . . .'

She cracked open another Slim Jim – they were minis – by way of celebration. Jones continued to stare benignly at the road, but she saw something around his eyes, in his frown, that looked a little haunted.

She waited a bit.

'You weren't joking,' she said. 'Were you?'

'No,' said Jones. 'I was trying.'

'You were funny. Sort of . . . inadvertently.' After the highway had gone by for a bit more, uneventfully, Bree continued. 'Knock knock jokes aren't really funny, anyway,' she said. 'They're more like corny. So it's funny when they're not funny?'

'I know that,' said Jones. 'I know other people find things funny. It's one of the concepts I find difficult to understand. Funny is what?'

'Do you not laugh, Jones?'

Jones thought quite hard about this; as did Bree, who was trying to remember if she'd heard him laugh since they'd met.

'No,' he said eventually, in a tone of voice that suggested that the question was an odd one.

'Not even if I tickle you?'

'No,' said Jones. 'I think that reflex is attached to anticipation. I don't have that. But I don't laugh. I know a lot of jokes. I remember every joke anyone tells me. I remember everything anyone tells me. I have an eidetic memory. It's one of the things that allows me to function. Someone tells someone else a lie and they laugh. I know that's how it works. But it doesn't work for me. If I know the joke, I know what's going to happen. If I don't know the joke, I often don't know it's a joke. It's just – nonsense. It confuses me.'

Bree remembered, suddenly, the way her own daughter had been when she was five or six. That was when they'd been living in Washington, again, in the long narrow apartment with the air-con unit in the window at the end of the hallway that made all that noise.

Bree remembered Cass saying two things, the two things connecting up. First was when she had overheard Bree talking to Al, when they were still talking, and Al had said something that had made Bree laugh. A joke, not one of his dirty ones. Bree had been a couple beers in, probably laughing harder than whatever Al had said deserved.

'What, Mommy? What?' Bree had repeated the joke, but Cass had just looked confused. Did that really happen? Why not? Why did you say it did?

That phase lasted months – a curiosity about jokes, matched with a total failure to understand them. They seemed to be everywhere. Suddenly her schoolmates were all telling these jokes and Cass would bring them home, wondering, almost to the point of tears.

Cass – prim with indignation, hands behind her back in the blue dress, toe of the red shoe pivoting on the linoleum. 'No, Mommy. That's not true. No. That's a lie.'

The problem was that Cass didn't understand the difference between a joke and a lie – and Bree, though she knew there was one, had not been able to explain it to her daughter. She had not, come to that, even been able to explain it to her own satisfaction.

Later, when Cass started to lie in earnest, the thing recurred from the other end. 'Did you do your homework?' 'Did you study for the test?' 'How was school?' These routine questions would be answered yes, and yes, and lovely thank you, Mommy. It was only when the teachers called to ask why Cass had failed the test, why she'd come to school without her homework, why she'd bitten another child so hard she'd drawn blood, and Bree confronted her, that she'd protest, 'I was joking! It was a joke!'

'Cassie, did you take Mommy's keys, honey?'

'No, Mommy, I promise. Daddy took them.'

And Cass would have a blazing row with Al. And then the keys would show up, in Hampton Bear's bear house in the corner of Cass's room.

'I was joking, Mommy! I was joking!' she would shriek as Bree, especially if it was late in the evening, smacked the backs of her legs red. Long time gone.

'What's the matter?' Jones said.

'Nothing,' said Bree. 'Bit of my Slim Jim went the wrong way.' She coughed and thumped her chest and wiped her eyes on her sleeve and went into the glove compartment and came out again.

'OK, Jones,' she said. 'Irish knock knock joke. You say knock knock.'

'Knock knock.'

'Who's there?'

'Mister.'

'No, it's –' she started. Jeepers he was hopeless. Then she realised he was, earnestly, trying. That made her feel . . .

'OK, Jones,' she said. 'Don't bother. Just drive.' Trying, she thought.

The light was going down ahead of them, spreading out over the sky. It was cloudy in that direction. They drove on through Birmingham without stopping, at Bree's suggestion, and got takeout from a Wendy's on the outskirts, also at Bree's suggestion. Jones ordered what Bree ordered, which was one fewer burger than she would have liked. Bree liked Wendy's. The hot foil wrappings felt classier than Mickey D's, and she liked the way the burgers were square even though the buns were mostly round. She liked that you could nibble the corners off, salty and greasy and chewy and hot.

They ate leaning back against the doors of the car where it was parked in the lot. The restaurant was light and the light spilled into a kids' play area with a slide in the shape of an elephant and a see-saw anchored to the PlayCrete by a spring. It had a smiling plastic Wendy face, with ginger bangs and braids, atop the central boss. Wendy's eyes were dark.

Bree felt tearful. She slurped her big orange soda. Jones, on the other side of the car, smoked gratefully, and the drift of the smoke smelled good.

As they drove, afterwards, Bree stopped trying to establish what went on in Jones's head. That was Jones's business, she reckoned. She liked him.

They drove on from the Wendy's and kept going to Tupelo, where when Bree saw the illuminated vertical beacon of a Motel 6 glowing she asked Jones to pull in and they decided to stop for the night. They would contact Red Queen in the morning. Bree wondered what had happened about the disappearing case – the one he'd had at the airport and then hadn't had.

They booked two adjacent rooms, both for cash. Jones helped Bree with her small travelling bag, put it in her room for her then came out to the walkway. It was round ten thirty, maybe eleven.

'Jones,' she said. 'Sleep well.'

'Yes. Thank you. You sleep well also.'

There was a moment of neither moving. Jones seemed to be looking for a cue.

She stood opposite him a minute, and thought of hugging him and then laughed aloud, a little nervously, and turned round and went into her room before she had time to register his quizzical expression.

Bree lay on her back on her bed in her clothes and looked at the ceiling. She thought of Cass. It was some time before she went to sleep. She wasn't aware of falling asleep at all. But she woke still in her clothes and with the lights on, where she had been lying earlier, with a disoriented feeling. That meant she had been asleep. The clock on the wall said it was 2 a.m. She could hear a noise.

Cheap thin motel walls, she thought, as her startlement abated and she got a sense of where she was. Barely more than partitions. It would be some couple going at it. But the noise wasn't the grunt and huff of sex, not even the stagy wailing some women seemed to put on when they found themselves in motel rooms with thin walls next to Bree when she was trying to sleep.

It was the high, animal, keening sound of someone in distress. Bree rolled her feet onto the ground and reached into her bag for the small, light handgun she carried and had never had to fire. She knew that this was a serious job. If this thing was as powerful as she understood it to be, she knew the DEI would not be the only people looking for it; they probably weren't even the only government agency looking for it. There were interests at work in it that would use violence. Red Queen had as much as told her so.

She sat with the gun in her two hands, getting her breathing steady, listening. The sound rose and fell, came and went. It wasn't the sound of someone being hurt. It was the sound of crying: the jagged hee-hawing of someone winded by grief. It was coming through the wall separating her room from Jones's. It sounded too high to be a grown man's voice.

Bree got up, rolled on the outsides of her feet to her door, and slowly turned the handle. Outside the air was still muggy. There was a dirty yellow halogen light illuminating the porch, and mosquitoes blatting against it. She eased the door behind her closed – a soft click, and a moment of panic before she remembered her key card was safe in her pocket – and she could no longer hear the bellow of the air conditioner.

She took a couple of steps down to Jones's door. It was closed. The sound was coming through the thin plywood. She kept the gun in her right hand, but let it fall down behind her thigh. She knocked, softly, with the knuckles of her left hand on the door.

The sound stopped, abruptly. She stood breathing there for a minute, then knocked again.

'Who is it?' It was Jones's voice. She had, momentarily, a flash of remembering the knock knock jokes.

'Jones?' she said.

'Bree?'

'Yes.'

The door opened. Jones was there, and from behind him there came a gust of old cigarette smoke. He had his trousers on, and no top. He was well muscled. In one hand he had a toothbrush and in the other a lit cigarette, and his eyes were red and sore. He looked at her a moment, winced, and resumed brushing his teeth. Foam appeared around his mouth.

'Jones?'

'What?' he said, removing the toothbrush. He put the cigarette up to his mouth and took a pull. The end was dabbed with shiny foam when he took it out. Then he turned round and went back into the room. His room was exactly like Bree's, except that beside the laminated no-smoking sign on the bedside table was the polystyrene cup from the bathroom, filled with butts.

Jones tapped his ash into this cup, went into the bathroom and spat noisily.

'I was just going to bed,' he said.

'What the hell's up? Was that you crying?'

Jones looked at her as if slightly affronted.

'Yes,' he said.

'Easy, Jones,' Bree said. 'What's the matter?'

'My mother is dead,' Jones said.

'Oh, Jones. I'm sorry. Shit. You should have said. What happened?' Bree moved in, awkward because of her bulk and because of Jones's semi-nakedness and his being a colleague and being covered in toothpaste and waving a cigarette. She thought she ought to hug him but contented herself with reaching up and squeezing his shoulder. Jones's face crumpled, then recovered. He sat down on the bed.

'Jones, look, we'll – where's home? Do you want to drive there? Did you just hear?'

Jones sat down on the bed, and Bree sat down with him.

'No,' said Jones. 'My mother has been dead for twenty-four years.'

Bree didn't say anything for a bit, then she said: '*Twenty-four years?*'

'My mother has been dead for twenty-four years.'

'I heard you, Jones. I mean: what? What's making you cry? Twenty-four years is a long time.'

'She's still dead,' said Jones.

'Jesus, Jones. Of course. I know, but it's like you just found out –'

'It *is* like I just found out. I always cry before I go to sleep,' said Jones. 'I have emotions. I don't have an imagination: I can't see things that aren't there. But I have emotions. I had something and it made me happy and I lost it and now I don't have it.'

'Tell me about her,' said Bree. Bree thought of Cass again, and then stopped the thought. 'What do you remember about her?'

'Everything,' said Jones.

'You're –'

'I remember everything she ever said to me. Everything she ever wore. Every time she touched me. Every smell and taste of her.' Jones sighed. 'I have an eidetic memory. That is my condition. Everything that ever happens to me I remember it exactly. If I didn't have that I couldn't function.'

'But.'

'Why would I not be sad when I am alone?'

'Jones, people get over things. They have to. You can't just –'

In the light from the wall lamp, Jones's face was a sick yellow. He looked miserable. He got up and went to the sink, rinsed his toothbrush and stood it in the other polystyrene cup.

'I can't. I know that this is not like other people. It's not important. It is what happens to me. But I have no way of "getting over things". I have no expectations, no desires that live in what you call the future. That is what apsychosis means. Everything I want is in the past. Everything I want to happen has already happened. Everyone I love is already gone, and I can remember everything about them.'

Bree didn't know what to say, so she didn't say anything. Jones lit another cigarette from the butt of the last. Bree felt sad and annoyed and a bit awkward.

'Would you like me to leave you alone?' she said.

'I don't . . .'

'OK, I get it. You don't know what it would be like. But you must know – from your experience – if you're happier when you have someone with you or if you're happier when you're alone.'

'I'm happier when you are with me,' said Jones.

'OK then,' said Bree. And she kicked off her shoes and lay down on the bed. When he finished smoking he turned off the light and lay down, apparently without self-consciousness, on the bed next to her. The keening noises he made rose a little, then settled, as Bree put one of her arms over him and held him as he fell to sleep.

Isla walks up between two rows of beanpoles towards the cabin. She thinks: nobody is here.

A cane chair, empty, sits outside the cabin. The windows are shuttered. There is an outer door, with a gauze screen in it, that looks like it once had some paint on the wood. It's very slightly ajar, and she pulls it open. She waits a minute, listening to nothing, then knocks on the inside door. She waits, turns on her heels and looks around her. There's no reply, still, from inside, so she walks round the side of the cabin. There's a sloping roof coming off the wall a bit below shoulder height – mossy slates, sheltering a pair of tall red gas canisters and a neat stack of chopped wood.

The back of the cabin is windowless, and faces an escarpment – there'd be room to wriggle past, but not comfortably. As she peers round she sees a cat vanish into the crawl space under the cabin. It smells of sawdust and wet earth. He's in the woods somewhere, presumably. She wonders about leaving a note, decides against.

She puts her face up against one of the windows, cups her hands around her eyes so she can see in. The room looks bare – there's a dark rug of some sort on the floor, some sort of pallet up one end, drifts of yellow paper stacked on and around a table on the blank wall. On the table is an old-fashioned hurricane lamp.

The yellow paper . . . This is it. The letters all came on long sheets of ruled yellow paper from legal pads. The writing disciplined, intense, very small. She is remembering the first letter she had: two years ago, out of the blue, apparently in response to something she had written about him.

'Dear Miss Holderness,' it had begun. 'The order of things is changing.' The letter was written in English, albeit some of it curiously constructed.

It had been addressed in scrawled block capitals with her first name gone over several times in ink, care of 'EtUdes/RecOltes', University of Nice. On the back was a poste restante address in Carcassonne.

He had read, he said, the short introductory commentary she had written – there'd been some sort of dodgy French transla- tion – on the value of his work to number theory for this small mathematical journal with its tiresome capitalisation.

She hadn't believed it at first. Clearly Mike was winding her up. But would even Mike write forty pages just for the sake of a joke? And Mike didn't know the maths well enough, she realised as she went on, to have written some of the material in the letter. Then she thought that it meant something momentous: if it was Banacharski, and he was still reading journals, it meant he might still be doing maths.

A subsequent page suggested otherwise. He had bought some artichokes at the market, and they had been wrapped in a photo- copy of her article. This, Banacharski said, was of tremendous importance.

'I ate these artichokes. There were four of them. And I counted each one the number of their petals, and counted each one the number of the fibres around their hearts. This took me several days. I have started to see what you are talking about. Your article shows a deep grasp of theory. Not in the mean- ings of your words, which are banal, but in the patterns of your words. You know this. I am now starting to learn. The problem is in disorder.'

Isla had been taken aback by this. She'd thought her article sensible enough.

There had followed – taking up most of the letter – a long, long string of numbers – a series with no apparent pattern to it. Then there were operations on these numbers. Some of these, as far as she could make out from the marginal notes, were derived from the number of letters in the successive words of her article; some had to do with the frequency with which given letters had recurred in the article; some had to do, in a complex way, with artichokes.

Banacharski was trying to sieve some sort of order out of the randomness. Nobody could do this. He was constructing equations, finding relationships, whittling the number string down . . . he was – as far as she could tell – trying to wrestle the data into abstract algebra. He was trying to use it to describe a shape in space time, or a manifold of that shape. He digressed, occasionally, into some impenetrable speculation about the symmetries of the artichoke.

His letter closed: 'Write to me. There is not enough data. The work I am doing is important.' Important was underlined three times.

Isla had tried to follow what was going on. He was mad, that was clear enough. It was a scarily powerful mind, she thought, in deep distress. She had been halfway through writing back when the second letter had arrived. It had been shorter, with moments of lucidity. 'I am fighting with devils,' it said. 'Forgive me.'

She had written back, finally, with her home address in Cambridge – he never used it, continuing to write care of the magazine, whose name he sardonically recapitalised, she noticed, in every letter. She said nothing about artichokes. She was chatty, factual, friendly – and did everything she could to flatter him. She told him about work that had been done on his work. Two major conjectures, she said, had been proved. He hadn't been active for seven years.

His letters had gone in and out of lucidity. None was shorter than twenty pages. The longest was eighty-six pages. They appeared at intervals of anything between two and ten days. One or two of the letters contained fragments that made straightforward mathematical sense. In most, the equations seemed to be somehow . . . bent.

Isla discussed them with a few colleagues, including – though she came slightly to regret it – Mike, but was shy of showing them to anyone. She felt somehow protective. She had a sense that Banacharski trusted her.

Frustration started to infect them, though, as time went on. For the last six months, things seemed to be gathering pace. He underlined heavily, used confusing ellipsis, the ascenders and descenders on his letters becoming longer and angrier. Some of his choices of word seemed odd, stilted – and he started to capitalise words at random within the text of his letters. He went on and on about something he called '*the churn*', or the '*in-between space*'. It was as if she was supposed to understand something he was trying to communicate and was failing to.

His last letter – all of them, previously, had been signed, simply, 'NB' – was signed off 'Affectionately, and in despair, Nicolas'.

All this has led her here. And she is looking, now, through the window of what must be his shack as a cloud passes over the sun and brings, in this high place, a slight chill.

She takes her face from the window and turns round and there he is. He is standing at the end of the wooden wall of his cabin, smiling at her. The first thing she takes in is the skin of his face. It is blotchy – a pattern of brown freckles alternating with a cross pink colour like sunburn. His eyes are deep-set. His lips are fat, old-man lips. His beard is dark grey, with a badger-stripe of white down one side, and spreads wide to his chest, across a striped and grubby shirt, open three buttons down.

Around his waist, higher than his trousers, is a length of what looks like baling twine, snarled in a scraggy version of a bow knot. He salutes her, then casts his eyes down and away, then

looks up at her again. He beckons, flapping one hand while looking at his feet.

His feet are in flip-flops. His toenails are filthy.

'*Alors, oui, entrez donc,*' he says, shuffling round the corner and
opening the screen door then the other one.

'I'm Isla,' she says.

'Of course,' he says, as he opens the door and ushers her in.
There's a strange look in his eye, she thinks.

'Honestly?' said Hands. 'I think you have a problem.'

The interview had gone on late into the evening, though
you would not know in the unchanging light of the room that
it had done so. Functionaries had been and gone. Hands had
spent several hours looking through sheaves of photocopies:
selections from Banacharski's letters, classified reports from
Directorate sources in MIC, what scraps of intelligence were
available.

The coffee in the cup marked Starbucks had been replaced
by more coffee in another cup marked Starbucks and Hands
had been given a very large cookie containing very large raisins,
which he had eaten hungrily. The atmosphere was near enough
genial.

'The way you might want to think about it is this,' said Hands,
cupping his left elbow with his right hand and rubbing it thoughtfully. 'If what you've described to me is correct, and I must stress
if, then this device, or engine if you will, is going to be highly
unpredictable in its behaviour. Highly unpredictable.'

Red Queen let him run.

'There's a point at which mathematics and advanced physics shades over, in a way it's hard for laypersons to understand,
into philosophy. It's not the fact that it's hard for the outsider to
understand, no. It's more the *way*. Laypeople, you see – laypeople
very often get the wrong end of the stick. Headline writers,
arts graduates, pompous novelists. They get very attracted to

metaphors, you see. You know how it is: they thought Einstein had proved that "everything was relative"; whereas actually he proved something much more interesting than that. Then there was quantum mechanics and the stick they got hold of the wrong end of was the wrong stick altogether.' Hands allowed himself a professorial little chuckle at his own joke. 'Then chaos theory. Dear me. What I mean to say is: it's not that all this mathematics is a metaphor. It's the other way round. It's that – sorry, I'm not explaining it very well. What we do doesn't reflect the universe. It describes it. See? There isn't a realm of ideas and then the world . . . it's more like . . . ideas are part of the world. And if this machine does what you seem to think it does, it's possible that what has happened is that something that ordinarily belongs for all intents and purposes to the realm of ideas is, effectively, acting in the world.'

'Are you going to tell me what this machine might be doing, Professor?' said Red Queen.

'I'm getting round to it. You'll have to forgive my thinking aloud.'

Hands was leaning forward and the elbow-rubbing was slowing and increasing in time with his diction. He paused.

'Mind control?' said Red Queen.

'No. I don't imagine so. Probably rather the absence of it. One of the big mysteries is consciousness. What is creating what I'm thinking, and what – assuming, that is, that we're not all brains in a jar, or the hallucination of some being in another universe altogether – is creating what you're thinking and what does it mean to think? Consciousness, ideas, imagination, selfhood – all the things that make you you and me me. These obviously arise from electrical impulses in the physical brain. And the best accounts of consciousness we have – which is to say, no real accounts at all – speculate that the ghost in the machine, so to speak, may be a function of these impulses interacting at a quantum level.'

'OK.'

'So the brain – consciousness itself – isn't separate from the system of matter and energy in the rest of the universe. It's part of it. Maybe a very tiny part of it, but that doesn't matter. Chaos theory says that something very, very tiny in the data of a system that feeds back through itself can create very, very dramatic results. So it's not theoretically impossible that some-thing that started life as an idea might have an effect in the world.'

'What are the chances?'

'Well – we don't know, obviously. I'd say it would be very, very unlikely. Very unlikely indeed. It hasn't happened before, as far as anyone knows. But then, if Banacharski has found a way of making a machine that affects probability – which would be odd because probability doesn't itself exist, necessarily; at least not in the sense that most people might understand it . . .'

'Then you're supposing,' said Red Queen, 'he made a machine with his brain. And this machine made it possible for his brain to make the machine. Isn't that a bit circular?'

'I'm speculating,' protested Hands. 'That's all I'm in a position to do.' He looked a little hurt. 'I'm a professor of mathematics, anyway: not of yet-to-be-discovered physics.'

Red Queen stood up, walked round the desk, returned to the chair, performed a lazy roll of the neck.

'So it won't look like a machine, necessarily?'

'I don't suppose so, no.'

'No knobs, buttons, flashing lights, wires?'

'I doubt very much it runs on a battery.'

Red Queen's watch said it was a quarter to midnight.

They were interrupted by a rap at the door of the room, followed before either had the chance to respond by a man of medium height, with a splash of grey in his hair, wearing a dark suit. His manner was brisk.

'Porlock,' said Red Queen.

The man bowed his head slightly. 'Word from Our Friends. They think they've found the suitcase the boy dropped at the airport. They're bringing it in.' Our Friends was Directorate slang for what might have been called the executive branch. Friends got things done. Theoretically, they were partner agencies. But Red Queen regarded their involvement in this – in anything – as at best a necessary evil.

'What was it? Where was it?'

'He didn't leave it. He passed it, as you thought, to someone in arrivals.'

Hands sat on the sofa mutely watching the exchange.

'Who?'

'Courier.'

'For who?'

'An agency. His name was misspelled on the manifest. That's why the initial sweep didn't pick it up. The client was MIC.'

Red Queen tensed, looked at Hands, then went out into the corridor with Porlock. Porlock pushed the door to behind him so that Hands could no longer hear their conversation.

'What was it?'

'An encrypted hard drive.'

'How did you get it?'

'The courier had an accident. Not the boy, the pickup guy. Non-fatal. Best Our Friends could do. We thought you'd want it.'

'I do. Put everyone on this. People with big brains and eyeglasses. Tell me when you've cracked the drive.'

'Could this be it?'

Red Queen shrugged. 'Seems unlikely if the analysts are saying the thing's on the move. Something's making the weather out there.'

'Weather?' said Porlock.

'Figure of speech. I mean something's stirring things up. And whatever it is, this hard drive is the best clue we have to what it is and where it's going.'

Porlock turned on his heel and clicked off up the corridor. Red Queen went back into the room, where Hands was shifting in his chair, looking faintly grumpy.

'Professor Hands. I'm sorry again to keep you so late. Now, this is important. You said earlier you thought we had a problem. What did you mean by that?'

Hands sat back in the sofa and rubbed the bridge of his nose hard with his thumb and forefinger.

'Nicolas Banacharski was one of the most brilliant mathematicians of the twentieth century. No question. He had a very powerful mind. But he was – is, if he's still alive – cracked. That is often part of the way things go with mathematicians who work at a very high level. If this thing he's made is a leakage of that mind into the world, and if it's working like a feedback loop . . . it will get more powerful and more unpredictable the more it operates.'

'And it won't have an off switch.'

'I have no idea. I'm not imagining this thing as something that has an off switch. I'm imagining it as something that will tend to produce effects that have to do with human minds. The very fact that you say it's affecting probability is the troublesome bit.'

'I don't follow.'

'Probability isn't something you can affect like – I don't know – like a magnet affects iron filings. When you load dice you're not affecting probability – you're affecting physics. You're making one side heavier. Probability isn't a force. It doesn't *do* anything. The earth hasn't got a probability field in the way it has a magnetic field or a gravitational field. Luck –' He blew out through his lips. 'Luck is something that exists simply in the brain of the lucky or unlucky person. It's an *idea*, not an actual thing.'

'We have Gypsies,' said Red Queen. 'Down on the fourth level. We have cats on their tenth lives. We have lucky clover.

Rabbits' feet. The Pentagon stockpiled rabbits' feet during the first Gulf War. They *requisitioned* rabbits' feet. They were issued.'

Hands shook his head. 'No luck. Just things, so to speak, taking place. Your brain is programmed to notice things that seem strange, to invent correlations and to make theories about them. Winning streaks.'

'If I won the lottery, I'd be lucky,' said Red Queen. 'I'd be amazed.' Red Queen was not lying about this. Red Queen didn't play the lottery.

'Yes, you'd think so. But are you amazed every week when someone wins the lottery?' Hands answered his own question: 'No. Because someone always wins the lottery. The thing is: that's not surprising at all. That's just something happening. One person in a million, or however many players you have, will always win. You're only surprised when it's you. From the point of view of the universe this is not at all unusual. A coincidence isn't something strange that happens; it's something that happens that you think is strange.'

Red Queen looked blank, frowned.

'Let me try to explain again,' said Hands, his slightly frayed but pleasurably superior sense of himself reasserting itself; his seminar tone sneaking back in. 'So if this machine is, as you say, affecting probability, it is affecting something that doesn't exist in the first place. It's affecting an idea in someone's head. An idea about expectation, or even *desire*. And then that idea is affecting things – substantial physical things – in the world. Its operation is as paradoxical, so to speak, as its very existence.'

'I don't really have the leisure to think about this philosophically, Professor, interesting though that may be,' said Red Queen. 'I need to know how to find it, and how to get it under control.'

'There,' said Hands, 'I don't know if I can help you. If it has to do with ideas – and if it is tending to behave in such a way as to be so to speak "improbable" – what it does will get more and more improbable. It will begin to feed back into itself.'

'It will get weirder?'

'In all likelihood, yes. I was talking earlier about cascade effects. You know, like when a truck starts to fishtail on the freeway, and then . . . it just goes and it spins out altogether. Something predictable, after a certain point, becomes very, very unpredictable. At the ends of these series, very close to zero or very close to infinity, the line doesn't just curve slightly – it goes . . .' Hands's right arm wearily described a rocket taking off across some sort of imaginary graph. 'What I mean is that something that we know to exist but that is highly, highly improbable – something at the point where the rules really seem to break down altogether – is called a singularity.'

'Like a black hole?'

'Yes, a black hole *is* a singularity, in physics. When it comes to the laws of physics, all bets are off, so to speak. But singularity means something slightly different across different disciplines . . . Are you paying attention to me?'

Red Queen was not – was, rather, thinking about the patterns they'd been plotting in gambling odds in the big centres. Porlock's clever idea. They'd let the numbers Doppler off against each other – Atlantic City and Vegas and bootlegged data for Tijuana; all-night poker hands flowing through the big Internet servers; roulette on reservations; anything that might pick up a sort of after-echo of the effect, like background radiation. Porlock had looked as smug as all hell when he'd brought the results, plotted through the day. It had suggested, however approximately, a vector: a field of disturbance heading due west from Atlanta, emitting a steady, Geiger-counter-like crackle of the unpredictable.

In Red Queen's head, a map of America. Porlock thought these gambling centres might be a way of plotting a course. But a line between Atlanta – the place where the boy had stopped and handed this package to his employers – and San Francisco – the place where the boy was apparently heading before he decided to go off-map . . . it went more or less through the Nevada Desert.

'Vegas. What would happen?'

'Sorry?'

'I'm thinking aloud. Let's say, sake of argument, this is a terror-ist action . . .' Red Queen got up from the desk again, paced down one side of the room, now ignoring Hands altogether. 'You have a coincidence machine. You want to cause maximum damage. Where do you go?'

'I don't follow you.'

'You go to Vegas. You go to – what would happen if . . . if . . . everything came up black all at once?'

'Well, I'm no expert on this, but generally casinos lay off odds. On average the people who bet red will cancel out the people who bet black. Rather as I was saying –' Hands was keen to get back to his lecture – 'the behaviour of a roulette wheel or a deck of cards – a straight one, so to speak – is perfectly predictable over a long period. That's why the casino always wins. The most freakish results all cancel each other out, and –'

'But *say*, Hands –' this was the first time Red Queen had not called him 'Professor', and there was a definite edge of impa-tience in it – '*say* everyone happened to have bet on black. Or nobody bet on black. Then it came black. Or say –' an image suddenly presented itself in Red Queen's mind – rows and rows of women sitting like tortoises in velour leisure suits, in front of the slots in the waxy yellow light – 'say every slot machine in Vegas paid out its top jackpot at once. What would happen?'

'Theoretically –'

'Theoretically hell. This would be – would be an act of war. It would wipe out companies, pension plans, stocks. It would cause chaos. This would be like dropping a coincidence bomb on America.'

'I suppose, in –'

'Professor, I need to make some phone calls, now. I would appreciate it if you were able to give us a little more of your time.'

'Actually, as I was going to say,' Hands returned, 'I see that gambling or stock markets would present a problem, economic-ally speaking. But I'm – when I said you had a problem I meant something rather more serious than that. A run of numbers in a gambling parlour is one thing, but a singularity is a problem of a quite different order of magnitude.'

'I don't see.'

'There is something that baffles physicists about the beginning of the universe. We know a little about what gravity was like, in the very first moments of time. And the chances of the initial state of the universe having arisen by accident are one in ten to the power ten.' Hands's eyes rolled up and right and his tongue appeared in the corner of his mouth. He remembered: 'To the power 123.'

'What does that mean?'

'That is fantastically improbable.'

'I thought you just said that there was no such thing as probability.'

'Not as a force, no. But let's talk as if probability exists as you understand it. For the sake of argument. The state of gravity at the beginning of the universe was so improbable that the odds-to-one against it are so great that if you wrote a 0 on every single atom in the universe, you still wouldn't be able to write it down. I'm saying this machine could do something much more damag-ing than bankrupting a couple of casinos or crashing the United States's economy.'

'There is nothing more damaging than crashing the United States's economy,' said Red Queen. 'Trust me.'

'No. I don't think you understand me. This machine could, if it – strange to put it this way – took a *shine* to the notion, pull our universe inside out through its own asshole.' Far from being dismayed by the prospect – in the way Red Queen was dismayed, deeply dismayed, by the prospect of explaining a threat to the economy to the boss – Hands seemed positively to perspire with excitement.

'Is that professor-speak?' said Red Queen.

'Yes.'

'Singularity,' said Red Queen thoughtfully.

'Yes.'

'Universe pulled inside out?'

'Yup.'

'Asshole.'

'Yes.'

'I wasn't asking. Professor Hands, we would appreciate it if you stayed in overnight. I'll have someone bring you a toothbrush. The universe being pulled inside out through its own asshole,' Red Queen repeated wonderingly. 'Nice. Well. That's a bridge we'll cross when we come to it. Keeping this thing from getting anywhere near Binion's Lucky Horseshoe Casino is the problem I propose to tackle first off.'

Red Queen got up and walked out of the room.

As Alex drove west, whistling on his way, little strangenesses proliferated in the world around him.

In one town in Nevada, the cashpoints malfunctioned. Hundreds and hundreds of dollars poured onto the pavements and were blown down the street by the wind. Children chased them. Adults chased the children. Some adults attempted to return the money to the banks. The banks blamed a lightning strike.

In Baton Rouge, a man in a tall hat removed it and a humming-bird flew out. He stopped in astonishment, not noticing the hummingbird, seeing nothing remarkable in the white sunlight on the sidewalk, overwhelmed only by a sense of déjà vu so powerful he forgot for an instant who he was.

Every narcoleptic in Mississippi went out at once. All of them were crossing roads at the time. People thought there was a plague. Cars backed up, honking, at pedestrian crossings as the pedestrians slept. And here, there and everywhere sleepers shared the same broken dream: of an old man in a shack in the mountains, a rainbow in the dark sky, a terrible wind. None of them remembered the dream.

11

Alex had the idea of going to bed in Memphis, but he realised not long after dark that he wasn't going to make it. So, just
around the time his eyes were getting tired and the road was
starting to seem strange, he stopped at a motel outside Tupelo.
He got a room, and asked the clerk where he could get food at
this time of night.

He drove the car down the road to a restaurant called Steak
Break. There – eyeing through the near-pitch-darkness of the
dining room the portion being eaten by a courting couple at the
next-door booth, he ordered just a starter – 'chicken tenders',
which turned out to be giant, volcanically hot kidney-shaped
chicken nuggets – and a baked potato, which came soggy-skinned,
waxy-fleshed, wearing a tinfoil leisure suit and a pompadour of
whipped buttter.

It tasted comforting. Beer came in a large, fridge-cold glass. He
had two sudsy pints as he ate. The waitress said something about
his accent, and he wondered briefly, flattered, if she was trying
to flirt with him.

The couple left and he was the last customer there. The waitress
followed the couple to the door – dark wood, four patterned-
glass panels, tiny curtains on a brass rail – and flipped over the
wooden 'We're Open!' sign on its chain.

It was only quarter past ten. As he sat in the restaurant his
phone pinged. He looked at it. Two messages. One must have
arrived earlier in the car, while he was driving.

The first one was from Rob. It said: 'One for all and all for
one? (3, 3, 2, 3, 4).'

For Alex and Rob, the crossword game was a sort of distant intimacy, mixed up with showing off, mixed up with competition. They'd been doing it since a drunken evening in their second year as undergraduates. Months could pass between them, but then one of them would think of one and the other would get it.

The first one after that evening had been a scrap torn from an A4 pad in a college pigeonhole: 'Cows hidden from Nazis? (3, 6, 5, 2, 4, 5).' Alex had scribbled 'The Secret Dairy of Anne Frank' on the note there and then in the porter's lodge and popped it back into Rob's pigeonhole.

Latterly they'd come through as text messages. Never a proper letter or an email. Never, since the first days of it, in person. The rule – though again, it had never seemed to be actually formulated or discussed – was that until you'd guessed the last one you couldn't send one of your own.

Rob was better at it than Alex. Alex thought about this as he chewed his potato. Something something in something something? Something something of something something? Something something to something something? The something something something something?

That set him off thinking about the sentence Rob had once asked him to make sense of: 'Dogs dogs dog dog dogs.' When Rob had explained it – *dogs that other dogs pester (dog) in turn pester other dogs* – Alex had tried it on Carey. She'd failed to be as impressed as he'd hoped. She'd said, with a sad sigh: 'Yeah. That's about the way it goes.'

Rob had been interested in the way the sentence was jointed. Carey, having had it cracked open for her, had simply lit on the meaning – the least important part. Rob had been interested in whether it also worked for fish: fish fish fish fish fish. Carey had said that was stupid because fish didn't fish – and if let's suppose they did, the ones that had been fished would hardly be in a position to do any fishing themselves.

Alex had let it go, pleased simply to be with her on a summer lawn by the river.

The second text message, the one that had just arrived, was from Carey. 'Where are you, boy? Weird things are happening. Have a good afternoon. Miss you. Talk tomorrow? Night.'

Alex wondered what he'd say. He'd phone her. If he did, would the dial tone, or caller-ID, tell her he was in America, though? A payphone? Would that be different? He didn't want to freak her out. He didn't want to spoil the surprise.

The box with the ring in it – he hadn't felt comfortable leaving it in the room, with its flimsy door – dug into his hip as he leaned forward to flag the waitress for the bill.

'Could I get the check?' he said, enjoying the American words coming out of his English mouth, resisting doing an accent.

The something of something something.

When he got back to the motel he was tired and turned straight in, setting the alarm on his mobile phone for seven thirty. In the middle of the night he half woke up. The room was cool, and through the flimsy curtains he could see the moon over the parking lot. He could hear crying from the next-door room. Then he frowned, turned over, and sank back into sleep.

'There have been disturbances in the mass media,' Red Queen said. 'Running up to this. That was one of the things that caused us to keep the file open on what seemed to many of us like a lost cause. It seemed perfectly possible the machine was just imaginary: something Banacharski had made up – though, remember, we have some partial material from his communication with Holderness. And, well, some of that material either demonstrated that this machine existed, or it demonstrated the opposite. He was very paranoid. It's possible some of what he told Holderness was disinformation, especially towards the end. But ...' Red Queen trailed off. 'Then the thing with the airplane. The thing with the frogs ...'

'Frogs?' Porlock said,

'You didn't hear about that?'

Porlock looked slightly irritated.

'Downtown Atlanta? It was on CNN. It led Fox. Frogs fell out the sky. Thousands of them. From very high up. Several citizens were killed.'

'I've been working a lot of double shifts. That's been known to happen, though. Don't the frogs get sucked up by tornadoes? We've just had not one but two hurricanes . . .'

'The killed citizens: 60 per cent of them were Atlanta-stationed employees of MIC Industrial Futures, Inc.; 40 per cent of them were Atlanta-stationed employees of subsidiaries or affiliates of MIC Industrial Futures, Inc.; 10 per cent of them was a postman.'

'A postman?'

'Yes. We think he was just unlucky. As opposed to the other citizens killed by falling frogs.'

'What sort of frogs were they?'

Red Queen admired that sort of attention to detail.

'Mostly the sort of frogs that are hard to identify when you drop them from a mile up. Almost all of them − that is, the epicentre of the frog event, or whatever you call it − fell on MIC's Atlanta offices. They took out the glass roof of the atrium. It was over the cafeteria. A lot of people in hospital with very nasty cuts. The offices are still closed.'

'Our Friends are sneaking in and planting more bugs, then . . .'

'Yes. Lots more. MIC, as I don't need reminding you, is the company that was paying Banacharski. From a good way back. They were funding his chair at the Sorbonne. When he resigned in protest at being funded by an arms company it looked like he was resigning in protest at being funded by an arms company, but everything we've since learned suggests that actually he was resigning in order to work directly for the arms company. The letters to Holderness talk about a man, Nieman, an operative for "the firm", who's clearly Banacharski's liaison for his research.

He lived for several years with no visible means of support. So MIC are all over this. We think it was their freelances who went after the guy they found in the plane.'

'What about the guy in the plane?'

'Still in hospital. Still a waste of time.'

'You know MIC has links to government.'

'What arms and baby-milk company doesn't?'

'Very serious links. We are, theoretically, on the same side.'

'We are on the same side – but in this, no. This machine is a game-changer. If they get it they'll be their own side. And the frog thing. It can't be chance. As I was saying, though: the mass media.'

When Red Queen talked about the mass media, that didn't mean newspapers and television. It meant the hundreds and thousands of the psychically sensitive, wandering mad. To most people, they were a disaggregated army of street-corner crazies, but for the DEI they were an underground railway, an early warning system, a giant biological radio tuned to sketchy transmissions from . . . well, that was the question. Red Queen preferred to remain sceptical, but running the mass media was Sosso's department, down in the underhangar. Red Queen didn't have to worry about it in detail. It was valued. Funding depended on it.

Sosso's theory of it was only ever going to be a theory: whenever anything became empirically testable, it lost its Dubya status and was transferred out of DEI. Dubya was the Directorate nickname for any file coded UU, for 'Unknown Unknowns': double-U. But Sosso's theory was this.

Old-style 'mediums' – Victorian charlatans in robes and false noses, wired up to jerry-rigged table-knocking devices – purported to have some control over their gifts. But media, to use the correct plural, were actually as passive as air and relatively common. The Chinese were rumoured to be 'training' them in very large numbers; harvesting Falun Gong and the Tibetan monasteries and 'repurposing' the prisoners in permanent detention. That gave even Red Queen the creeps.

What made media media was that only a mind slightly hanging off its hinges could let whatever it was through, and the way it came through was garbled. Low signal, high noise. Any single medium would produce indecipherable gibberish. Yet in aggregation the signals had yielded suggestive results. A hobo in Palo Alto might mumble 'Harra fugg . . . a-budda. Zzzzally! Mmmrgfff' at precisely the moment that a heavily medicated paranoid schizophrenic in the Bowditch Hall at McLean's would exclaim, from swampy dreams: 'Paternoster! Carthago delenda est! I am Caligula!' And if you combined the sounds of their voices the recording might throw up a fragment of a word in Aramaic.

Sosso, a true believer, liked to use the image of each medium being a single string on a huge harp; you'd hear one note but you needed to hear the chord. Or the assemblage being a pipe organ: the more pipes you could hear the closer to the tune you got.

In a system they'd grimly termed 'tag and release', operating over more than two decades through homeless shelters, outpatient mental health units, combat veterans' trauma units and addiction clinics, thousands of potential media had been identified and fitted with transponders, typically hidden in the fillings of their teeth, or in metal pins fitted somewhere in the skull or jaw where they could benefit from bone conduction.

The second generation of these devices were able to tell when the medium was asleep or unconscious, and flag the signals received accordingly. It was generally believed in the Directorate that sleep – or catatonia, states arising from hypnotic or psychedelic drugs, alcoholic dementia or near coma – was the most likely to yield what Sosso called 'accurate' or 'high yield' material.

Sosso's team worked on these. They used bleeding-edge voice recognition and translation software to sieve the data, compiling and noting sentence fragments and unusual or foreign words.

They combed different overlays and combinations of voices, experimented with staggering inputs according to the different time zones or lunar phases, squelched the bass or treble, speeded and slowed the recordings, even played fragments backwards on the off chance of backward-masked messages. Mostly, they came up mud.

They also tracked the frequencies of particular phonemes – according to time logged and geographical concentration. This was often what yielded the result.

Sosso had a piece of software that allowed her to mouse over a satellite map of the States. On the top-right side of her desktop were two panels – one a ticker tape of sentence fragments that had been tagged as of interest; another a dynamic list of the most common utterances, ranked in order of frequency, available for the last year, last week, last twenty-four hours, last minute.

Marked on the map with mobile red dots were tagged media – mostly, they were concentrated in western California and Florida. Manhattan was red. There was a scarlet dusting over Oklahoma and Montana, too.

If Sosso moused over a dot she could pull up a file: personal history and utterance history broken down statistically. A ticker tape of current utterance could be displayed, over the voice, in real time. The signals from Montana were always lousy, crackly as hell, but in the big cities, they freebooted on the cellphone networks.

Media who said the same thing as each other within a two-minute window would be colour-tagged blue for affinity. They'd return to red if a twelve-hour period had passed without a recurrence. If there was a recurrence, or something else significant to suggest a synchronicity, they'd go a brighter blue and slightly increase in size. A very thin blue line would connect them on-screen.

The usual global utterance rankings tended to have mushy collections of sibilants, non-signifying smacky-lip noises, belches and high whinnies of anxiety at the top. Few words made it in.

The less imaginative obscenities sometimes made the top thirty. 'Kill' and 'help' and 'mama' occasionally nudged into the top hundred.

In the days preceding the arrival of the Intercept, the patterns had been altogether stranger. Usually, no more than a couple of blue lines at any one time appeared on Sosso's map: a sketchy dark blue diagonal would connect the Mission District in San Francisco with the French Quarter in New Orleans for, maybe, forty-eight hours. A disconnected line would strike from Fire Island to Key West, flicker, evanesce. Accelerated to the one-second-to-six-hours timescale they used to scan manually for patterns, it looked like a broken 1980s screen saver: a dusting of red dots jittering like midges in the summer air, blue lines appearing at random and then disappearing a second or two later. Rarely, very rarely, one of the blue lines would sprout another line from one end, like an elbow, or two lines would intersect at a non-perpendicular vertex. Then that would go.

In the run-up to the Intercept, lines had appeared and stayed. Sleeping madmen were babbling the same things thousands of miles from each other, at opposite ends of America. These lines on the map formed a double-looping cat's cradle with two huge empty patches. The lines intersected in Atlanta, where an unnamed vagabond – he had signed himself 'Nobody' in a smudgy scrawl when he'd been admitted to the Salvation Army shelter where he'd had the seizure and been tagged in '98 – was saying, by the look of it, the same thing as his brother lunatics coast to coast.

The utterance charts for the media involved in this event were highly unusual. Underneath the noise, some consistent patterns were emerging: Nobody was producing them most consistently and urgently, but fragments of these utterances were uniting media on a sweeping continuum of tangents up the south-east.

A disyllable or trisyllable that seemed to be 'Meat hook', 'Me door', 'Meet her', 'Ammeter', 'Umma' or 'Ramada' was coming up. 'Ankara', 'Gon' and 'Nameless'. 'Wadis', or 'at ease', or 'hotsy', too. Nobody had been able to make any sense of it and, in truth, Sosso would probably have been as freaked out as anybody else if they had. Most of the time Sosso – who was a true believer but inclined to the comforting notion that whatever signals came through from wherever would be deliberately impossible to understand – would affect excitement if they could coax half a line of a Kraftwerk lyric out of the whole of the continental United States.

It was the pattern and consistency of the affinity tags that was striking. It seemed impossible to account for by chance alone. And perhaps, Sosso had speculated, that was all they could hope for.

But in the last twenty-four hours, the blue dot that was the crossing point of the weird figure of eight started moving west – in fits and jerks. Right at that crossing point – still, apparently, ranting like a champ – was Nobody. The transmitter showed he was on the move, and his direction and pace seemed to be shadowing the data from the casino numbers.

12

The point of the journey, for Alex, had become the driving itself. He felt as if he had left his old life – not for a holiday, or for a week, but entirely and irrevocably. He had moved deeper into his solitude. Even while he was moving forward towards Carey, he felt as if he was moving further away from everything else.

Road sadness crept up on him. He used the car stereo less and less. At first, he had driven with the windows down and the air rushing in, but as the hours passed he found the noise not exhilarating but distracting, and he stopped it. He wound the windows up, put the air con on. It made a gentle whoosh. When it got too cold, he turned it off. Then as the car heated he turned it on again. He did this automatively, unthinkingly, until day cooled into evening and he left it off altogether.

The road sadness was half pleasurable: less sharp than his initial homesickness. But it was what was going on, and he gave himself to it. The America he was driving through was familiar to him from films, but it wasn't the America in the foreground of films but in the background: the highway America that was endless and the same everywhere.

He woke up in Tupelo and drove into Memphis. It was late morning and he followed the tourist signs to Graceland but he didn't go in. He drove past without seeing any Elvis impersonators. He stopped mid-afternoon, that day, for food and petrol. And he pressed on.

He got used to the rhythms. His mornings were startled by the brightness of sunlight. He'd wake up in a room in a chain motel, and get up and shower and check out and head onto the road when the sky was still whiter than blue. His mornings were full of optimism. Any time before midday he felt in command. He felt the star of his own film.

He'd stop early, sometimes, for lunch; or he'd have a late breakfast and skip lunch.

The wheels turned and the car hummed and the petrol needle made its half-daily journey across the dial on the dashboard. He would eat fast food, or food from gas stations. He tried monster bags of pork rinds – pretty horrible, actually; giant, chemical-tasting puffs that were to pork scratchings as popcorn is to sweetcorn – and grazed on sour-apple liquid candy. He ate microwave sandwiches and Jack in the Box burgers, nacho cheese and Gatorade. He browsed in chillers, with heavy doors, full of Vitamin Water and cardboard carry-packs of longneck beer.

The vastness of the country impressed itself on him. The road, when he was in between cities, was worn pale grey and yellow: and was only two lanes in either direction. An image came to him of the roads – arteries they call them – as the country's circulatory system. He imagined himself swept along them like a blood cell, a platelet, shouldering past the big trucks, pumped by a huge heart somewhere miles away. That made him think of cells dying, DNA unknitting, fraying, counting down.

He drove for hours and hours in a near trance, adjusting cruise control, watching the road ahead vanish under his car, thinking about Carey and trying to imagine a joint future. Again and again, his imagination failed him.

He could imagine their past well enough. Drunken scamperings in college. Their becoming a fixture of the scene, 'Beauty and the Geek' – they'd gone to one fancy-dress party as that. But the future was a blank.

He started to drive into the night. As he crossed over into New Mexico the landscape changed. The neon minarets of the rest stops thinned out, became less frequent in the big desert, in between cities. It was just the ribbon of road and the car and the scrub to either side.

He felt calm but alert, as if he could go on for hours without sleep. Then, as time went on, he felt a little dislocated – as if he had gone on for hours without sleep, but hadn't noticed it. He couldn't tell how fast time was passing, or had passed.

There was a period of about an hour – was it an hour? – when he became hypnotised by the road in his headlights. There were no other cars around. The car seemed to be floating – just ahead of it fifteen feet of tarmac rushing in a blur in the yellow light. No sense of forward motion or acceleration. No sense of time or space passing. He was barely aware of the wheel in his hand.

Far, far ahead in the distance he could see red tail lights, but no road or horizon line to orient them against. They rose slowly, as if levitating into the air. Then they winked out and it was dark as far as he could see.

Alex eased off the pedal a little. The speedo kept steady. He had put cruise control on without noticing it. The red light reappeared – higher than it had been, and still climbing, moving off to the left. Alex started to wonder whether it was a car at all. Had there been mountains?

He looked down in front of him, saw the road coming into existence a car's length or more ahead, churning monotonously towards him, vanishing as it hit the lower sill of the windscreen. Alone, he thought. He raised his eyes.

The whole of his consciousness seemed, now, to be zeroed on that little red light, miles in the distance. Would he, one day, remember this moment? The road fell away underneath him. Nothing was funny. Nothing was sad.

If you moved far enough out, for long enough, you lost your bearings.

The red light vanished again. The car started to climb. Alex imagined around him, unseen, trains creaking and lumbering through the night. Sleeping families. Empty forecourts. Rough sleepers mumbling. In his pocket was the ring that was going to link him to Carey, whoever she was, whoever he was.

A little later, as the Pontiac crested a rise of some sort, Alex saw a glow in the distance – not the sharp point of red that had been the lights of the car in front – rather a diffuse, blue-grey lambency announcing itself on the horizon.

It got closer. It was big – not a building but more a pool of light – huge, by the side of the road, with darkness and the empty land all around it. It was a car dealership, out in the middle of nowhere. There was nobody there. The windows of the building itself were black. It rose up from the car park like the bridge of a container ship. All around it were cars, hundreds of cars, parked hull to hull, with halogen lights burning bone white above them.

It made him think of an elephants' graveyard. Not white bones tanning in the sun, but empty windscreens, roof props, the scratchproof paint shining under the cold arc lights.

Alex rode on, until it vanished behind him, an island of light, unpopulated, in the enormous desert night.

Isla spends the week with Nicolas. At first, he doesn't say much at all, though he behaves as if he was somehow expecting her – an affectation of serene foreknowledge that she doesn't know whether or not to trust.

He ushers her into the shack. She ducks her head under the lintel as she enters. He, behind her, nodding courteously. The shack has a smell of wood and something sweet and dusty, like a church. He follows her in, gestures at a wooden chair that's pushed in against a desk. On either side of the chair are tall stacks of yellow paper. The stacks of paper are everywhere. He sees her looking at them, waves dismissively as if brushing them away, shuffles to the chair and pulls it out, turns it round for her, busily nods and points her at it.

'There, there – please . . . sit.'

The old man smiles encouragingly, nodding again faster as she advances.

She sits, nervously. She still has her backpack on so she teeters on the front couple of inches of the seat, smiling back at him, hands on her knees. She keeps suppressing an instinct, like someone meeting a nervous dog, to extend a low palm, gently.

He turns round, fumbles behind one of the piles of paper and fishes out an ancient kettle on the end of a snaking orange extension lead, then fills it from a large earthenware jug. He mumbles to himself in a sing-song voice under his breath as he does so.

As the kettle starts to rattle and cough, he moves over to an arrangement of shallow wire baskets hanging one above the other from chains. She can see a couple of leeks just going dry at the ends, a red net of cashew nuts. The whole assemblage wobbles as he rummages in it, and two handsomely sized eggs, smeared with a dab of dried brown, loll against each other in the bottom basket.

He pulls something out and returns, his tall body hunched over a little as if half out of shyness, half to save himself the effort of standing up only to bend again. On the floor he puts a dark green mug. It is the colour of old copper, she can see, on the inside. He produces a cloudy tumbler from somewhere else, puts it down too, and as the kettle passes its crisis of excitement, drops a pinch of some sort of herb into each and tops it with boiling water.

'I don't get many visitors,' he says, stirring each with a spoon before handing her the mug, punctiliously, handle first. The infusion smells very strongly of sage. He sits down cross-legged with a great crack of the knees and looks at her, then downwards into his beard, whose ends he worries at absently between finger and thumb.

He begins with a cough, and a shrug. 'I've been gone a long time,' he says. 'I know . . . I know . . . I'm very – touched – that you have come to see me. My last letters – I must apologise for . . . well, let's . . .'

He pauses and shakes his head quickly from side to side.

'We'll talk about that later, perhaps. Yes. I'm glad you came.'

Isla simply sits there with her face glowing. She tells him how much he is admired, how much she has longed to meet him. After several minutes of this he starts to respond more than monosyllabically.

'Oh, it's a long time since I did mathematics, really. A child's game. A means to an end. My work now is very different.' She can see the flattery working on him. 'But you know that, don't you?'

He is still reluctant to meet her eyes for more than a moment. But she keeps talking, tries to keep him talking. She picks up on points in their correspondence, passes on faculty gossip – to which he listens with what she suspects is feigned interest, apart from the odd light of recognition, sometimes hostile, when the name of a mathematician of his own generation is mentioned.

At one point during their conversation – this is when Isla thinks she has made a breakthrough – he sees her eyes drifting over to a netting bag of some green vegetables by the pallet where he sleeps.

'Ah, yes,' he says, and the twist of his mouth seems almost self-mocking. 'Artichokes.'

Occasionally she feels something spiky in his mind pushing back at her. He'll ask a question about a point of mathematics, as if testing her, checking she's understood. Sometimes the look when he raises his eye is minutely sharper, more appraising – then the sentences will again trail off and the combing of the fingers through the beard will increase. He continues to sit cross-legged, without apparent discomfort.

As they talk, he hauls over a pottery container filled with pea pods, takes a handful and pushes the container over towards Isla. They shell and eat the peas, which taste woody, but less horrible than the sage tea – and to Isla, who is both hungry and nervous, they are a welcome opportunity to do something with her hands.

That first night, she keeps talking to him till the sun sinks. He lights the hurricane lamp and moths loop in crazy eights around the table. They pass a point where impoliteness has become moot. Only when he notices her start to shiver a little, and tries to give her his blanket, does she make a move. The blanket, she guesses, is the origin of the dusty smell.

'I'm sorry. You are too kind. I must leave you . . .' She dares his first name: 'Nicolas. I have to go and pitch my tent.' She asks if she can set up her tent down the slope from his house. 'Perhaps we can talk some more in the morning; if I'm not intruding?'

'No,' he said, wanly. 'You are intruding, but you are not an intruder. Perhaps a helper. A sharer.'

That night she sets up her tent, laboriously, in the pitch dark. She dreams of goats bleating, and the following morning she is woken by the sound of chickens pecking about at the entrance to her tent. It hasn't rained. Shivering from the dawn, she pokes her head out and sees Banacharski, bent over in his corduroy trousers, scrubbing at something in the dirt up by the front of the shack.

That is how Isla Holderness's week with Banacharski starts. She quietly slots into his life, and he lets her. That first morning, she offers to make him breakfast and he, affecting to be startled by the emergence of this woman from the dew-steaming tent at the foot of his garden, nods. 'Come.' She uses the eggs she saw – they are fresh enough, and finds a couple more in a dirt bath under the house, one still warm.

The gas canisters she saw outside heat a little tank of hot water Banacharski uses to wash. But he also has a single-ring burner on a bottle of gas and she finds a skillet.

'I don't usually cook,' he says.

She makes omelettes, seasoned with chervil she finds growing at a short distance from the house, and they eat them. He, again, insists she take the chair while he sits on the floor.

For most of that morning she helps him potter around the garden, pulling weeds. He does this more than she, but he

133

points, occasionally, and grunts. She doesn't know anything about gardening; she has always lived in big cities. As it goes on, prompted gently, the older man starts to talk a little more – about himself, about the disappearance. He won't say much about it, but when she says something about being overcome by 'pressure' he turns to her sharply.

'I am not mad,' he says, looking her very directly in the eyes. 'I know that that is what they want everyone to think. And it suits me – for my own purposes, for different purposes. But I am not mad. I know exactly what they are doing. EXACTLY.'

He turns his head from her and roots at the foot of the hedge, turns back – looking cross, with a dandelion leaf tangled in his beard. 'Exactly what they are doing. I am not mad.'

That is followed by another long silence and a furious bout of weed pulling.

It is early afternoon when he declares that he has to work. He does so in a sudden snap – a violence of gesture that takes her by surprise. She senses, suddenly, that he's long past when he'd have started ordinarily, as if his gardening has been a distraction he has affected until it has become intolerable. The weeds he has been pulling are some way from his garden. They were there for a reason.

He walks briskly into the shack and shuts the door. Isla goes for a walk. The weather is pleasant enough. She walks a contour of the hill behind the shack, descends into a valley and marches up the other side until there is a pleasant ache in the tops of her legs, thinking all the way. She thinks how to approach him, how to coax him out. She has never done anything like this before.

Will he be finding her attractive? The thought has crossed her mind. He did have girlfriends when he was younger. He probably hasn't had a woman since . . . unless . . . Why should she speculate? He's an old man. She knows Mike would say: is it safe? She feels safe. He's an old man. He's reedy, pot-bellied. If he tried anything she could, with these strong thighs and these arms she goes swimming with . . . she feels safe.

But she wonders, just in the abstract, if he finds her attractive.

And so it goes. She returns later in the afternoon and knocks on the door. He lets her in. He has been in the chair at the table, writing on a yellow pad. He seems in a good mood.

'My new work,' he says, tilting the pad towards her. It's in prose, very densely written, studded with what look like algebraic notations. She makes to peer more closely at it, but he snatches the pad away and puts it face down on the desk.

'Tell me, Isla Holderness . . . what do you think happens to us when we think? When we want something?'

Isla raises both her eyebrows, opens her face, looks deferentially blank. Banacharski snorts. They don't talk about his work again that night. But, as last night, she asks whether she can stay in her tent, and perhaps help him tomorrow and he assents with a courteous gesture.

And so they establish a routine. Isla helps him to cook, makes a few efforts to clean up the shack – though she knows better than to touch his mouse-nests of paper, let alone order them or be seen trying to read them. And, gently reasserting her interest, she piece by piece steers him into talking about his work. It is a slow and elliptical process.

'I put it another way,' he says one evening, apropos of nothing, and in the middle of what has so far seemed to be a conversation about the virtues of eating raw vegetables (he says he lived happily through one summer eating cow parsley and soaked nettles). 'If everything is perfect – if our measurements add up, if we can measure that, and that, and that –' he points with sudden violence to the verticals on the wall of the shack, just in the shadow of the hissing hurricane lamp – 'and that angle is so, and that line is so, and that force is so . . . we can build a house. Yes? So when the winds blow, when the hurricane comes, we will be safe. You see?'

Isla learns simply to ignore this sort of thing, not to startle, to go with the sudden shifts in his conversation. His speech is like the patchwork prose of his letters. She had assumed they were written discontinuously, at different times of day and in different moods, as the storms of his madness blew themselves out, as signals swept from nerve to nerve in his brain and clarity came and went. It seems, though, that the shifts are almost instant. It is as if he is participating in half a dozen conversations, and simply tunes in and out of them – sometimes responding to her, sometimes to some cue elsewhere.

'Now in here –' He points to her head. 'Now out here –' He waves at the air. 'A pretty fantasy. You can measure nearly. Very, very nearly. But you can't measure precisely. True knowledge is impossible. I measure this once, then twice. Which is right? Then a third time. This is – what is the word? An analogy.'

Isla asks, is he talking about subatomic particles?

'Not that – yes, that is part of it, but I mean something bigger than that. I mean that everything we are is a mistake in the measurement. Everything. This mistake – this is the devil's gift to us. The devil broke the clockwork. Now . . .' He looks at her, suddenly exultant, and raises his hands, palms outwards by the side of his face. '. . . CUCKOO! CUCKOO!'

Late another night, they are talking about time. It is something that Banacharski seems agitated by, a subject he returns to.

'Imagine, see. Time is not a thing, not a thing that flows from one thing to another thing to another. It is a direction – a dimension. Does north flow? Does sideways flow? No. You can't measure time because what do you measure it with?'

At another point he draws a circle on one of the sheets of paper and shows her. 'Here and gone do not mean anything,' he says. 'Look. Make this axis time. This axis space. Here –' he marks a sort of triangle inside the circle, shades it roughly in – 'is the map of Alexander the Great in the world. And here. He is not "gone": look. He is here: on the map between such a place and such a place and so-and-so BC and so-and-so BC.'

He draws another blob on another part of the circle. 'And here is the map of Nicolas Banacharski in the world. In this world. And here –' he draws another blob, this one overlapping the last – 'is the map of Miss Isla Holderness in the world.'

That night he becomes a little tearful. 'You have to understand, Isla,' he says. 'When I was a child I was a displaced person. Whenever you have a war, you have displaced persons, shifting from place to place. They are victims of chance. For me, there was the chance of where I was born and when I was born, and the chance that I was born at all. Everything was chance. What my mother saw. Where my father died. It was chance. One lived, one died. Chance that I was born, and not somebody else. I am trying to repair that. Do you understand? Think, like a play on words, perhaps – another chance.'

She touches his arm, and she sees wetness on his lips. 'I am an old man, Isla Holderness. I am an old man.'

Later, he mumbles something she doesn't think about until much, much later.

'Nobody wants me,' he says. 'Nobody is coming for me. I promised nobody anything . . .' he says at one point. He seems distressed. Isla takes a risk, and puts an arm awkwardly around his shoulder, and a charge seems to go through him. The yellowy whites of his eyes roll sharply towards her. He seems not just self-pitying, but scared.

13

Alex sat up in the bed under the thin motel sheet. He reached over to the little MDF unit screwed to the wall by the side of the bed and found his mobile phone in the half-light. It was the small hours of the morning, though he didn't bother to check the display on the big digital alarm clock. The answer to the crossword game.

'The set of all sets,' Alex typed into his mobile phone, and pressed 'send'.

'In your *face*, Mr Rob,' he said aloud, even though he was alone. He felt immensely comforted. Rob would be on his way to work, he thought. He pictured Rob, on the Noddy Train, as he without fail called the Docklands Light Railway, heading in to the job he boasted about but hated at PricewaterhouseCoopers or DeloitteDeLaZouch or whatever the company was called.

Rob had made such a noise, when they'd been together as students, about not becoming what he called a 'spamhat', his blanket term for anyone richer and older than himself whom he suspected of having taken a lucrative job because they had been – deservedly – bullied at school. Rob had been – deservedly – bullied at school.

Alex imagined – no, knew for a certainty – that his text would ping, or zoing, or chirp onto Rob's BlackBerry or iPhone or whatever he now had as he swayed along on the train, and that Rob would be excited by it, and affect to have had his day ruined.

Alex, even though it was late, waited five minutes before sending his next text. It was as well to affect not having been saving it up – but at the same time taking a few minutes to imply a plausible albeit startling facility of mind.

'Inexperienced butler? Sounds like an old film. (3, 5, 3, 2, 5).'

He was woken fifteen minutes later by his phone – on silent – burring against the hard surface of the bedside unit. He reached for it, bleary now, and thumbed the unlock sequence. The little square screen was fish-green. New message.

'Cnut,' said Rob's message.

Alex smiled and sighed, replaced the phone on the bedside table and settled back into a happy sleep.

Red Queen's encryption team worked on the hard drive they'd recovered from MIC – the drive the boy had couriered across the Atlantic for them and dropped off in Atlanta. The drive was exceptionally hard to crack, but – the cryptologists reported – not impossible. Progress was being made by brute-force computing. Red Queen regarded that as somewhat suspicious. So did Porlock. Still, they persevered. Resources were diverted. Compartment by compartment, data started to come off the disk.

It bugged Red Queen, though, that the casino metrics suggested the device itself was still on the move. The data coming off the hard drive didn't make much sense, as yet – it certainly didn't resemble, as Red Queen had initially dared to hope, backup blueprints for the machine. So what did it have to do with anything?

Ellis, MIC's head of security, had been working on the hard drive too, or rather working on its absence. MIC couriered several items of varying sensitivity between its offices in London, Washington and Atlanta every day; to say nothing of the material it moved between narco states in South America and AK-infested government buildings in Lagos, Freetown, Mogadishu and Khartoum. If any of those packages went missing, Ellis was informed.

Commercial competitors – as senior management insisted on calling the private interests, most of them governments rather than companies, and most of them clients rather than competitors, that tended to be interested in ripping MIC off – needed to be discouraged from obtaining sensitive data.

Ellis's anti-theft policy was twofold. The first side of it was straightforward. They used a dozen or more different courier companies in each country, randomising each job and booking them independently and at late notice. All electronic data that they couriered was encrypted and tagged; and all disappearances were investigated.

The second part of the anti-theft policy was slightly more complicated. In the first place, MIC couriered something in the order of five or six times as many packages as it needed to. Only very select personnel knew which contained the important data and which were heavily encrypted dummies. These were what Ellis liked to call 'Barium Meal Experiments': they'd tie up a lot of time and expertise, and once broken would yield complex, useless or deliberately misleading information. Their chief purpose was to cause their interceptors to give themselves away by acting on a red herring – a piece of bogus market-sensitive information that might cause a greedy dictator to tilt at a stock, or a hint that the opposition had bought a surface-to-air missile package for which MIC sold the only effective countermeasure. Sometimes it was more important and more profitable to know who was ripping you off than to prevent them doing so.

They were also, most of them, laden with the sort of high-end Trojan viruses that would install a nice back door, for MIC, in their hosts' computer systems.

They knew, for instance, that the Atlanta package had travelled by air to New York within a few hours of its disappearance from the courier company. But the signal from its tag had abruptly cut out on arrival. It had either been discovered or encased in concrete, or discovered and then encased in concrete.

In New York, the tag had not been discovered, nor had it had been encased in concrete. But it was deep underground, with the DEI's cryptographers. And it was nearly a day before those cryptographers fully cracked it. And a bit over a day when they realised what had happened.

'Like something gift-wrapped in a cartoon,' Porlock said without a trace of mirth when he made his report. 'Black on face. Hair sticking up.'

'Swine,' said Red Queen.

The quarantined network they'd been using to open the drive had quietly suffered the computer-virus equivalent of Ebola and would take more time and energy to cure than it had taken to break the encryption in the first place. Among the effects of the virus was that every computer in the network was quietly trying to get in contact with a remote ISP – almost certainly one of MIC's secure nodes – four times per second. They were doing so in vain, since the network wasn't wired to the outside world. But it made Red Queen think of the magic harp in the fairy story, screaming and screaming from under Jack's coat that it had been stolen.

The data on the drive had been mud. One programmer speculated irritably that the extensive personnel file for a company named 'Herring Enterprises' – they checked: it had no personnel; it was a Cayman Islands shell – was a private joke.

The DEI's programmer was right. It was a private joke. But it was not a private joke that Ellis was much laughing at. Ellis, too, had missed a trick. When he was first told about the missing package, he had given it little thought. Let his subordinates work it.

He was more preoccupied with trying to find this probability machine, and the routine loss of a BME – as, on checking, he saw it was – was neither here nor there. It was only when it occurred to him that it was Atlanta and that it was about the same time this kid had given those idiotic thugs of his the slip there, that he went back and wondered about a connection.

Could the boy have stolen the package? Could the machine have caused the package to be stolen?

Ellis looked at the loss of the package. It had gone through the airport, routinely, with no problems. The representative of the courier company had picked up the briefcase with the hard drive. But the closure of the Atlanta offices after the incident with the frogs – another thing that had installed the flickering jelly bean of an incipient migraine in the corner of Ellis's field of vision – had meant that he'd returned with the package to his own company's offices with a view to putting it in the safe. Where he'd been mugged and relieved of the suitcase. Two muggers – he didn't get much of a look at them. The loss had been reported to the police, but Ellis didn't hold out much hope of recovering it. Not with someone flying it instantly to New York, which was not what normal muggers did.

Ellis couldn't see a way that the boy, even if he had had an accomplice, could have known about this package arriving at the same time as him; nor where it would be going; nor why he would be interested in it in any case.

Ellis found out which courier company MIC had used, and telephoned their UK office. He was rude to a series of dispatchers until a senior manager looked it up on the computer.

'His name was Alex Smart,' said the manager. 'Yup. First time we've used him, according to our records. The usual thing – student or something, no criminal record, answered one of our ads online. He got a short-notice flight to Atlanta. We got your parcel sent. Why? Is there a –'

Ellis hung up. Well. That explained how the kid got to Atlanta. MIC bought him a ticket.

If Ellis had been more puckish, he would have said 'Swine', but Ellis instead swore unimaginatively, hammered the phone cradle with two fingers and then started to dial again.

'What I have been trying to do,' says Banacharski later in the week. His sentences, still, are not always coming out entire. 'To build a machine. To undo – these knots.'

They have spent a long day together. As usual, Isla has been circumspect. She has tried to make herself useful – has cleaned, even, where the opportunity to do so without looking rude has presented itself. She has retreated when it seems right – particularly when he has insisted that it is time for him to meditate. It hasn't been a problem for her. She has taken herself off on a walk.

She has started to get used to his moods. She doesn't think that she's going to learn from him what she'd hoped – still less, get him to come back to civilisation. This was the thing that, though she didn't admit it fully, she'd fantasised about: she, as Perseus, with the gorgon's head to show off. When she was little her dad taught her how to fish. She liked the idea, always, of the skill of bringing something in that was stronger than the line by which it was caught. She has an ego, Isla.

So she doesn't think she's going to bring him in. But she has started to feel for him. She reproaches herself. She always felt for him – even when she'd only read about him she felt she understood him. But now, she feels like she has a responsibility. She sees his mind, like a boat straining at its moorings in a heavy tide, and she feels sorry for him. She wants to soothe it.

'In the war. My father died. My mother lived. My little sister died. I lived. Chance. How do we live with that? How, Isla Holderness? How do we live with it? It is impossible. Nobody can. Nobody can do that.' He seems half to be talking to himself.

Then he changes tack again. 'There are walls in the air.' His hand, in a chopping motion, comes down between her face and his. 'Everything is so close to us. These walls: a membrane's distance. We think – our physics, already, almost shows it if you know how to look. Every moment spawns infinities – new universes. A sparrow falls, a sparrow doesn't fall – you know that?'

'The Bible,' Isla says.

'Yes. The Bible. Every sparrow, a new universe. Every feather, a new universe. Every wingbeat. What happens –'

'This is the parallel universes idea you're talking about?'

Banacharski waves, impatiently. 'Not parallel. No such thing as parallel. That's what the devil, as I told you, made impossible –'

'You're talking metaphorically?'

'Yes! Metaphorically. Yes, I am. Exactly that.' He looks, riddlingly, pleased with her – but not as if she has said something he agrees with, she thinks, so much as that he knows she didn't understand. 'What he does to the measurements, the devil, that's it. Everything curves. Not parallel. Like soap bubbles, these infinities. Everything touching everything else. You could just step through. If you could only see the walls. If you could hear what all those versions of you are saying, just on the other side. Think of what happens. How do you think of it? You go forward, yes?'

'Ah. Yes?'

'Look.' He wiggles his hand like a fish. 'Your choice, this or that. Your chance, this or that. You jump out of the trench and the precise angle of the bullet from a machine gun two hundred metres away –' he dashes the tips of his fingers on his temple 'finished. You are hiding in a house, and your baby daughter then – just then, as the guard comes by – she hiccups or she starts to cry – finished.'

Isla just looks, keeps looking at him.

'You think this is a chance in a million. This: what kills you. What lets you live. But go back. How you got there. Every tiny chance builds on another tiny chance before it, and before that, to the beginning of the universe. Why are you there then? Why do your parents meet, and why do their parents meet, and how does that one sperm in each one meet that egg? If you look at it like that, look, it is impossible, no? Impossible. My speaking, like this, to you, how did we get here? Start back then. It is like a maze. Take any wrong turning of an infinite number and look: we are not here.'

He rocks, now, back and forwards a little on his haunches. His right hand turns and turns in his beard. Isla sits on the chair. She catches sight of herself with her hands folded over each other in her lap, primly, like a figure in a medieval painting.

'The only way that what we have here – something as improbable as you, and me, sitting in this room together – can take place is if everything that could have happened, somewhere else, already has. You follow me? So this is what I am working with. How do you solve a maze?'

Isla feels the length of the pause. He is looking at her.

'You follow the left-hand wall?'

Banacharski wheezes with laughter.

'Backwards! You start at the end. Then every fork, it is not a problem – it is not a thing that can go two ways. It is just a node that is leading you back home. I mean this –' he waves his hands again – 'metaphorically.'

He stands up, now, and takes a step or two – agitating his hands.

'I mean that chance is an illusion,' he says. 'We think one thing happens and not another. But really everything happens. No time passes and nothing is lost and nobody dies. They are living in an infinity of universes, at every moment, for all time . . .'

His eyes look at her, as if from far away. Isla feels creepily, sorrowfully, a sense of how broken his mind is. She knows, then, that she can't stay. She shouldn't have come.

'Just here –' He fishes, again, at his imaginary wall in the air. His lips are moving into a sad smile, and his eyes are wet. 'So near. Imagine if you could pass through these walls. Imagine something that would make everything exist at once. Imagine if at every little point you weren't seeing universes splitting off, but universes coming together. You will see the maze entire – it will be not a maze but a pattern, you see? Like on wallpaper. A decoration, not a prison.'

Isla's cheeks feel stiff. She smiles at him, arranging her face somewhere between quizzical and accepting.

'Everything that is lost is present,' he says. 'See? If you can just reach through, with your mind, through the wall, into the place where something never happens, or doesn't happen yet . . . Everything that has gone is here. Anything can happen because everything will happen. Everything true, everything existing, everything here, now, always . . .'

He looks at her almost imploringly. 'Nobody dies. Nobody goes away. Nothing is ever lost.'

The following day, Isla tells him that she has to leave. Banacharski looks momentarily stricken. Then he shrugs.

It is a bright morning, chillier than the previous one.

'Walk with me,' he says. They set off up the hill behind the house. At first Banacharski says nothing; then, to her surprise, he links arms with her. The slight tang of him on the air makes her not revolted, but a little sad.

'I have enemies, Isla,' he says. 'You know, when you first came here, you wanted to know why I left the Sorbonne? That was one of the reasons I had to go. I had the real fear that they would kill me. No joke. They would kill me before my work was finished.'

'But, Nicolas — why would anyone have wanted to kill you? Your work was abstract. You were a mathematician, an academic. You're just being —' she dared it; after a week, she dared it — 'paranoid.'

'No!' he snaps. 'That is how they try to discredit me. How they try to make me lower my guard. *Paranoid!* Tchoh! Even then, I knew my work would have — implications. I let something slip in a lecture, and one of their agents — Oh, believe me, Isla Holderness. They have agents everywhere. Everything is connected to everything else, and in this spiderweb there are good spiders and there are bad spiders.'

He has lost his thread.

'You said something in a lecture.'

'Yes, yes. Somebody wrote to me. Frederick Nieman, he called himself. Some kind of joke, I think: *Niemand*. "Fred Nobody." That was how I was to know him. He said he was interested

146

in my researches into causality. I was not working on causality, then. Not openly. I was still a geometer. But at the time I had started to think about these things: about geometries that were not strictly mathematical: geometries of desire and intention. Nieman had happened on my work by chance, he said. He understood some of the implications. He foresaw a great future for me, he said. And he would pay.'

Banacharski huffs, a little, as they reach the top of the hill. She feels him leaning more heavily on her arm.

'They wanted what I was doing, for them and them alone, but they did not understand what I was doing. They thought I could make them a weapon: something that would change outcomes. Make magic bullets. If you sell weapons, you know, everything looks like a weapon.

'I knew, of course – he did not even need to say it – that if I did not do what they wanted they would kill me. I was afraid. I told him that I would share my work with them. This was a company that had done great wrong. It worked, during the war, with the Nazi government. Many, many people were killed with their weapons. But I was scared.' He looks ashamed, but at the same time a little defiant. 'I told them I could build them a probability bomb. For that, I told them, they needed to pay, and I would need isolation.

'So they paid me, helped me disappear. I disappeared – this was the big joke – after I resigned in protest at the discovery that their money was funding my chair at the Institute. They liked that. Double bluff.'

Something in Banacharski's face changes, like when a shift in the angle of the light turns a transparent surface opaque. 'I became my own ghost,' he says.

'The statement you gave, though,' says Isla, 'about the systematic corruption of science by the military?'

'Yes,' says Banacharski. 'They let me attack them because they thought it would help. I was telling the truth. Triple bluff. There is no bomb. There never was. I am engineering reality – not assembling some toy out of nuts and bolts.'

They walk on a bit. Isla watches a small brown bird prick and preen in the grass, the beak and head moving sharply.

'But Nieman,' he says, as if more to himself than Isla, 'I think Nieman is coming back.'

'Back? He's been here?' Isla asks.

'No,' says Banacharski. 'We haven't met. Only letters. He writes to me on yellow paper. Always yellow paper. Like the paper I use. I am afraid about meeting him. But I think he is coming for me anyway.'

'What did you do with their money?' Banacharski looks at her sharply. She worries, for an instant, she went too far. She sees something of cunning in his expression – a decision to say something almost taken, then a decision not to.

'You must concentrate, Isla. I stalled them. My work is nearly finished. But they may come for me. They have been losing patience. You know, you need to take care for yourself . . .'

He is now looking down at his wrecked flip-flops.

'There is something I would like you to have of mine, Isla. A gift. You have been someone who has shown me kindness.'

Banacharski reaches into the pocket of his filthy trousers and produces something. Isla sees it glint, and then she startles at the pressure as he presses it into her palm. As he does so he looks furtively about him, into the distant trees, the empty ground between.

He withdraws his hand and she looks into her own. It is a ring, right where her lifelines cross – a simple silver thing, with a figure-of-eight design sweeping over the top of it.

'It was my mother's,' says Banacharski. 'I have nobody. Now I give it to you.'

'I can't.'

'I have nobody. You take it. That ring will be – how should I say it? – a lucky charm for you.'

He gives her a strong, fond look. 'Borrow it, then. Think of it as a loan. Come back at the end of the summer. Bring it back to me. God keep you safe.'

Isla sets off for home the following day, walking down into the local town, from where she arranges a taxi – it takes her half a day – to get back to Toulouse. That is the last time she sees Banacharski alive.

As Hands described to Red Queen, they continued to exchange letters. But Banacharski's letters had become wilder. Isla, back in Cambridge, felt uneasy – as if there was someone shadowing her. When she went out every morning to get the newspapers, she found herself casting suspicious glances down the aisles at the Co-op. There'd always be someone holding up a pot of yogurt or a tin of sweetcorn, fondling it abstractly, reading the label with studious distraction.

She thought for a time that she might be going mad – that Nicolas's paranoia was rubbing off on her. The magazine continued to forward his letters. Sometimes, the way they were folded in the envelope, a certain looseness about the glue, made her feel like they might have been tampered with. She took to hiding them.

At the same time, other letters started to come – more personal ones, addressed directly to her. The handwriting on the envelopes of these was different – more restrained – though the writing inside was the same.

In the last of these, he wrote: 'Don't worry. You have my love. I am nearing the centre of the artichoke. Do not trust. Destroy.'

Something, she thought, had started to confuse him. The letters were in the same handwriting, but they seemed to be from two different people. The letters that came through the magazine raved about this 'machine', which he said was 'nearly built'. She puzzled over that.

In these letters, he promised her that 'when the time was right', he would share his discoveries with her: she was, he said – and here it was triple underlined – 'the custodian of his legacy'. But he said the time was not yet right. He said he was 'storing some parts of the machine' in a place known only to him.

The other letters, the ones that she told nobody about, were love letters, of a sort. That is, they did not profess love directly. But they were personal. They were trying to make a connection. And they talked at length – great length – about his childhood, and what he remembered about the war. Much was about his mother, Ana, the presumed owner of the ring he had entrusted to her. She had lived through the war but cancer got her while Banacharski was in his teens. He talked about his first memory of her, rocking in a chair with him, sitting in her lap wrapped in a woollen blanket. That was at his grandparents' house in Allenstein, what is now Olsztyn in northern Poland. He said he remembered how the blanket had tasted: of dust and pine.

Banacharski enclosed, in these letters, pages from a manuscript he said was 'my mother's testament'. It seemed to be a memoir of some sort, but it was told in the third person, annotated in pencil by Nicolas, and quoted from in his letters. Between the two narratives – and what of the history of his life remained on the public record – Isla was able to piece together the sequence of events.

One fragment described Ana Banacharski's courtship with Nicolas's father, Sergei Mitrov, in Berlin in the late 1920s. Mitrov was a Russian anarchist who had fetched up there after fleeing the Bolsheviks. She had moved to the city as a student, and they met after she attended a meeting in the radical bookshop where he was staying. She had fallen pregnant, and they moved through Europe together living, unmarried, as a family.

Then came the Spanish Civil War. Mitrov joined the International Brigades, and Ana moved back to her parents' in

East Prussia. Nicolas would then have been seven. Three years later, when Germany annexed Poland, and the persecution of Allenstein's Polish-speaking minority began, Ana fled with Nicolas to France. Ana's story described the old man, her father, waving from the door of the town house – his moustache, his mild smile and the turn-ups on his trousers. It was the last time she saw him.

Mother and son spent the war years in a series of refugee camps. 'Her Nicolas, her little Buddha, her watchful child,' her narrator wrote. 'Ana knew she would have to leave him.'

Nicolas's own narrative picked up here. He talked about his memories, the watchful child reporting. At some point they had been reunited with Mitrov. He remembered his mother, terribly distressed, in the camp outside Paris. He had worked out afterwards, only from his mother's memoir, that he had had a sister who was stillborn at about that time.

But in 1942 Mitrov was separated from Ana and his son by what Banacharski called 'a malign chance'. His letters stopped coming. He did not survive the war. Nicolas wrote, curiously, that he had no memories of his father at all.

These communications resembled love letters not in anything explicit, so much as in their intimacy of address, their notes of tenderness, the parallels they drew between past and present. There had been a girl he had known in the refugee community at Chambon-sur-Lignon, he said, called Kara. Isla reminded him of her. She had resembled Isla, he said, though he did not say in what way. He sketched out a chaste friendship between the fourteen-year-old Nicolas and sixteen-year-old Kara, complicated by longing. Her father was Danish – a wealthy man in the antiques business. He had not encouraged their friendship. They'd been separated, though he'd had letters from her after the war. She hadn't died. But she had disappeared. In his early twenties Nicolas had tried to find her without success.

'Gone,' he wrote. 'Another gone. Another lost to time.'

His letters seemed confiding, tender, anxious that what had happened to him would be known, and his connection with her maintained.

'Chance – or the illusion of chance – is what divides us one from the other. It is chance that carries us apart. Chance that kills us. But what if chance could make us live? What if chance brought us together again? It is just a matter of seeing it right. Of turning it around.'

Isla wrote back, in one letter: 'Nicolas, you say it is chance that divides us. But is also chance that makes us live. You lost people by accident. But you also found them by accident. You found me by accident. Every human being on the face of the earth is here – you said it yourself – by chance.'

'You misunderstand. Deliberately?' he wrote back. 'For everyone who is born hundreds of millions of people – real people – are never born. Who speaks for them? They are nobody. Who will rescue them? What if you could imagine a world in which those people live and are not alone and do not grow old and die? And what if by imagining you could make it so?'

In early autumn, via *EtUdes/RecOltes*, came another letter, sharper in tone than any of the previous. It wondered, with crude sarcasm, whether she was in the employ of 'the other side'. It asked her to come and visit him. It said he had something to give her. But before, it said, she needed to answer him one simple question: 'Nobody has been reading my letters. I have proof positive. I need to know that you are who you are. So answer me this: what is a metre? Reply quickly.'

Isla called her colleague Mike about this. She was worried, she said. She sat in the kitchen of her house in Cambridge and showed him the last letter from Banacharski. What could he mean? Mike shook his head. 'Buggered if I know,' he said. 'Your boyfriend is, let's not forget, mad as a badger.'

'A metre,' she said. 'It's a measurement. He's preoccupied by measurements. And he's trying to build a machine. He says he's finished it.'

'Clear as flaming mud, love. I'd leave it. Write back and tell him it's something to do with Napoleon. He probably thinks he's something to do with Napoleon.' Mike seemed moderately pleased with the witticism. He fetched himself another of Isla's biscuits and moved on to some faculty gossip.

'What is a metre?' he said as he left. 'A hundred centimetres, eh?'

Isla did not show Mike the letters she had got privately. And she did not tell him about Ana's ring. She was still turning it over in her mind two days later. She was leaving for her 10 a.m. seminar, running late and with her hair still slightly wet against her neck, when she picked up the post from the tiled hallway. There were two letters, forwarded from Nice. Both were bulging, as if there was more paper in them than their envelopes were strictly designed to bear.

She tucked them under the arm of her duffel coat as she stepped out into the street. She slipped open the first one with a thumbnail, her bag on her lap, as she settled on the top deck of the bus on the way in to the faculty. She felt her cheeks grow cold as she read.

The yellow legal paper was in some places torn with the force of the handwriting. Block capitals alternated with lower case, no one letter joined up with another, and words of German and French mashed into English sentences. The ruled lines on the paper were only ever a loose guide when Banacharski was excitable – but here the lines of his script were flapping off them like an untethered mainsheet in a gale.

It was a wad of incoherent fury, calling her a 'thief', a 'liar' and a 'Judas'. It accused her of working with 'the enemy, the murderers, the Moloch'. The second letter was shorter, and barely in prose at all. On the first page, her name was written in block capitals, dead centre, and a series of numbers scribbled underneath – separated by dashes and subject to a whole succession of transformations that brought them out to new numbers.

She leafed through. He was using the letters of her name – it would be Kabbalah, she guessed; he had spoken to her about using Kabbalistic practice for, he said, exploring 'the relationship between speech and number'.

On the following pages the letters of her name had been anagrammed, and further manipulated into numbers; or, the letters of her name were written out as a matrix, and multiplied by another matrix constructed from the same letters. Her eyes started to swim. He couldn't have slept. Nobody could physically have achieved the rate and ferocity of work in these letters – would not physically have been able to write them down – in the time between them.

They were both dated the same day, though they bore different postmarks and had clearly been held up a few days between Paris and London. Isla, scouring her memory, couldn't swear to it that they hadn't been written on the same day as the original letter posing the riddle. The final page of this second letter ended: 'Nothing comes of nothing. Nobody's here. We are divided by nothing. Forgive me.' His signature at the bottom was also bristling with numbers, all of them cancelled to zero.

She missed her stop. She was twenty-five minutes late for her seminar by the time she got there and she noticed her hands trembling as she wrote on the whiteboard. She felt very afraid. She cancelled drinks with Mike and Jude. She spent the afternoon talking to the faculty and the college about a temporary, emergency leave of absence. The first flight she could get to Toulouse was the following lunchtime. It would cost her. She didn't think about that.

The following morning, a third letter arrived. On the envelope it said: 'To the Supposed Isla Holderness.' She read it on the way to the airport.

'You are not who you say you are. I am not who I was. Nobody is here,' it began. Almost every other sentence contained a sarcastic intimacy – 'my dearest "Isla"'; 'my trusted "Miss Holderness" ' – as if parodying the man who had written her those private letters about his life over the past couple of months. The brusque kindness she remembered from the shack was gone. She found it unbearable.

It ended with a signature: not 'Nicolas' or even 'NB' this time, but 'Fred Nieman'.

And so, fast-forward to Isla, walking round the final curve of the approach to Banacharski's shack, feeling that she knows what she is going to find.

The fire had long gone out, doused in cold rain. But the smell of burning came through, wet burned wood. Droplets stood on melted plastic. The shack was gone – a black stain on the ground, a couple of jutting teeth of carbonised wood. Across the wet grass to either side were wisps and fragments of cinderated paper, the odd rag of sodden yellow in the fingers of the green.

The Calor canister under the wall of the shack had obviously gone. Half of it was there, its skin twisted and blackened. Its shrapnel had half dug turves out of the ground, and the grass was radially scorched on that side. The wooden floor of the shack was gone from the centre, where the fire seemed to have started. There were threads of rug towards the outside – where the stump of a piling emerged from poured concrete foundations. A stick of table leg was there.

The wind had blown the fire away up the hill, drying and burning the grass in patches up behind the shack. The beanstalks, the ones nearest the hut, were scorched but those towards Isla were intact, if more overgrown than when she had been here. The leaves were blowsy, the season long gone. Isla walked closer.

Too late, she thought. She had run out of time. He was gone.

She twisted a pod off one of the beanstalks, and thumbed it

open. Inside, a broad bean – the only one full-size – sat in its velvety white cushion like a ring in a jeweller's box.

She walked round the shack, looking for him. She thought of calling for him, but it felt wrong, somehow, to raise her voice. He was gone. She knew that. Not dead – she didn't know why she was so sure of that, but she somehow felt confident of it – but gone. Beyond her help. Nobody could help him.

Her good Gore-Tex boots kept the wet out. She remembered him drawing his diagram: 'And here is the map of Nicolas Banacharski in the world. And here is the map of Miss Isla Holderness in the world.' She understood now why this was strangely comforting.

In among the bean shoots the chickens picked, pecking morosely at the wet grass, shivering their wings. Had he left them? Their henhouse was intact. She peeked into it. There was straw in there, and the hopper was dry, and full of grain.

Isla walked back down into town, and caused the police to be called. They came up, took a statement – Isla struggling a little with her French – filed a missing persons report, and late that evening told her she was free to go home. She spent the night in an auberge, and set off the following morning, early, resolute, sad: telling herself she had done everything she could and not believing it for a second.

When she arrived back in Cambridge, she came home to find that she had been burgled. Her laptop had gone, as well as her video recorder, the contents of her underwear drawer and medicine cabinet, and the nearly full bottle of vodka she had kept on the dresser. A pane of the front bay window had been smashed. A creditable but, finally, unsuccessful attempt had been made to remove the television.

Also, her jewellery box was gone – and with it, which somehow at that moment felt more important to her than even her own christening presents, Ana's ring. Isla had sat down on her living-room floor and, before she called the police, cried for a long time.

Three days later, Isla's house was burgled again. This time, it was Banacharski's letters to her that went. It happened during the day, while she was at the library preparing a lecture. No glass was broken. Nothing of value was taken. Nobody was spotted at the scene.

14

Isla Holderness never saw Ana's ring again. Her laptop, having been sold in a grimy pub on the outskirts of town, was eventually recovered by the police.

Its thief was seventeen-year-old Ben Collings, who was picked up not two weeks later while attempting to prise open the back door of the Co-op at 4 a.m., in the mindset of exuberant criminal incompetence that a gram and a half of his brother's home-made amphetamine sulphate and a litre of white cider could be relied upon to produce. His fingerprints matched the ones he had left on the door of Isla's fridge, and his teeth – as the Cambridgeshire Constabulary's equivalent of the CSI lab was proud to report – precisely matched the profile of the two-thirds of a miniature Melton Mowbray pork pie that he had not stolen from inside it.

Mr Collings, as the PC who returned Isla's laptop to her explained, was 'a worthless little toerag' of precisely the sort who formed the cop shop's most loyal client base.

Collings had offloaded most of Isla's possessions onto his big brother – a toerag of some seniority – who had in turn dispersed them among the pawn shops and market stalls of the town. Ana's ring had ended up in an antique shop the quality of whose merchandise was belied by the tweeness of its name. Herbert Owse's Antiquarian Omnium Gatherum stood on Burleigh Street, and was manned by a rubicund numismatist with a wild beard and a liking for checked shirts and moleskin waistcoats. His socks, though this is of scant relevance here, were held up with suspenders. His name was not Herbert Owse.

It was into this shop, however, that Alex Smart ducked while cutting down Burleigh Street one afternoon on his way from the cinema – where he had been spending the afternoon not working on his PhD and not thinking about the fact that he wasn't working on his PhD – to the pub where he was meeting a friend in order to continue doing same.

Alex, who was not in the habit of browsing in antique shops and would not have been able to afford antiques even if he had, had gone in to escape a sudden shower of rain. The shower of rain proving unusually persistent, he was obliged to make a furious pretence at interest in the shop's contents. Away he browsed, under the jovial eye of the proprietor, occasionally asking questions.

'This piece,' he said. 'Eighteenth century, is it?'

'Art deco,' the proprietor replied.

'Hm,' said Alex, opening and closing a cabinet door. 'Very good . . . hinges, it's got. Are they original?'

'Yes.'

'Very good. I was thinking of something like that for my mum. Likes hinges, she does. How much is it?'

'Eight hundred and seventy-five pounds.'

'Oh. Oh my. Really?'

'Yes.'

'Well – bit more, you know. Embarrassing, but a bit more than I was actually thinking of, you know. Spending.'

The supposed Owse made brisk play of returning his attention to the notes he was making in a ledger with a stubby pencil. Alex walked the shop's narrow aisles, keeping one eye on the rain through the bow window. The shop exuded a considerable aura of brownness: wooden floorboards, patches of curly-cornered carpet, brown cabinets and brown bookshelves and brown leather books.

Alex inspected an umbrella stand in which a number of pawky specimens shuffled their spokes. He read the spines of some of the old books, most of which were the sorts of things you might expect to be bought and sold by the yard rather than for their titles – volumes 4 to 8 of something called *The Cyclopedia of Practical Agronomy*; the second volume of a Victorian translation of *Don Quixote*, with illustrated plates.

Then, peering into a glass display cabinet at a selection of silver-black necklaces and brooches with topaz and coral in dented settings, he saw the ring. As he looked at it he thought – in a way that felt light and easy – that perhaps he would ask Carey to marry him, and that this was the ring that he would present to her.

It was sitting upright in a cheap jewellery box. He liked the design, the antique look, the silvery sheen. The ring set his chain of thought in motion, there, while he waited for the rain to stop. But once he had thought it, it seemed right and natural. It was a thought that had been waiting for a thought-shaped slot in his head to occupy, and there it was. They would get married. He would get a cheap flight to the States, and he would go to San Francisco and surprise her with a ring.

The ring was two hundred pounds. Alex could find that. Just. He'd be eating pasta with butter for a bit, but he could find it. He asked the supposed Owse to put the ring aside for him. Wrote his name and mobile phone number, promised to come back the following day. And by the time he stepped out of the shop into the lane, the bell above the door dinging sweetly, shaking a few drops of rain onto Alex's head, the sun was just breaking through the clouds.

And so to Jones, and to Bree – our two supernatural detectives – hot on the heels of this fugitive device. Jones was driving, and Bree was eating.

Bree had worried about Jones driving. The worry started not long after they had gone over a large and tricky interchange through a just-red light that Bree wouldn't have risked. She had read the cross traffic – three lanes of impatient metal, a terminal moraine of shining chrome, pregnant with the intention of surging over their carriageway at the first click of their light to green. They had seemed to heave. Jones had piloted their car serenely through.

'Jones,' she had said, her thigh cramping with the effort of pumping an imaginary brake, 'with your condition . . .'

'Uh-huh,' Jones had said.

'How good are you at anticipating things?'

'Not very,' Jones had said. The speedo had been nudging eighty.

'Things like cars pulling out suddenly, or appearing from dips in the road while you're overtaking . . .'

'Uh-huh,' Jones had said. He had appeared to have no idea of the drift that the conversation was taking.

'Are you good at anticipating those?'

'I don't know,' Jones had said. 'I don't think so. Which cars are you talking about?' He had looked around, scanning the road, meerkatted into the rear-view mirror, peered ahead down the road, as if to see what Bree was referring to.

'Not actual cars *here*,' Bree had said. 'I mean, any cars. Cars you might anticipate. Cars that might pull out or appear from nowhere.'

'Cars that don't exist?'

Bree had realised the problem, and fallen silent. Jones's relationship with time was not, she remembered, the easiest thing to navigate. Nor his relationship with notional cars.

'Jones, your head is a strange thing.'

'It is the only head I have,' Jones had said. 'I have nothing to compare it with.'

Bree had thought of a better way of putting it. She had asked: 'Have you ever crashed a car?'

'I have fast reactions,' Jones had said.

'That's not answering the question,' Bree had said.

'Yes,' Jones had said.

Bree had shrugged. She had let it go. Someone believed Jones could drive. Someone had given him a licence. They hadn't crashed. And Bree hated to drive.

So here they were. Jones driving – slowly, at Bree's insistence – and Bree eating an egg-salad sandwich and a big bag of Doritos. It was a beautiful morning. Everything felt light and good. It was one of those mornings when Bree felt a lightness. The weird thing with the crying had shifted Jones in the way she thought about him. She had thought, at first, that he was handsome. But Bree reckoned she thought everyone was handsome. She hadn't been with anyone for a long time. Then she had thought he was freaky, which he was. But now she felt maternal towards him – and she was surprised to find that feeling warmed her.

'Look at that,' she said, holding up a Dorito. 'That orange. Nothing in nature is that orange.'

Jones looked at her Dorito.

'An orange is that orange,' he said.

Bree ignored him. She put her feet on the dashboard. 'Damn,' she said, munching happily. 'What did they do before Doritos?'

Bree and Jones continued west, stopping to use landlines, where they could, to contact Red Queen. Data points came back: here, a probable sighting; there, a CCTV image of the Smart boy in a gas station forecourt. They were going in the right direction, feeling their way half blind after their quarry. They discovered, only twelve hours afterwards, that he'd been in the same motel in Tupelo.

Bree did most of the talking. Jones almost never originated conversation, but Bree poked and prodded. Bree had become curious about Jones. She asked him what he did when he wasn't doing what they were doing.

'I'm not usually a field agent,' said Jones. 'I work in a small department in Washington. I go through data.'

Bree raised an eyebrow. 'Most of the Directorate's desk work is in New York,' she said.

'I work for different agencies,' said Jones. 'I work in a small department. My condition is useful to agencies looking at data. I can find inconsistencies. I don't suffer confirmation bias.'

'What's confirmation bias?' Bree asked. Bree was smart, but Bree couldn't fill out a tax return. When she'd been at school, statistics and math had swum before her on the page. They'd role-played a business class when she'd been a teenager, and when presented with a pretend balance sheet she had gone red and found herself giggling with fright and embarrassment.

'People see patterns that aren't there,' said Jones. 'They see what they want to see. I don't. I see only what's there.'

'Is that rare?'

'They say so. Much of the work I do is with tax. But also climate data. I check the algorithms used to identify terror suspects.'

'Sounds interesting,' said Bree, thinking otherwise. Sifting data. Jeezus. 'You get bored?'

'No,' said Jones. 'Never.' Bree had lost the ability to be surprised by this.

His tone was light and his eyebrows remained in position.

'What do you do to relax?' Bree said.

'I smoke. I do Sudoku. I cook.'

'You cook?' Bree said. Her interest was piqued. She couldn't imagine Jones cooking. Bree loved to cook. She cooked a lot. It was one of the things she did to pass the time when otherwise she would have been drinking.

'I was told I needed a hobby,' Jones replied. ' "Take your mind off things." I cook every evening and on weekends I cook twice a day. I like food.'

'What you can taste of it through all those cigarettes . . .' Bree interjected.

Jones didn't sound in the slightest defensive. 'I have a good sense of taste.'

'What do you like to cook, then?'

'I've cooked all of Julia Child and *Larousse Gastronomique* and Robert Carrier's *Great Dishes of the World* and Delia Smith's *Summer Collection*. I am on number 467 of Marguerite Patten's *Cookery in Colour*.'

Bree had an image of Jones, solemn and methodical, dressed in an apron and a chef's hat, in the kitchenette of some anonymous and undecorated apartment in which he would be entirely at home. She imagined him holding a burger flipper. He would look like an illustration.

'Black Cap Pudding,' said Jones. 'Put a good layer of stoned prunes or blackcurrant jam at the bottom of the basin.'

Bree burst out laughing. 'What?'

'That is one of "More Steamed Puddings". After that I will cook "Castle Puddings".' Jones looked almost happy.

'Castle puddings, eh? Whatever floats your boat, I guess. You a good cook, then?'

'No. My food is not always good. The instructions have to be exact. I am not good at guessing. I know a "lug" and a "pinch". But what is a "good layer"?' Bree resisted cracking wise. 'I have been finding Marguerite Patten difficult. Delia Smith is very good. I like Delia Smith.'

'My favourite food,' said Bree, apropos of nothing, 'is . . .'

And then she started to think about what her favourite food was. Once again it had eluded her. Every time she played this game – usually imagining herself on Death Row – it changed, but never that much. She had once looked online at a list of actual last-meal requests, and she realised that she had all the same favourite foods as most prisoners on Death Row. Gray's Papaya hot dogs. White Castle sliders. Fried chicken. Pancakes with bacon. A pint of vanilla ice cream with cookie dough. Cold toast thickly spread with salted butter. Banana cake.

She let her sentence trail off. Time and landscape passed.

'You cook for friends, then, Jones?' Bree said a little later. Picking up a conversation with Jones was easy. It was as if you could put him on pause, like a VHS. 'Throw parties?'

'No. I cook for myself. I don't socialise,' Jones said matter-of-factly. 'People find me unnerving. I have assessments with a specialist, Dr Albert, and a socialisation worker called Herman Coldfield. Herman works for the government. He tells me to think of him as a friend.'

'Do you?'

'No.'

She almost said: 'Got a girlfriend?' but then had second thoughts. Of course he didn't. But did he have sex? Even thinking about Jones's sexual needs, if he had any, creeped her out. She had started to think of him as a child, almost. The idea of him as a sexual being repulsed her. But presumably he did – well . . . something. Everybody did. But sex without imagination; without fantasy; without thinking about what the other person was thinking . . .

Bree pushed that aside, and pictured Jones's life, and felt a little sad. His half-life. That unfurnished apartment – clean, drab, anonymous – in which he would be at home. The bedroom in which he would do his crying, the kitchenette in which he would do his cooking, the shoes by the door each morning waiting for him to step into them and go out into the world without fear or expectation.

That was how it had felt to her, the first months sober. I'll be your friend, Jones, she thought.

And so, across country, the three cars proceeded. There were Bree and Jones, making shift with each other. There was Alex, making lonely time – thinking, driving, enjoying the pleasurable melancholy of the road, listening to the Pixies and Talking Heads over and over again, wondering how he would remember this journey, how he would describe it to his children.

And there were Sherman and Davidoff, making no progress, wondering why their iPods didn't work.

'My name is Bree, and —'

Bree had liked drinking. She had been a good drunk. A happy drunk. When she took the first beer of the afternoon — never before noon; never, at least not till towards the end — and felt its coldness scald her throat, its warmth blossom in her chest, she had been suffused with . . . what? A sense of generosity, of well-being, of peace with the universe.

That was the best bit. Of course, she'd smoked then too, just the odd one. So the cigarette, the first hit. That was good. But the drink was where the action was. A six of Michelob, pearled with frost in the top of the refrigerator. Crack and sigh as the cap came off. The bottle sighed too. Then a big pull from the neck and it was like the lights came up.

Bree had been sociable. She and Al had gone out in the evenings, taken Cass when she was tiny. They couldn't afford a sitter in those days. Nobody was buying Al's paintings, and though he got a bit of work here and there hanging other people's stuff it wasn't enough. Bree had stopped being a cop and was pulling down one quarter of jackshit working part-time at the Pentagon.

That first beer, yes. That had been the kicker. Bree tended to make a point of not thinking about it too much. It had been a long, long time and the craving was weaker. But sometimes it still surprised her, like an old ache. And when she did turn and think about it, the taste of that first mouthful was still fresh in her memory as if it was just gone midday.

Level and confront. My ass. What would you give for just — just once more — the taste? Just once more. No such thing as just once. We know where that leads. But before you die, don't you want to feel that again? The cold filling the mouth, the eyes closing, the eyes opening to an easier world?

166

It was only later that it got harder. Al got less fun. Bree still maintained this. She knew – she fucking knew, OK, by the end of it – that things had got out from under her, but that didn't mean that she was necessarily wrong about Al getting less fun. She'd started staying out when he'd gone home, and they started to row about Cass.

That always hit a nerve with her. That was when it got vicious.

'You dare say that, you fucking piece of shit. I love that girl. I love her more than anything. I'd kill for her. Kill. I do everything for her.'

'Who got her up for school this morning?'

'I was *sick*!'

'Bree, you're drinking too –'

'My drinking has nothing to do with –'

'You were sick because –'

'I got *day flu*.'

'You got –'

'I got her up yesterday, and the day before and the day before, and, 'cause one time –'

'It's not just the one time, love.'

'Love' stung her. The softness of it.

'Al, do you even think, ever just think, just once what it's like to be me?' She'd hear herself slur on 'ever', losing the second vowel, but she'd plough on. The thought of what it was like to be her made her eyes prickle but she wasn't going to give him the satisfaction, and the emotion was redirected into anger. 'I'm holding this damn family together while you try to sell your piece-of-shit paintings.' That would wound him, and she'd see him suck it down. Looking back now, it still made her hurt somewhere remembering moments like that when she'd see how hard he was trying. Turning the other cheek. That holier-than-thou stuff enraged her.

'I work, and I cook, and I come home and I look after our damn kid, and if one morning I get sick I'm what, I'm a bad mother? I get a drink – yes, maybe I have a couple drinks because I damn well need to unwind and now you're going to sit in judgement over me?'

'I'm not sitting in judgement.' He looked miserable, utterly defeated. Bree had always been strong, always stronger than him. 'I love –'

Doors would slam, tears come. 'Fuck you, fuck you, fuck you.' And Bree would show him what was fucking what by going out and necking a couple.

'I love her more than anything.' Bree wondered. You had to say it. You had to feel it. What if it wasn't true?

Bree could look back on all this now and know she was wrong. She didn't like to think too clearly about how wrong – she'd been through that, and you'd go crazy if you spent the whole rest of your life fifth-stepping, Bree reckoned; you'd get addicted to shame.

But what was odd was that as she accessed the memories she didn't feel wrong. She remembered not just what she did and said, but what she felt. And as she inhabited the memory she felt it again. She felt indignant. She wasn't that bad then. Nothing worse than millions of normal people who bring their kids up fine, and whose husbands didn't get their panties in a twist if they had one bourbon over the line most nights. She was dealing with it.

That was what she thought of as her double vision. That indignation was still a part of her. But so was the part that saw something else. And even back then, the part that saw things as they were was there. It simply didn't seem urgent. I'll keep an eye on that, she'd thought.

She knew that her morning routine wasn't great; wasn't how it had always been. She'd make sure she was in the bathroom alone, Al out of the house preferably. Then she'd run the shower and before she got in it she stood over the sink with her hands gripping the sides and she arched over it and retched. She had learned to do this silently, for the most part, feeling her diaphragm spasm. She had to do this for somewhere between thirty seconds and a minute. Most days, a few tablespoons of bitter yellow bile slicked onto the white porcelain. She'd ride it out. That, too, passed, and the nausea left with the bile.

Then she'd breathe in and breathe out. And she'd stand up straight. The shuddering and the retching gone, she would feel a lightness, as if she'd been purged. She'd swill her mouth and the sink with water, and step into the shower, almost bright, ready to face the day.

And even though her work at the Pentagon was paper-shovelling, she kept at it. She arrived on time and she left on time and she worked damn well. Until Al left she was keeping it going. She thought of Al's mousy, too-long hair. The yellow tint to his sunglasses and the brown leather jacket he loved and always wore. The speed and anger of his going.

Bree looked out of the car window. America was passing. It was warm, but the air was thick and the sky was the colour of ash. A couple drops of rain fell on the windshield.

Al was still there when she'd started to lose time. They'd had so much time back then, when they were young and new-married, that Bree barely noticed it going missing. When it did, it had been funny – Al shaking his head at how Bree couldn't remember getting home from parties and feigning theatrical outrage when Bree would ask: 'Did we . . .?'

'You've *forgotten*?'

Later, though, she lost time more easily, more unexpectedly, more disconcertingly. Time started to vanish in the way that dollars would vanish from her purse – just a tentative five minutes here or there, surreptitiously, calculated so she wouldn't miss it but not calculated well enough. She'd find herself in a different room than she had been, tips of her fingers grazing the door jambs, mouth open to deliver a sentence she had no idea of. She would frown and withdraw. That, at least, early on.

The thefts became more blatant. Money from the purse was not an analogy. Money really had been going missing from her purse. And it was hard to be sure, at first, how much and when. But it was clear Cass was stealing from her. Finally, she confronted her about it and Cass reacted as she always did when cornered: with the sort of indignation only an eleven-year-old can muster. Her whole face shone red as she screamed back. Bree slapped her – not on the face but on the legs.

Al had gone by this time. Had he? Bree couldn't always remember the sequence of events. But that would explain why she was so angry – he'd left them both in the shit, the way he walked out. She was under such pressure then. She couldn't afford childcare. And her money was going missing. And Cassie was bed-wetting and Bree was exhausted and her good-for-nothing husband had meanwhile lit out for the territories with an armload of his own paintings. It was the first time she'd hit her daughter.

'Never steal. Never steal from your mommy, never. You hear me?' Blood thumping in her ears, rage misting everything. Cass's yell, as the blows landed – suddenly turning the corner into a shriek, even shriller and even louder.

It was about this time that the sneak-thief started to get bolder. Money started disappearing from the bedside table. And drinks – the emergency half-jack in the wardrobe; the old miniatures of vodka in the ice compartment. And time – great chunks of time would have been pocketed, spirited away. It was very confusing.

Was the same person who was taking the money taking the time? That's all money was, Bree had once heard someone say: frozen time. It became impossible to keep track of things.

The thief was eventually apprehended.

Bree never felt that the Bree who had been doing that stuff was another person, one who had died at those meetings to make way for the shiny new person who was now sitting in the car with Jones. That Bree had continued. In another life, one where Bree had spent a lot less time sitting in smoky, talky rooms on jittering plastic chairs comparing war stories, she was living on, still drinking. She'd be deathbound by now, living through blank, real spaces, passing hours and days into her blackouts like someone patiently feeding a furnace: there, but not there.

And she was here, but not here. She followed this Bree around with the tenacity of a shadow. She was long when the sun was low; almost invisible in the bright of the day. Bree could lose touch with her for just a second, by jumping – but then gravity intervened and Bree wasn't a great one for jumping up and down these days, in any case.

Stupid analogy, Bree thought. Raindrops, an unexpected shower, gathered and ran on the windshield. They felt like another analogy, and she wondered what it was like to be Jones, who had shown no signs of making conversation since lunch, and for whom the slick of water running down the windshield would never be anything other than rain.

Bree thought about not-Bree, drinking Bree. It was as if she had acquired a twin. In that life, this Bree would be shadowing her. Sober Bree, in that world, would be not-Bree: would be just there, hanging around, waiting. The thing that was your deepest, darkest terror: the thing you longed for.

Snap. Cheers, sister.

Except in both these worlds, they had taken Cass away, and Bree wondered momentarily in which of these worlds she was living and why.

15

It was the morning of the third day that they got a sure fix on Alex. It was pure good luck.

Red Queen remembered that the Directorate had a long-gone field agent by the name of Doc, living in the New Mexico desert near the Texas border. Doc was semi-retired on medical grounds after spearheading the Directorate's intensive 2003 investigation into the effectiveness of ayahuasca trances as an intelligence-gathering technique.

The verdict of the investigation – reached not by Doc himself but by those observing his experiments with a clearer head – had been 'not very'. Doc was loco in the brainpan, no two ways about it.

But Red Queen reached out to Doc anyway, and Doc – who did things, if he did them, for reasons of his own – agreed to drive his tangerine-coloured pickup to a bluff overlooking the I-40 and wait for 'this cat with the magic ring'.

'Magic ring?' Red Queen had said.

'A snake told me about it,' Doc had said.

Red Queen had made a mental note. 'And his licence plate. You have it?'

'Wrote it down. In-scriibed it.'

'With a pen?'

'It's cool,' Doc had said. 'I see auras. He's going to be lit up like a Christmas tree on the Fourth of July. He'll be haloed in rainbows. It'll be like the Northern Lights. I'll see him.'

'The licence plate . . .'

'It's cool,' Doc had repeated before ringing off. But true to his word he had perched above the highway and watched the westbound traffic with lizard eyes. And to Red Queen's voluble astonishment, had not only got a tail on the boy but confirmed that the boy was himself being followed. 'Couple of wolf-like cats. None too smart. Violent men. Big one and a small one. Keep losing him. And there's something else. Somebody else. A very old man. He's here and he's not here. Like John Barleycorn or an old shaman I know. I'm moving in,' he had added. 'Do me good to get within a sniff of civilisation. Reckon I've got a fix.'

He had left Red Queen listening to the staticky burr of an open line, then Doc had rolled his old wagon down onto the highway, and followed them at a leisurely distance. And it was as that orange car, with its big, bald, white-sided tyres was lumbering onto the great artery heading west, that Alex had exclaimed, aloud and to himself: 'Don't forget your toothbrush.'

Doc said, also to himself, musingly: 'Something about a toothbrush . . .'

And two hours later, Doc found a payphone and called Red Queen, who called Bree on her cellphone, and directed her to a superstore in a roadside mall on the east side of Albuquerque in the early afternoon.

'He's there,' Doc said. 'I'm just not sure when.'

Bree and Jones showed up, and did two circuits of the wide parking lot, and weren't able to see the boy, or his car, or anything of that sort.

'Had a feeling, this guy, apparently,' said Bree, with a shrug. 'Another hit for the Directorate. Still, best we've got. We proceed,' she added philosophically, 'through hints and accidents.'

Jones went to get some tobacco. Bree ambled in to check out the store. She walked the aisles, found nothing. No sign of the kid. Near the door there were a couple of girls with too much make-up, wearing long coats. They were chewing gum. With them was a middle-aged man in a cheap suit, pretending not to be watching her as she came in the door. He had something concealed in his palm. She saw his thumb work at it, and he turned his hand, looked surreptitiously down at it. It glinted. Bree didn't like it.

She turned round and headed outside, intending to take up a position where she could watch the front entrance unobserved. She took a trolley. A trolley would be good. Make it look like she was shopping. Who was that guy? Where was the boy?

Alex ran his tongue around his teeth. His upper incisors were pleasantly slippery. He was worried about the lower set, though. They felt furry, clagged. He had a stark visual memory of his toothbrush, sitting red on the white sink at the last motel. He had left it there, hadn't he?

It was about lunchtime anyway. He'd stop. Two birds with one stone.

'Don't forget your toothbrush,' he said aloud to himself, before pulling into the supermarket car park. He slammed the car door, hopped out, and set off for the entrance to the shop.

The store dominated the parking lot: a wide glass frontage that could have done with being cleaned more recently, and big scrolls of paper yellowing in the windows advertising special offers, on beer and cleaning products, mostly. Next door were two smaller shops – a tobacconist and a pizza place.

A dirty great sign, hoisted above the entrance like a hat, announced simply: 'SUPERSTORE'. The letters were picked out in broken light bulbs. A nondescript cartoon character – it looked like a smiling chocolate button – was giving the world an unwavering thumbs up from next door to the letter E.

MIC's guns for hire had lost Alex's trail again, and Sherman had morosely assented to Davidoff's insistence that they stop driving and get some food. A roadside sign half a mile back had promised pizza. Davidoff used a hand on the roof to haul his big frame from the car and they stood there scanning the scene like children at the gates of Disneyland.

Sherman saw the kid before Davidoff did, and nudged the bigger man. He saw the recognition bloom and take hold in his face like a pilot light. Davidoff's eyes scanned the parking lot, and Sherman knew what he was seeing. There was a hedge down the left-hand side. Maybe a hundred metres of asphalt between the kid and the entrance to the store, twenty metres between the two men and the boy they were chasing.

A fat woman in a T-shirt was pushing a shopping cart out of the store. Nobody seemed to be here other than that. A tall grey-haired guy, a couple of hundred metres away, was leaning up outside the door of the tobacco store next door, smoking. A handful of cars in the lot, empty. Sherman picked up pace. Davidoff broke right, out on a slight trot, as if he was someone jogging to get a parking ticket while his family waited in the car. Sherman closed slower.

Ninety metres, fifteen metres.

The boy was moving on a diagonal. Across the front entrance of the store there was a snake of trolleys – what had once been bright pink plastic faded to brittle white in the weather – shucked into each other. To reach the entrance, the boy would have to walk round the right-hand end of them and up the wheelchair ramp.

If Sherman took the straight line – went left of the trolleys and vaulted up the wrong end of the ramp – he'd get there about the same time as the boy.

Eighty metres, ten metres.

Davidoff way out to the right. Scan left – that angle covered. Was there a back entrance? Probably. Best not let him get into the store in the first place if at all possible. Best not let him bolt.

Seventy metres, ten metres. Easy. Easy.

Ouch! Shit. The fat woman – not at all where he'd expected her to be – had barked her trolley against his shin. Stupid fat –

'Sorry, sorry,' she was at once muttering, fussing: 'Oh gosh, oh gee. Sir, I'm real sorry – I didn't see where you were . . .' She started, inanely, trying to brush down the lapels of his jacket with her hands . . .

Sherman struggled to keep his temper. He could see the kid reaching the end of the ramp, and here was this woman right in the –

'It's fine, really,' he said.

'Oh, you're so kind, I'm sorry, I'm sorry.'

'It's *fine*,' he repeated, jerking away from her. A bit too snappy an emphasis. She was startled, suddenly looking offended.

'Well, there's no call –'

Oh for fuck's *sake*. 'Dammit –'

He pushed her trolley to one side roughly – it clattered to the tarmac, lighter than he had anticipated; he didn't have time to wonder why she was pushing an empty trolley – and hopped past, breaking into an angry trot for a couple of paces, enough to carry him to within nearly grabbing distance of the kid. But as he did so the kid heard something and jerked his head round – saw Sherman looking straight at him, read the tension in his face.

Alex Smart didn't recognise Sherman but something in him knew instantly and viscerally that the man behind him was after him. He gasped, stumbled over on one ankle, recovered, hip-checked the back end of the line of trolleys and sprinted up the ramp for the entrance of the shop.

Shit shit shit. Sherman abandoned all pretence of stalking him and just went flat out. A fraction of a second of indecision – go right and round the line of trolleys, or try to hurdle them – resolved in favour of cutting the corner.

He grunted and put one hand out to grab midway down the caterpillar of trolleys, pushed off the tarmac and swung his legs up to vault – the kid whipping back his head to look with candid fright at the man cutting the corner off between them – feeling as he left the ground the trolleys sliding under his hand, his trailing foot now not clearing but catching the steel railing on the other side – angular momentum bringing him round faster than he could compensate for.

The electric doors of the supermarket whooshed open and Alex ran inside. Sherman crashed down onto the top of the ramp behind him. His left hand broke his fall at the cost of an impact in the heel of his hand so hard the pain detonated in his elbow. He lost a smear of skin – he didn't feel it – then first his left then his right knee crashed onto the hairy black-and-red plastic mat that said 'WELCOME' in big letters.

Nothing was broken, but the physical shock – a charge of adrenalin and humiliation – made Sherman very, very angry. The electric doors had half swiped shut behind Alex, but then Sherman's face broke the beam, and they jolted open again. Sherman scrambled to his feet and stumbled through the doors.

He got his head up just long enough to see, confusingly, what seemed to be the bottom half of a girl in a bikini before his forward momentum drove his head into the soft part between her bikini top and her bikini bottoms. There was a shrill squawk, interrupted by the sound of the air being driven out of her lungs by Sherman's head. She went down and so did Sherman, rolling off sideways and sprawling on his back.

It *was* a girl in a bikini – two of them. Both blonde. One of them now on the deck somewhere, the other shying above him on her platform shoes like some sort of horse. As Sherman tried to get his footing and his dignity back, there was the sound of an air horn and his field of vision was obscured by an avalanche of something coming down on him – colours, red, white and blue . . .

He threw his hands up to protect his face, and yelped. Sherman was engulfed in something soft and multicoloured and swirling. The air horn gave another great asthmatic hoot and Sherman found himself spitting out something dry in his mouth . . . little bits of paper.

The girl on the floor was crying – or wailing, anyway – and Sherman was sitting in a small snowdrift of red-white-and-blue confetti, half of which seemed to be wrapped in flakes round his tongue. The air horn went off again.

Sherman scrambled to his feet. There was a guy in a white button-down shirt with a tie on, trying to help him up and grinning inanely in his face.

'—tulations! Sir, yes, sir, sorry. Sorry, sir, let us –' the man in the shirt sweeping confetti from Sherman's shoulders, the one girl helping the other girl up – 'quite unprepared, quite an entrance, ha ha, but no harm done, no, sir, let me extend the compliments of the store to you, yes, sir–'

'What the *fuck*?'

'Ha ha, sir, no, I'm sorry, sir, there's no need for that kind of language, I think you'll be pleased, sir, to learn – let me help you up with that – sir, this is a very proud moment, a proud moment I say, in the history of this store, to be able to say you are our one MILLIONTH customer!'

And with that the man in the shirt and tie extended the open palm of friendship to the man from MIC and the man from MIC hit him in the face.

Alex heard all this – or some of this – behind him as he ran through the store. He dodged a startled sales assistant, brought down a revolving rack of tennis shirts, gulped air, hurdled a low stool on which until moments before someone had been trying on a pair of trainers, and then seeing half concealed between two racks of off-brand sportswear a beige fire door with a bar across it at waist height rammed his hand into the bar so hard his palm hurt.

The door slammed open and disgorged Alex into a corridor of whitewashed breeze blocks and grey floor tiles. It smelled of stale air and long-ago bleach. Alex let the door shut behind him and ran down the corridor and round the corner, grabbing at a bit of pipework to swing himself round as he went.

He heard his own trainers squeaking on the lino, and his chest hurt at the Y-shaped bit where his lungs met.

There were what looked like storerooms off the corridor to one or other side – grey doors, with wired windows in them. He wondered about hiding in one but the fear of being trapped was too strong. Besides, his body – he didn't know who that guy was, but he knew he needed to get away from him – seemed to be taking these decisions for him. He carried on running. At the end of the corridor there was sunlight leaking in round the edges of another door with a bar across it. Alex bet that would be the outside door.

He didn't know how long the guy he'd heard fall over behind him would take to be on him and he didn't want to find out. He barrelled into the door. It resisted the first bump, but then he pushed again and the bar yielded and the door opened. He spilled out into the light. He was by an open loading bay of some sort – a thin and inexpertly laid strip of tarmac led round to the far corner of the building and back out.

Ahead there was a shallow bank of scrubby grass, a low wall, a patch of waste ground. Further away, in the distance, the highway. He stopped for a moment and looked around. If he could sneak back down between the outside wall of the store and the hedge he could maybe make it to his car. But he'd have to cross the car park. That guy had moved fast. If he hadn't seen where he'd gone would he have doubled back to try and ambush him? Or would he even now be making his way through the back corridor of the building?

Before he had the chance to speculate further, Alex flinched: in the shadow of the loading bay he thought he saw something move. He turned to face it, but his eyes were still adjusting to the brightness. There was something there, though. Definitely something there. He stepped a bit further back –

At that precise moment the fire door banged open again with some force. Out of the door came Sherman, looking as he was:

furious. The door itself swung out and struck Davidoff – who had been unfortunate in the moment he picked to pounce – hard on the top of his forehead. Davidoff, behind the door, went down like a rail of shirts, but not before the momentum of his charge had sent the door slamming back onto his colleague. Sherman, weighing not more than three-quarters what Davidoff did, himself fell over, again, right at Alex's feet.

Alex, not sure at all what had just happened, looked down at the crazy man – who, he noticed, had a gun in his sock and looked like he was proposing to start pointing it at Alex just as soon as he got round to not being on the ground again – and bolted for the corner. If the bad guy was now behind him, the decision where to run had become a whole lot more straightforward.

Jones had caught up with Bree outside the superstore. Jones was smoking and Bree was wondering what to do when Alex emerged from the gap between the low trees and the left-hand side of the store running at full pelt across the parking lot towards them.

Bree looked at Jones, whose expression was perfectly blank. Let him go, thought Bree. This was too public. They knew what car he was driving. The brief was to follow. Protect.

'Like a bat out of hell,' Bree murmured as the boy closed the gap between them. She felt a stirring of anxiety in her gut as to what was following him, then quenched it and put on her best bovine bystander expression.

Like a bat out of hell. She wondered about the origins of the phrase. Why were bats, especially, keen to leave hell? The boy ran right between the two of them, legs pumping almost comically high, breath coming in rags and tatters.

Something occurred to her as she watched him go.

'You have no idea,' she said to his departing back, 'what's going on, do you?' He took a corner – Scooby-Doo legs – and was fumbling at the door of the silver Pontiac and then was in it, overrevving the engine before he got it in gear, then taking a wide loop round the near-empty parking lot and grounding the undercarriage with a scrape as he bounced down the awkward gradient onto the street. He was gone.

The guy Bree had hit with her trolley earlier came out from the same place more or less as Alex was getting into the car. He had something in his hand that he stowed quickly inside his jacket as he saw Bree. At around the same moment, the front doors of the store slid sideways and out came – to Bree's considerable surprise – some sort of store detective in a brown uniform, along with a pair of cut-price beauty queens and a really distressed-looking guy with a wad of crimson toilet tissue clamped to his nose and nosebleed all down his cheap shirt and what looked like confetti in his hair.

The guy with the gun in his jacket clocked them. Bree could see him making a swift calculation. He broke into the sort of awkward, loping run that someone who has just sustained a crunching blow to the coccyx might adopt. First he seemed to be making for the road on foot, the store detective making a half-hearted attempt to lumber in pursuit and the nosebleed guy waving one arm and shouting something from the safety of the doorway. Then, a way away, Bree could hear something that sounded like a siren and the man thought better of it and swerved towards a car parked near the entrance to the lot. He was gone before the store detective got halfway across the space between them.

The guy's car was a rental. Bree shrugged. Everyone's car seemed to be a rental. She had the plate. Red Queen would run something up.

' 's go,' she said. 'I made the plate. Did you make the plate?'

Jones nodded. 'Every one in the lot.'

'Jonesy,' said Bree. 'There is a use for you after all.'

'There was another man,' Jones said. Bree looked at him with eyebrows raised. 'He came past me when I was buying cigarettes.

I saw them talking.' Bree was thinking – what with them both having been standing in the middle of the parking lot for the last ten minutes and the guys in the stripy cars about to show up – that it was time for them to be off.

'Wait,' said Jones, and vanished at a run towards the far side of the building.

'Jones!' said Bree.

A police car rolled, siren blipping off, into the parking lot and pulled up outside the line of trolleys in front of the store. The store detective and the nosebleed guy mobbed the window as the cop got out. Arms were waved. Bree couldn't afford to stay still and risk becoming somebody's witness so she moved off, fussing ostentatiously with her trolley, and then stood behind their car pretending to do something in the trunk.

When that got boring, she sat in the passenger seat and started to eat Jolly Ranchers from the stash in the glove compartment, two at a time. She liked to combine the cherry and peach ones. Thinking about recipes kept her calm, she had discovered.

Where the hell had Jones gone? The cop had gone into the store with the nosebleed guy and his entourage. He had his note-pad out and was writing as he went. He looked, from his body language at least, bored. Good. Bree waited some more. She ran out of Jolly Ranchers. She thought about calling Red Queen but then thought she better be safe and wait for Jones and wait for a landline. She wondered if there were some Reese's Pieces at the back of the glove compartment. There were not.

Then the door opened and Jones climbed into the driver's seat. He smelled of stale smoke and something else. He pulled a rag out from the compartment in the door and wiped at his hand. He was looking dead ahead. Under the level of the steering wheel Bree could see –

'Is that *blood*? Jesus. Jones: what the hell? Are you hurt?'

'No,' said Jones. 'The other man is dead.'

Bree was speechless, for a moment.

'You're joking.' She felt dizzy.

'Don't joke,' said Jones. A fact about himself. He showed her a cellphone. On the screen was a picture of a man's face. He looked startled. There was a penknife sticking out of his neck. His mouth was slightly open. Very little blood. The background was tarmac.

'He was unconscious,' said Jones. 'I was searching him and he woke up. I didn't know what to do so I killed him. No documents. Only phone. Took his photograph. Might be helpful.'

'You killed him?'

'I didn't know what to do.'

Jones looked intently ahead, turned on the engine, drove the car out of the lot.

Alex was freaking out. He spent at least as much time looking in his rear-view mirror — for *what*? He barely even got a look at the guy — as out of the windscreen. Within thirty seconds of joining the freeway he'd come so close to rear-ending a truck (he reckoned his front bumper had been about four inches from the sign reading 'I Brake For Pussy', which would have been fatal had the driver done as advertised) that he'd given himself an even bigger fright than he'd had round the back of the supermarket. He'd had one nasty near miss as he'd become confused as to what was the inside and what the outside lane when you're driving on the other side of the road. A wailing horn had reminded him.

A panicky attempt to fish his mobile phone out of his left-hand pocket — he was still sketchy as to who he would call but he knew he'd rather have it on the passenger seat than in his pocket — had nearly ended in the sort of disaster they show on the news.

Who the hell was that man? With a gun! An honest to God gun. As he drove, he started to calm down. Just a random lunatic. Another one. America was full of those. But what had happened back there? It looked like the door had bounced off something and hit him. What had the door bounced off?

Alex's appetite for his road trip was dwindling. What was causing him especially strong palpitations was the thought – he didn't know from where – that he recognised that man. Could the man have been stalking him or something? He thought of Rutger Hauer's character in *The Hitcher*: a blond, amused lunatic killing his way through the desert and always, as in a nightmare, seeming to get ahead of the hero. Wherever you showed up, he'd already be there, and would have marked his arrival with some dead bodies or a severed finger in a bowl of chips.

Alex kept going west.

He stopped, two hours later, when his petrol gauge started to wag into the red zone. He found a service station, a busy one. And only when he'd been standing in there for twenty minutes, affecting to browse the Doritos under the reassuring eye of the CCTV camera, watching the arrivals on the forecourt, did he set out on the road again with something like a restored sense of calm.

The guy couldn't possibly be following him. Too much time on his own was affecting his imagination. Even so, he came within an ace of calling Saul, just to hear his brother's voice, sleepy and annoyed, at whatever time it was in England.

16

They'd risked sending the photograph of the dead man in over the dead man's phone.

Red Queen had spent fifteen minutes talking Bree down.

'I did not sign up for this,' had been the agent's first words when she'd got a line to the Directorate. 'Your guy killed someone in cold blood. We don't do that. We don't do things like that. We have no –' Bree flapped her hand – 'no – we have no – we're not –'

'Don't panic,' said Red Queen. Red Queen was panicking.

'– we have no jurisdiction. If we were – we're not –'

Bree was hyperventilating, nearly. The DEI wasn't a judicial body. It didn't have any jurisdiction at all. It just had a remit.

'Did you know? Did you know he was going to do that?'

'Don't panic –'

'*Tell* me.'

Red Queen left a silence a bit too long. 'No, I didn't. He wasn't supposed to . . .'

'You – what – who told him? He's . . . this, this "thing". He's like mentally ill, and you've got him –'

'We thought. Our Friends thought –'

'He's what? He's what? Our Friends are involved?'

'Of course they're involved. This is very big. Of course –'

'Jesus, RQ. He could go to jail. I could go to jail. He *murdered* someone. In a Kwik-E-Mart parking lot. With a frigging squad car outside.'

Bree breathed in and out, raggedly, gathering breath to continue, goggling at the telephone cable. She felt sweaty.

'Where did he get a knife? What was he doing with a knife?'

'Bree – half the people in this country carry a *gun* –'

'So why didn't he use a gun? What's wrong with him? He's a Friend? Are you saying he's a Friend? I thought he was Directorate –'

'On loan. Their asset.'

'Well, how do you know? Was this part of *their* plan?'

Red Queen exhaled.

Bree said: 'You don't know, do you?'

The silence lengthened.

Eventually Red Queen said: 'None of that matters. You know how important this is. Keep your head. Stay with it. Do your job. We'll look after you. Trust me.'

Bree didn't say anything to that, put down the phone, went back to the motel room.

The dead man, as Red Queen had feared, was linked to MIC: off-books payments over five years. Frederick Gordon Noone. Forty-one. A British national, ten-year veteran of the UK's Parachute Regiment, where he was known as 'Davidoff' for reasons unclear to Red Queen.

Noone had got his boots sandy in Iraq and Afghanistan. Clean service record. After leaving the regiment he had, along with many like him, touted for private hire and found himself doing a similar job for much more money and with the rules of engagement tilted in his favour. He was on Blackwater's books, briefly – then left. The payments from a slush fund linked to MIC had started shortly after.

The trail pointed to sub-Saharan Africa, some time in South America – training FARC, probably, thought Red Queen. The run-of-the-mill end of MIC's operations involved arming and training terrorists and their opposite numbers in government in most of the major conflicts around the world. Creating customers, was how they thought of it.

No family, apparently. Good. His employers weren't going to be reporting this guy missing any time soon. He'd entered the country on his own passport, a guest visa, but that wouldn't send up flags from USCIS for a while. He'd booked a return ticket, no doubt just for the sake of form, but that was still a fortnight away. Hotel? Car? His partner would probably take care of that.

Good.

That they were fielding someone – one of a team, presumably – with traceable connections to them, travelling under his own name, suggested haste and urgency. They were taking very big risks with this thing. So either they were counting on some powerful protectors or they were starting to flail. More likely the former.

This wasn't Red Queen's usual beat. Not at all. The Directorate seldom if ever staged interventions. It soaked information up, spread spiderwebs, moved as invisibly as possible through the world. If it did something stagy, like bringing in Hands, it called in a favour from Our Friends. But this situation was beyond the usual thing. The executive branch, so to speak, needed the DEI's knowledge. And DEI needed the executive branch.

There was still at least one more guy loose on the ground.

Red Queen spoke to Porlock. Explained the situation, though something about his manner suggested he knew about it already.

'Go to Our Friends. Tell them it's their mess. They need to go, find this dead man before anyone else does, and make him disappear. This needs to be contained, agreed?'

'Agreed.'

Sherman waited in the car park of their motel for three hours for Davidoff to return. Better safe than sorry. Then he risked a call to Davidoff's pay-as-you-go.

The phone, on the side table of Jones's room in the motel, trilled and its screen lit up. Jones picked it up and got a pen and wrote down the number but did not answer it.

Jones waited. The phone went again. Same number. Jones carefully wrote it down underneath where he had written the number the first time.

Sherman frowned. He knew the big fella would be pissed off that he'd bolted, but there was no great percentage for Sherman in standing around to make friends with Mr One Millionth Customer and the meet-and-greet girls, and Davidoff could take care of himself.

He'd last seen Davidoff at the front of the shop before it had all gone tits skyward. He'd slipped off, Sherman assumed, to go round and cover any back exits. Much use he'd turned out to be. How the little sod had managed to hit Sherman with the door, he didn't know, but it had done his shin a mischief and from then on in Sherman hadn't had much of a chance to do anything but follow his nose.

This was a crap job, he thought. A crap, crap job. Everything that could have gone wrong had. And now, when he'd like to have been safely indoors having a chod and a read of the paper, he was sitting in some backwater in the middle of America surveilling his own motel room from a car park – he seemed to spend a lot of time in car parks – or feeding crap tin money into crap tin payphones. Lost idiot wanted. Please call Ed Otis, answers to Sherman.

He didn't know what was keeping Davidoff. He thought about phoning Ellis but then thought about not phoning Ellis and preferred the second thought. He thought about returning to the shop, wondered about whether the car had been seen. He thought not. As far as they were concerned he was just a violent nutter who missed out on a free trolley dash and the chance to have his photograph taken with a couple of village idiot beauty queens.

Finally, he decided he'd rather just go than keep sitting here. He waited till after dark, and then drove. The forecourt and the neon sign were still illuminated but the glass front was shut.

Sherman parked the car a couple of blocks away, and walked back to the shop.

The snake of trolleys, locked and chained in the black light, looked like something's spine. A single car, seemingly abandoned, gleamed grey-white in the middle of the car park. The display windows of the shop faced blankly over the asphalt, eating the dark. Sherman shivered, pushed his hands into the pockets of his jacket and broke into the beginnings of a trot.

There was nothing outside the building. Sherman spent a few minutes in a pool of shade near the exit, watching the windows of the building for the sweep of a flashlight – anything that said 'night-watchman'. Nothing. He circled towards the back of the building.

A sign directed deliveries to a roughly laid tarmacked strip down the side of the store. He trotted down under the shoulder of the building, into the dark. He could smell diesel and grass. He walked round – down a long wall, one locked door and a shuttered loading bay. All quiet. On the other side of the loading bay was the fire door that had knocked him over that afternoon. There was a dim, hooded light over it. He shuffled down the wall towards it.

He was startled, then, by a rustle in the bushes and froze. A tousled figure – not tall enough to be Davidoff – was standing still out there in a pool of dark, seemingly looking in his direction. As Sherman's eyes adjusted he could see the outline of a rough beard. He'd disturbed a hobo. Dumpster-diving probably. There was another rustle, and the old man stepped back and was gone. He wouldn't have been able to see much of Sherman, not from that distance and with Sherman in the shadow of the building. Probably just heard him.

Sherman waited, then went on. Screened from two sides by the low bank and the hedge, he risked the light, tried the door. There wasn't a handle – just the bar on the inside, and the shop may not have had a nightwatchman but it was bound to be alarmed.

If Davidoff had got trapped in there, he supposed, he could have decided it was better to wait the night out than risk tripping the alarm. He didn't have a car. But that didn't make sense. Davidoff hadn't gone into the shop, not from the front, anyway. And if he was in there he wouldn't know that Sherman had taken the car. And why would he have got locked into the shop in the first place? He had a phone . . . No. Sherman had a bad feeling about his partner.

It was just as he was thinking about this bad feeling he had, about his partner, that Sherman heard the sound of a motor idling outside the front of the shop, then coming closer. It sounded like it was coming down the side of the building, where he'd just walked. It stopped. Then there was the sound of a car door opening, and closing. What made Sherman freeze was that the noise of the car – throatier, a van of some sort – and the noise of the voices sounded like someone trying to be quiet. His route back was cut off.

He moved quickly, scrambling out of the light and over the wall and up the slope into the foot of the hedge. He wriggled down into a long, ditch-like concavity he found in the earth. He could hear low, purposeful voices. The foliage was good above him. He risked raising his head.

Four men – all in dark overalls. They had penlights on them, and they were sweeping methodically, stealthily, down the back of the building and up the slope towards where he was hiding.

Shit. He could bolt onto the waste ground behind and risk running for it. But an image came into his head of being shot efficiently in the back. He stayed, put his head down. If they rolled him, he'd pretend to be a sleeping drunk.

He breathed as shallowly as he could. The dancing penlights, he was relieved to see, were moving up towards the ditch a little further along from where he was. Then one stopped, there was a sharp whisper, and the others converged on it. They'd found something. They were maybe six feet away.

There were now two torch beams. Two of the men had clipped off and stowed theirs to free up their hands. In the play of the light Sherman saw the men haul something up, something heavy. As it came, Sherman knew what it was. He'd seen these things hefted like that often before. They yanked it awkwardly out of the ditch, then each man hooked an arm briskly, professionally, under each armpit – another man picking up the legs. No hesitation, no alarm. One man directing.

The head flopped back as the torso came up. A splash of light flashed over it. Mouth open, eyes open, a slick darkness down one side of the neck. That was where Davidoff was.

The four men bore him away, head jouncing, round the corner of the building at speed. Sherman heard a car door close – quietly, but firmly, then another one. Then the motor started and retreated and he was left alone in the hedge in the dark. He waited there for a very long time, and then he got up, walked a long route back to his car, and drove to a new motel.

It was 4 a.m. He found a payphone and he phoned Ellis.

The first thing Ellis said was: 'We know.'

17

Bree and Jones hadn't said very much since the incident. Bree, because she was nervous. Any second she expected a siren to hiccup and whoop, and blue-red lights to revolve in the rear-view. She didn't know how far Red Queen's reach went, but there was only so much you could do. Someone would have found the body, she thought. Made their car from a security camera at the store – as usual, she'd ensured Jones parked with the plate towards a low wall and the car well away from the store, but there'd been only one way in and out of the parking lot.

Jones had killed. And Red Queen was leaving him in the field? Leaving Bree with him?

It made Bree feel faintly sick to think about him. That large-knuckled hand settled on the steering wheel had pushed a penknife into a man's neck a few hours previously. And if he was upset by that he wasn't showing it. She'd thought – when she'd found him in distress – that she'd been getting somewhere with him. She'd started to feel something towards him – protective-ness, even.

Bree looked at him as they drove through the city's backstreets in search of somewhere to lie low. His face was expressionless and his eyes seemed to be watching something out of sight. They scanned the road; his right hand passed the wheel round to his left hand as he turned corners. He blinked, occasionally. He didn't talk. It was as if, since the incident, there was nobody there. She felt like she was sharing the car with a ghost.

They had eaten separately and Bree had insisted they check into separate motels, a few blocks apart. She said she'd collect him in the morning and they'd go on. He could cry all he liked.

She dropped him off, took the car back, found her way into another of those rooms. It had low yellow light, like all the other motel rooms in America. There was a bedspread that made you feel sad, and the sort of mirror that turned even a young face into a landscape of pits and pocks and defeated skin. Bree could feel her DNA fraying, her cells ticking down and closing in. She looked at herself in the mirror and wondered what it was like to have fun, not to be scared, not to have to work from the time you got up until the time that, gratefully, you whimpered into sleep. She felt very, very sober.

Not that she'd sleep. The incident at the store, the sight of the dead man's face, was going to see to that. Ever since she had been tiny, Bree had been terrified of dying and death. She hadn't been able to visit her father in the hospital. She'd never seen a dead body. Didn't know how anybody could do so and carry on. The very thought of it was enough to bring up a small tremor in her hands.

Whenever you read about dying in books or films it always seemed to picture it as the world darkening and growing silent and getting further away: an old television dwindling away to a white dot, starting at the edges; an inky inrushing in the vision, and the volume going down. That, Bree thought, would be nice. A nice rest.

Bree's night terrors cast it differently. What Bree was frightened of was that far from the world going away and shutting the door politely behind it, the opposite would happen. She was worried that the drab world was the only thing standing between her and something much, much gaudier – like the flimsy curtains they put round hospital beds. When that ripped, she knew deep in her bones, the murmur of daily sense data would rise to a screaming hurricane and she would be overwhelmed, drowned, vanished, obliterated but somehow still there just to take it all in like someone with their eyelids stapled open in a violent cartoon.

When she'd gone to the Freaky Fields with Jess and Anton and taken acid in school – and boy oh boy, was that ever one of her less bright ideas – she'd had a glimpse of it, what it would be like. It had started with a lemony creeping up her cheeks – something like a grin, and they'd been talking and throwing the red ball around until her teeth started to taste funny and she heard sentences a fraction of a second before she spoke them.

The burr of the light in the yellow grass, the too several voices of her friends, the panoply of facial muscles she was expected to find uses for, the way reduplicative fragments of nonsense words and phrases started muscling into the side of her mind ('undefunnady', 'downshudder', 'slidewise') . . . she felt panic rising around her like the puddles of silvery water around her hips.

It felt like she'd been flying the light aircraft of her consciousness for years without incident, on automatic pilot. And here she was suddenly and abruptly switched to manual: strapped into the cockpit of a 737 and seeing bank after bank of winking lights and switches and multiple joysticks and tiny dials: far too much information coming in. She hadn't needed to think about how to smile, or to pronounce the word 'funny', or to separate out the different information coming in from her ears, her eyes, her skin and her own thoughts.

Now the filters had been removed and she was overwhelmed. She knew then, as she set in for the long haul of a catatonically bad, never-to-be-repeated trip, that this was what dying would be like – only an infinite progression of powers worse.

She hadn't been able to explain it well to her ex-husband, when he'd found her sweating and shaking beside him in the still hours of the morning. She hadn't been able to explain it to the therapist he'd made her see before he'd given up on her and gone.

She hadn't been able to explain it to her mother when it had first struck her. Everyone's frightened of dying. Everyone. But not everyone thinks about it all the time. It was the first thing she remembered from her childhood. Fear in the bones.

She had been six years old. She knew that, because her younger brother Gill had just been born. He was lying there in his cradle up the corridor, asleep already. Bree had had her bath like always and now, with a too-big, grown-up's towel around her shoulders and her flannel pyjama bottoms on, the pale blue ones, she was brushing her teeth in front of the mirror over the sink in her bedroom.

The sink was too high. She could rest her chin on the edge of it only, so she stood on the orange plastic toy crate like her mother had shown her. Now the porcelain was cold on her belly. Her dad had come home and her mother had gone downstairs to fix him a drink.

She reached up to the toothbrush holder fixed to the tiling behind the sink. The holder had a flat plastic cartoon of Snoopy's kennel, with Snoopy and Woodstock sitting on the roof. The body of the kennel, like Snoopy, was white. The roof was red. Woodstock was a splotch of yellow. Bree's toothbrush was red and had a little picture of Snoopy on the handle.

She squeezed a pea-sized burr of toothpaste onto the bristles and started to brush around her front teeth in the conscientious circles she had been taught. She remembered, or perhaps imagined, looking at herself in the small mirror, her short blonde hair dark from the bath and tousled and her mouth foaming.

Milk teeth, little round pearls. Soon grown-up teeth, she knew. Then what? Round she brushed. I am Bree, she had thought, looking in the mirror. Nobody else is Bree, only me. It struck her as strange. It had occurred to her that she was a person, a separate person from everyone else, that she was alone in her head – she hadn't expressed it to herself this way, she thought, not at the time; but she could remember the feeling and it corresponded to that – and that she was moving towards something like abandonment. She felt suddenly overwhelmed, like when she was lost in the supermarket. She knew too that she couldn't, having once had this thought, ever unthink it.

The Snoopy toothbrush holder wasn't friendly. It was inert: just a plastic thing, a small object in a huge universe. Bree's mother had come upstairs to find her crying disconsolately, still moving the toothbrush in automatic circles across her teeth, and powerless, with a mouthful of peppermint foam and no vocabulary for it, to explain the feeling.

She had learned to explain it later, to herself. And she had learned to distract herself from thinking about it; but it was there knocking under the floorboards in her apartment, winking at her from the back of the refrigerator, waiting for her in the closet.

She found herself goggling, occasionally, at the people who walked past her every day, wearing their haircuts on their heads and going about their business, and seeming never to have stumbled on this dreadful thought – or if they had stumbled on it, having forgotten it.

In her twenties, she had developed a recurrent half-dream: something that would creep in between her being awake and the little mischiefs of sleep starting to derail her mind. She had learned to control it with pills and rituals and work, but the dream was essentially a dramatisation of what was going on in her conscious mind. In these dreams, she died. And instead of things getting quiet and dark and receding, Bree had the sense of something rushing in on her: something that had always been there, but had been hiding – held at bay by the walls and floor and sky, by the surfaces of things. Now her protections fell away. There was a sudden undoing of reality: something unpicking the angles of the corner of the room, the sky unzipping, the floor's tessellations of atoms untoothing and a downflooding of light.

At the same time, the sound of something approaching from a very long way off that would also somehow be just the other side of the walls: a gathering roar, which would make it physically impossible to think, but would be recognisable as it overwhelmed your ears as the sound of a million million million million individual voices – everyone who ever lived or could have lived – whispering a single word.

Bree used to wake with the sound only of her own blood in her ears, and the sheets wet, and the walls and their vertices in place.

Now the dead man was going to bring that back. Bree wanted a beer, now, very much indeed. More than she had wanted one in the many years she had been going to meetings. She made some strong coffee, took two Dylar, waited for breakfast.

18

Ellis told Sherman: 'You finish the job. You finish the job, you get it back to us – you'll get paid Noone's bounty too.'

Sherman thought about telling Ellis to have some respect – that a man was dead – but he thought Ellis might actually get off, a little, on acting the tough guy about that, so he didn't. He instead looked with distaste at his mobile phone.

'What am I supposed to do with this kid? He's a British national.'

'You do whatever you need to do.'

Idiot. Sherman diced up telling him to shove it, but decided on balance that that could backfire badly.

He said: 'You're the boss. Where do I start looking?'

Ellis said: 'He's going west. He had an onward ticket to San Francisco. You know his car. Assume that's where he's going. There's only one road he's likely to be on. All you have to do is follow it.'

So Sherman did. But at the same time, Sherman made other precautions.

And when, the next time he called the number he had for Ellis, he heard only the long 'bleeeee' of a disconnected line, he put those precautions into action.

He had not been surprised. Whatever Ellis had said, things had got too hot. MIC were gamblers, and like any good gamblers, they had decided to quit while they were ahead.

Sherman remembered what, long before he had thumped him, his father had once said to him when drunk: 'Life is hell, most people are bastards and everything is bullshit.'

'Disavowed,' he said to himself. 'Hell, bastards, bullshit.' It remained to be seen whether, to extend the figure of speech, he was one of the losses that MIC would be interested in cutting; or whether they were relying on the lumbering local law to do that for them. He didn't intend to find out.

Don't assume anything, was what he thought. Options open. Keep some outs.

His iPod was working again. It was playing REO Speedwagon. He thought of Davidoff, mispronouncing the name, and felt an unaccustomed anger. Davidoff had been set-dressing for these creeps, safe at their desks in front of their computer screens, totting up the numbers, playing the percentages.

Sherman dropped the car, picked up another one across town, and headed as far and as fast as he could out of this story: making time, making distance, making – as he always had – his own luck.

Alex stopped in a Motel 6, sometime after dark, and called Carey. It was past eleven, but he didn't want to go to sleep without hearing another human voice. The phone rang once, twice, three times, and she answered.

'Care?'

'Hey, baby.' Her voice was croaky. 'It's late. Where you been?' she said. She said something in the background he couldn't hear.

'What?'

'Nothing. Just talking to someone. Wait up.' There was a readjustment. He pictured her wriggling to lodge the phone in the crook of her neck. ''Sbetter. Go on. What's up?'

Alex was leaning against the car. Now he could hear her voice, his earlier panic seemed to calm down. That guy was long gone. Carey's voice was sleepy. He pictured her in the pyjamas she wore when she slept alone, with the phone crooked into her neck, half paying attention to the television, or yanking open the fridge, or making gestures at him across the room while she talked.

'I'm in America, Carey.'

'You're *what*?' Carey spoke the second word in italics.

'I'm here. I'm in America.'

She seemed to take a moment to take it in.

'That's great. I mean – where are you? What? You're in San Francisco?'

'No, not quite. I'm more like – I'm in Albuquerque.'

'Albuquerque?'

'Well, I was. Few hours back.'

'What are you doing there?'

'I'm coming to see you.'

'Oh my God!' She sounded like an actress in a teen movie, he thought, the open vowel on the final word like g*aah*d. Then she said it again, catching herself – that was one of the things he loved about her – sounding like an actress in a teen movie and making herself therefore sound more like one.

'Oh my Gaahd!' she said. She was spontaneous the first time. Her voice sounded now like a smile without the eyes going. It was disconcerting.

'I thought I'd surprise you,' he muttered.

Now a peal of laughter, unforced. 'You have surprised me, crazy English boy. Oh my Lord, that is so romantic. And so –' her voice got muffled momentarily – 'sorry – shut up – not you – so . . .' She had lost her thread.

'Shit,' she said. 'What. I mean, romantic. But stupid. Seriously. What are you doing in Albuquerque?'

'I don't know,' he said truthfully. 'I was going to surprise you, but I got this flight to Atlanta –'

'Atlanta?'

'Courier. It was a hub. It was in the right general direction.'

'Courier?'

'The flight was really, really cheap. I just needed the onward ticket, and then I missed the connecting flight, so now I'm in a car.'

'You drove from Atlanta to Albuquerque?'

'I always wanted to go on a road trip.'

'You missed the flight is what. This is such a trip. So you coming to San Francisco?' Her voice sounded suddenly less sure, a little knocked off balance.

'I had this idea – you ever been to Vegas?'

Carey laughed. 'You said it like Vegas, without the "Las". What a player! Soon you'll be calling San Francisco "Frisco" and we'll know you're from out of town.' Alex felt a little deflated. 'I'm sorry, baby. You can pronounce Albuquerque Al-ba-kway-kway and you'll be fine by me. Yeah, I've been to Vegas. My folks drove me up there once when I was like thirteen or something to watch them gamble –' Carey always called her foster-parents her 'folks', never her mom and dad – 'but I haven't been since. Don't think I did much gambling.'

'You want to go? Meet me there?'

'Hell yee-ah. What made you think of that? Going to get us married in the Elvis chapel?' She laughed. Alex didn't. He hadn't actually thought of the Elvis chapel. Well, actually, he nearly had. Like with the ring, he wasn't someone who was very good at feeling his way into whether something was so naff it was cool or just naff. And now there was this awkward dead drop in the conversation. She'd been joking and he hadn't responded with the proper levity and now – oh God – it was like there was this fucking great dead badger sitting between them.

He had to say something. 'Of course,' he said, failing to prevent his voice from sounding serious.

In their relationship there was something, he realised, that caused them to strike each other at near right angles. They didn't quite get each other; from his point of view, it felt like he was always play-ing catch-up a little. She was hard to read, but he thought that was what made it work. They missed each other that little bit, and then when they caught up they found the misunderstanding funny. He knew he amused her: otherwise she wouldn't spend all that time giggling at him. And she amused him, he thought – though the more he thought about it the more he realised that probably he loved her more than he found her funny.

There. An unevenness. An unevenness he could live with.

'Yeah,' he said. 'In the Elvis chapel. Just like Chris Evans and Billie.'

'Who?' she said.

'Doesn't matter. Just – can you get the weekend off?'

'Sure. Yeah. I mean. Yeah.'

'Well, how long will it take you to get there? I don't – I mean, I think I'm about a day away.'

'A day? From New Mexico? That's a long day.'

'It's all I've been doing for days. Thinking about stuff.'

'Hold up,' Carey said. 'Just moving into the other room. I'm with someone.'

She covered the handset and he couldn't hear anything for a moment or two, then he heard a door close.

'Who are you with?'

'Nobody,' she said. 'Just a friend from work. So, Vegas. Let's do it. I've got air miles. I think they've got flights for like a hundred bucks. Wow. It's hard to imagine you in the States. You're so . . . British.'

She didn't sound overexcited. Alex, for an instant, felt that flatness he had felt at the start of his journey. Not lonely, just numb. Why did anybody do anything?

'So, er . . .' He couldn't think of anything to say.

'OK, sweetie, let's talk tomorrow. I'll see about flights, yeah? Vegas. I like it. Let's do it. Two day's time? Where are you staying?'

'Motels.'

'Uh-huh. OK.' She sounded distracted again.

He reached into his pocket for the ring, something concrete. He turned it in his hand, and he felt less alone.

★   ★   ★

By lunchtime the following day it was fixed. Alex pushed on to Flagstaff, arriving after night fell. He stopped, checked into a motel. The Grand Canyon was near. He imagined its vast absence as he lay on his bed, trying to get to sleep.

On his heels, had he but known it – had they but known it – were Bree and Jones, still heading west, still trusting – as instructed – to luck.

There was little said in the car as they drove. Bree, slightly giddy from not sleeping, was still thinking about what Jones had done, still seeing the surprise on the face of the dead man, still wondering what it would mean to have done the worst thing in the world and not understand what had happened – if, indeed, that was the situation Jones was in. His sunglasses might as well have been armour-plating. There was nothing in there; nothing Bree could understand.

When he was hungry, he would suggest they stopped, and they would eat in silence, standing by the car, Jones looking in whichever direction he happened to be facing; Bree looking in whichever direction Jones wasn't. After that, again, he just drove, eyes blandly scanning the world.

Bree realised, as the miles rolled past under the blank blue sky, that some part of her hated him not for killing the stranger, but for getting away with it. He had done the worst thing in the world, and nothing had happened to him. He didn't fear the consequence. He couldn't feel the loss of another's life any more than he'd feel the loss of his own.

And was it the worst thing in the world, even? No. The worst thing in the world was what Bree had done. Bree had done that years ago. Bree had lost her baby.

She couldn't remember much of the sequence of events. By that stage the memory thief had become brazen. Just flashes, disconnected points of pain, smeared routines. Cass getting her own breakfast and going to school – her spoon clanking softly on her bowl, audible through the partition wall in Bree's dark box of morning pain. Cass, more than once, helping Bree off the couch and into bed. Cass finding bottles and pouring them out, and later, Cass standing barefaced and shaking, chin up, fronting Bree's rage.

She never hit her. She shook her. Never hit her.

And then Cass's own anger – ever since Al had gone. There was bed-wetting first, nothing said. And then, after she started her bleed, the focusless rage of a teenager. Bree had done everything she could to direct Cass's anger at Al. It gave them something to share. It was Al's fault. Al had gone altogether. How could he do that? How could he abandon his own daughter to . . . to Bree.

Trouble at school. Bree hadn't bothered going in to see the head. Bree remembered screaming at the social worker. Marion – pig-faced Marion, with the flakes of dandruff in the dark greasy bit where her hair was parted. Bree hated her whether or not she was doing her job. But the whole machinery went on. Then there were her appearances and non-appearances in court, her desperation, her fantasies, her sloppy embarrassments of love.

Bree even tried to run with her – skip out and run to another state. She pulled Cass out of bed in the middle of the night. It would be like Thelma and Louise, just us girls, she said. She crashed the car into a hydrant, dead drunk, before they reached the end of the street. The seat belt left a purple bruise on the girl's right collarbone and across her sternum. Bree saw it through the bathroom door, set off by the white of Cass's training bra.

When they asked about her rock bottom in meetings, Bree always said it was waking up in the nuthouse: dawn growing blue in the awful window, and shaking with the need for something to make it go dark again. That was nearly a year later, the year she completely lost. She didn't talk about losing Cass. She couldn't share that.

She said to herself that that had been her real rock bottom – that had been the turning point. But what Bree could not turn to face was that losing her daughter had not been her rock bottom. She had loved her daughter, but she had loved drinking more. She had, in the early days of Cass's absence, almost been relieved. Someone else was looking after her; someone good. She could drink safely now. Nobody was watching her.

She hadn't loved her daughter enough to stop drinking, was what the bottom line was. That was a sentence she uttered to herself only when she was so drunk she knew she would forget it.

Every year, at the approach of Cass's birthday, June 29th, Bree thought: this is the year when I go and find her. She could track her through the care system. She could make the correct applications. This is the year, she would think, when I go and knock on the door of her foster-parents' home — she imagined some white suburb, somewhere warm, with a smell of oranges in the air and a clean SUV parked up in the driveway and all that baloney — and say: 'I'd like to see Cassie.' That would be the year when she would show the young woman who had once been her daughter a fistful of recovery medallions, and beg for her forgiveness. And then what?

She could see Cass — all the different versions, from the first sight of her. Purple face, whitened with vernix, screaming in the hospital. The double whorl in her hair. The surge of love and exhaustion as she first held her weight — her future coiled into that tiny body. The last words she had heard Cass say had been: 'Please. I don't want to leave my mom.' She couldn't see Cass now. She was a young woman and her face was nobody's, something indecipherable, unavailable to Bree's imagination.

Most years she went to two meetings that day, and didn't talk about Cass. One year, early on, she came within the crack of a screw cap of a bottle of brandy from relapsing. The thought that she couldn't do it made her desperate to take a drink; the thought that she might one day do it kept her from it.

But she had still never looked for Cass. She could not come face to face, not in that way, with the centre of her shame. She thought Cass would forgive her – and she thought that there was no way, no way on earth, that she would be able to bear that.

Are you ashamed, Jones? Can you be forgiven? Bree slept that night in a motel in Flagstaff, forty feet from where Alex Smart slept. She, too, felt the giant absence of the Grand Canyon out in the night, but exhaustion took her this time and she was almost grateful when she had the death-dream instead of any other one.

19

A day and a half later, Alex arrived where he was going. Las Vegas rose out of the desert like a mirage. Even from this distance, it looked like a place that someone had invented, or dreamed about after falling asleep with the central heating on too high and a belly full of Stilton.

Alex arrived in town early in the afternoon, and opened the windows to the dirty heat. He was wondering what the inside of the car smelled like. After the desert, where there was no direction but forwards, and no other cars on the road, he found himself again on multi-lane highways, being bullied by SUVs shouldering from lane to lane.

The movement of traffic pulled him down into the centre. He found himself travelling slowly, from stop light to stop light, down the broad, gaudy Las Vegas Boulevard. The Strip: it was a place at once new to him and familiar – a place that had lived, in jumbled form, in his imagination. He'd seen it overflown endlessly, by helicopter, in the title credits of *CSI* – the Eiffel Tower and the Montgolfier balloon traced in blue neon, the pyramid shooting a beam of light into the sky; the burlesque monumental lions outside the MGM Grand; the anonymous coppery curve of the Wynn. He'd zoomed in on it, too, in Google Earth: monumental schematics from the air; frozen images at street level; granular, gaudy and smeared with light.

Was it as he had imagined it? He didn't know. It seemed to come pre-imagined. But it occurred to him as he drove that he hadn't seen it in daylight before: it wasn't intended to be seen in daylight. The concrete and stone answered the sun with a wan brightness. It looked as worn and bleached out as Christmas tree lights discovered in the attic in summer.

He drove up to the top of town, and pulled into the stacked lot of one of the older-looking, shabbier-looking hotels on Fremont Street. He parked the car and an elevator took him to the lobby. There was an old guy wearing an honest-to-goodness cowboy hat leaning on the desk, staring past the waistcoated clerk at nothing. His face was a pained squint, and red thread veins pooled at the hinge of his jaw. Nobody was attending to him. His jaw tightened and relaxed.

Alex checked in. His room was on the eighth floor – it was shabby and small and brown everywhere and it smelled of old smoke. A double-glazed sliding window in a metal frame looked out onto a stained concrete wall gridded with identical windows, the other wing of the H-shaped hotel. Past that, the view towards the north – simmering low-rise, ribboned with tan overpasses.

He felt, at that moment, exhausted. It was another four hours before he was meeting Carey. He lay down on the coverlet of the bed, and fell asleep there without even taking his shoes off.

He woke up with a feeling close to fright. The air conditioner was roaring. His mouth was gummy, his head sore and sweat had chilled on his skin. The light outside was metallic, now, and when he went to the window the facing wall of the hotel was the colour of dirty brass in the old sun.

He should have been looking forward to seeing Carey but he was feeling, again, dislocated, unworthy, indecipherable. It made him panicky.

The problem is that when I'm alone I literally cease to believe that I exist.

He said the words to himself aloud, just to feel the air across his tongue. It was something he'd remembered from somewhere, not his own thought. He looked at his rucksack. It belonged to a stranger. He rubbed the back of his neck. His watch told him it was seven o'clock. He was probably just hungry.

★   ★   ★

They had arranged to meet in the Golden Nugget at eight. Alex had suggested meeting her flight, but Carey said that'd be a drag. She had heard that the casino contained the world's biggest nugget of gold. 'Let's meet there! Just you, me and a big gold rock. It'll be cute.'

Walking into the casino was like walking into an aquarium. The door – no, the entire wall – was permanently open to the outside. It gaped. The mouth of a whale. Not an aquarium. Not just an aquarium. An aquarium and its contents. A mechanical whale, trawling for human plankton. No need to suck: just leave the mouth open and let them wash in.

Even during the heat of a cloudless day, something seemed to stop the sunshine spilling from Fremont Street into the building: a filter in the air – an invisible baleen plate. Within a couple of steps the crisp hot light bouncing off the pavement outside would be gone. There was only the indecipherable carpet, the high ceiling, and slot machines arrayed in rows and islands under the buttery artificial light. It felt like cigarettes and acid stomach and the headachy buzz you get when you pass through tiredness into the unreal underwater feeling on the other side.

You turned round and the pleasant sunshine outside was a wall of white. Reality was oversaturated. It hurt the eyes. Safer in here. The second time you turned round you couldn't find the opening back to the outside world at all. And now, in the evening, the inside started to colonise the outside. That border was porous, after all. But the unreality inside seeped onto the street like smoke.

A shift in the current and you had turned round, lost your bearings. The direction you struck out in was wrong. The angles were wrong. That wall wasn't that wall. It wasn't even a wall at all. That bar was a different bar.

The slots fanned and pulsed. Through alleys of fluorescent coral, portly men in T-shirts lumbered like groupers. Some grazed on the machines, bland-faced and blissful as fish. Old women

209

perched on stools, human spider crabs, barking their yellowed foreclaws on the panels. Cocktail waitresses moved purposefully, dartingly, alertly. Clownfish.

Alex had somehow imagined the sound in the casino would be a cacophony, but it was soothing. He had expected to hear whirring and clattering – and that was there, if you listened for it – but in aggregate it was a sort of anaesthetising white noise, like the sound of the sea.

Over the top, the bleeps and squelches of electronic noise, snatches of tunes, here and there cataracts of imaginary money pouring into imaginary metal containers, digitally simulated. Behind, the purr of a million coins flipping, a million tumblers coming to rest and then starting in motion again, a million balls settling into sockets, a million cards burring into new configurations.

Alex remembered seeing a documentary, once, about a casino in America where women bought buckets of coins and sat, all day and all night, feeding them into the slot machines. There was something devotional about the act: patiently, unsleepingly, as if in a trance, they fed the coins into slots and pressed the button to spin the reels.

With every press of the button, there came a near-imperceptible tensing in the shoulders: a tiny jolt of hope. Then, as the wheels came to rest, came a readjustment. Every few spins, the machine would cough a handful of coins into its trough, and the women would look rejuvenated, freshened: hope satisfied. The coins would be swept back into the bucket, ready to be fed in.

The machines were playing the people, rather than vice versa, it had occurred to Alex. Nearly half the time, the women would have more coins in the bucket than they had started with – but a tilt of the algorithm, the tiniest pressure of a thumb on the scales, meant that the number of coins in the bucket tended, over the long run, towards zero.

Every small score was not a win, but a rebate: a contribution to the struggle, a prolongation of the period of time in which the player was able to believe that the impossible could happen. As they fed these coins in, whittling their chances down the long curve to zero, the same process was going on in every cell in their bodies.

But here there were no buckets, no coins. The clatter of money was synthesised. Just as the blackjack players, on their fields of baize deeper in the casino, exchanged their cash for plastic chips, the slots players now fed dollar bills into machines. You could see them, out of cash, approaching the machines peevishly, feeding ragged cloth bucks into the machines' mouths, having them whirr and spit back. Rubbing the dollars flat on the top of the machine, straightening out the bent corners, thumbing the face of the dead president, feeding them back in, hoping.

If the casino gods were smiling on them, their money would disappear and stay disappeared, and the machine would politely blurt out a white paper slip. It was this that they would feed into the machine.

Paper money was translated into electrons, which were translated into paper, which was translated into electrons, which were translated into paper, which was translated into electrons, which were translated into paper money.

That made sense. This was a place where money – never something strongly tethered to reality – slipped anchor and became altogether imaginary. And the more imaginary it got, the more like itself it became. This was money in its purest, most contingent form – owned, in the perpetual instant of play, by nobody. It existed in a field of probabilities – between the hope of the impossible and the knowledge of the inevitable.

Alex walked the casino floor. His dizziness subsided and a sort of calm came over him. Seven forty-five. Fifteen minutes to kill. He found the nugget glistering in a glass box. Really quite big – nuggets, as Alex had always thought of them, were no bigger than a Tic Tac. This nugget was supposed to look a bit like a hand, but it looked more like a bit of coral. It looked gaudy. It looked like a fake nugget – as if the gold had been sprayed on from a can.

He had just sat down with a rumpled ten to worship at a nickel slot machine when a hand on his shoulder and a voice hazy with travel said: 'Hey.'

He turned round and stood up and there was Carey, in the old Dead Kennedys T-shirt she used to sleep in, jeans frayed at the hip, hair down, brown-armed and smiling.

'Hey,' said Alex, and felt as happy as he ever had. 'You're early.'

'So are you,' said Carey. Her arms were warm on his neck as he hugged her.

He pulled back and said more or less without drawing breath: 'It's so good to see you. Look! Vegas! I'm playing a slot machine. What's up? How was your flight? Enough about you, let's talk about me. My God, I've had this weird road trip, I swear, every lunatic in America has tried to kill me or make friends with me. Where's your stuff?'

Carey lifted her pink vinyl shoulder bag by its strap. 'Travelled light. Underwear, change of T-shirt, lipstick in case I need to go hooking to earn back what I lose at poker.'

'Want to go back to my hotel and put it in the room?'

'Hell no! This is Las Vegas. Let's hit the town. Waitron! Bring me . . . a daiquiri.' There was no waitress anywhere in sight. She waved her arm as if twirling an invisible baton, then shouldered Alex out of the way and slammed the palm of her hand onto the fat SPIN button in the centre of the machine's console. It quacked and blurted, shuffled its numbers.

'I win!' said Carey.

'No, you don't,' said Alex.

'Oh,' said Carey. 'No, I don't. Does it make that noise when you lose? Imagine the noise when we win. OK. Cash out. Let's hit the town.'

'Hang on,' said Alex. He pressed the button again. The reels moved. There was a simulated cascade of falling coins.

'Magic hands,' said Alex, waggling his fingers.

'We won,' said Carey. 'Jackpot!' Three oranges. They were thirty-five cents up.

'We won!' Alex repeated. 'Go, us. OK, let's cash out and explore the' – his hand moved towards the CASH/CREDIT button but Carey swiped it away – 'town –'

'Are you crazy? We're on a streak.'

'There's only ten dollars in there . . .'

'Shhh.' She pressed the button again.

An hour and a half later, having never been more than $4.85 up, and having finally gone down to zero, they left to go into town.

Carey and Alex were doing what you do in Las Vegas. They sat at one of the bars in Circus Circus – Carey had demanded that they go in, claiming without a hint of sincerity that she had been frightened of clowns as a child and that it would be good aversion therapy – and played the video poker game embedded in the actual bar. Alex had won $100 on his first go, and Carey had then spent fifteen minutes losing it while they drank their watery screwdrivers.

Then when they got hungry they looked for somewhere to eat and realised that everything was either a cheap chain restaurant or an expensive chain restaurant, so they went to a cheap chain restaurant and had fajitas. The restaurant was dimly lit and noisy with pop-punk music with Mexican lyrics. Teenagers with glow sticks round their necks hip-swayed between tables, taking orders as if they had trains to catch and returning to drop the food off with casual violence.

The meat came on lethally hot metal skillets. The tortillas came in a plastic simulacrum of a wicker basket, accompanied by a plastic simulacrum of a saucer containing a plastic simulacrum of grated cheese.

They bought long, bulbed plastic horns containing pre-mixed margaritas dispensed by a machine, which were only drinkable because they were so tooth-hurtingly cold that you couldn't taste how sweet they were. They took the remains of them out onto the street and walked down the Strip.

When? Not now. Not now. Not now.

They continued to walk until their aimlessness started to become something palpable, an awkwardness between them.

Even ordinarily, Alex would be anxious in this situation. Nothing made him more anxious than the need or expectation of having fun. Vegas was a place devoted to the idea of fun. Everyone, everywhere you looked, was trying to have fun.

Alex had brought Carey here under the pretence of having fun. He worried he wasn't having fun. He worried even more that Carey wasn't having fun, or, at least, that whatever fun they were having – the food was OK, wasn't it? They hadn't lost all their money gambling – was deprived of sunlight and water by the enormous shadow of the fun they should have been having, by comparison with which their own meagre portion of fun was a wretched failure.

Oh God. What was he thinking of?

He looked over at Carey to see whether it looked like she was having fun. It was impossible to tell. She wasn't hooting with laughter and throwing her head back. She was just sort of walking down the street looking at stuff. She had a drink in her hand, at least. Good.

Alex had finished his own drink. Ever since he had started worrying about the aimlessness – that is, he had an aim, obviously, but the more he wound up to it the less he was able to communicate with the outside world, and until he had done so his companion would be left with the overwhelming impression of aimlessness – he had been sucking away on his margarita so as to be doing something even if he wasn't saying something.

It was a margarita in a brightly coloured plastic cup, a foot long. It said so on the side of the cup. Foot-long margarita. With a foot-long straw. That was fun, surely. That was drinks plus fun. Alex felt utterly adrift.

It was probably ages since he'd said anything. Had she noticed? Was she bored?

He knew he should say something. Say something. That was the thing. But the only thing he could think of to say was 'Will you marry me?' and even though that was the exact thing to say the moment was wrong. You couldn't just come out of the blue with it, could you? Just abruptly? She'd think he was a loon. Or, worse, joking.

Here? Not here. Not in the street. Yes. Why not? In the street. This is your life. This is your life, going by, and you're going to look back on this moment as the moment when you didn't take the decision that would have made you happy for the rest of your days on earth. With this American girl you love wholeheartedly.

You know you love her wholeheartedly. You have said so to yourself, and had you a diary you would have written it in your diary. You cannot always, when called on, feel the love as a wave of emotion – not in the way you could when you watched her sleep, before you were a couple, or the way you can when she's somewhere else and you miss her. But you know it's there. It's just – it's something you take for granted. Something you're so quietly sure of you barely examine it.

Action. For goodness' sake. Action. That's all. Just do it.

Alex thought about how he used to trick himself into jumping into swimming pools. You ran up to the edge promising yourself that this was just a practice run and that you were going to stop, and then when you got to the edge you simply kept running and took the view that you would apologise to yourself later for the white lie. Always, a great body-shocking spout of cold water to the chest and crotch, bubbles of air foaming up around the ears and neck, and limbs paddling at once, spastic with surprise.

'Carey,' said Alex. He looked past her shoulder. There was nobody there. The Strip was empty as far as the next corner and the sky above was a perspectiveless blue-black. It was warm, and away behind him he could hear the hiss and swish and flop of the fountains outside the Bellagio dancing their exhausted dance.

'Mmm?' Carey was distracted. She took another sip of her margarita and Alex admired with a little wave of desperation the way her cheek pulsed inwards as she drew on her orange straw.

Alex felt the ring, in its square box, digging against his hip. He was on the verge of action. He felt a little dizzy. He remembered that once he had tried the swimming-pool trick, a little drunk, in the shallow end of a pool with submerged steps. He had driven the little toe of his right foot into the corner of the lowest step, and gulped a lungful of water. Saul had pulled him out in time for him not to drown. For the next fortnight, his broken toe had been so painful that simply hopping downstairs on the other foot had, with every step, sent an inertial throb of blood into the digit that had caused him to gasp.

He went on, anyway.

'You know what you said about the Elvis chapel?' he said.

'What Elvis chapel?' said Carey, turning her eyes to his. She brought the straw back up to her lips and pursed them around it. She had a look of blank expectation. Alex looked at his feet.

'Well,' said Alex. 'I wanted to say. Look.'

Alex thought of getting onto one knee, here on the pavement, but he knew in this instant – with the certainty that he knew he would never climb Kilimanjaro, or emerge victorious from a fist fight, or play a significant role in the history of the human race, or be unconditionally adored by beautiful teenage girls, and with the faint, humming sadness that accompanied those certainties – that getting down on one knee in public was something he did not have the ability to do.

'Carey, what I'm trying to say is –'

216

And he could not meet her eye. And then he could. She was still holding her margarita, in its big pink plastic yard-of-ale tube, up in front of her chest. Her arms were slim and golden from the sun, and her big Dead Kennedys T-shirt was not quite formless enough to prevent the curve of her breasts from being visible.

She looked beautiful. Alex felt the moment freeze-framing into a memory. He felt as if he was looking back in time to this moment, from some point in the future. But he still didn't know what happened next. Carey slurped her margarita.

Alex glanced nervously over her shoulder. The street was no longer empty. Three men in white suits, walking abreast, were waiting at the crosswalk ahead. Something familiar about them.

Alex put it aside, turned back to Carey, took a deep breath, closed his fist on the sharp-cornered parcel in his pocket, made himself look directly at her quizzical, almost slightly peevish face. A face saying: yup, what? Get on with it . . .

'Carey. Love. Will you –'

Carey took another big slurp of her margarita. Evidently the last. The straw made a violently diarrhoeic noise in the crushed ice. Alex gave a nervous yip, and then barked with laughter. Carey looked baffled.

'What's funny?'

'Just – the noise your thing made. It's nothing. I don't know. Silly mood, I guess. I'm just happy being here with you. Sorry.'

'Don't apologise.'

'Sorry.'

'Are you OK?' she said. 'You've been acting a bit – just since we ate – a bit distant.'

'Oh, no, no. Shall we walk? No, I'm fine. I was just thinking about. What do you want to do next?'

The white-suited men were getting closer. As they approached Alex could see what was familiar about them. They were Elvis. All three of them. One fat Elvis and two thin ones. The white suits were jumpsuits. The fat one, disconcertingly, had a star-spangled

V-shape from shoulders to crotch. It was hard to tell how old they were, because they were wearing identical black wigs and identical fuzzy-felt sideburns and sunglasses the size of drinks coasters. But judging by the way they were walking they were epically drunk.

The fat Elvis lurched left, inadvertently shoulder-barging the thin Elvis in the middle, which sent him into the other thin Elvis, who pushed tetchily back.

'– even listening to me?'

'Yes, love, sorry. Look out. Those three drunks.'

As the Elvises ambled up level with them, Alex grabbed Carey's elbow and pulled her out of the way. Too late. Fat Elvis barged into the back of her. Carey's drink tumbled from her hand and bounced on the sidewalk.

'Hey!' she exclaimed. The Elvises rolled on, oblivious.

'Hey!' Carey said again. 'Why don't you look where you're going? That was my drink, you dick.'

Half past them, now, the Elvises turned round. Alex didn't like the expression on Fat Elvis's face.

'You say to me, girlie?'

'I called you a dick,' said Carey. She pushed out her lip. When she lost her temper, Carey had a tendency to forget that she was a slightly built woman in her early twenties rather than, say, a light-middleweight boxing champion.

'Don't call him an asshole,' said the thin Elvis in the Evel Knievel suit. ''S an accident.'

'I've hit a girl before,' said Fat Elvis. Alex believed him.

'I didn't call him an asshole,' said Carey. 'I called him a dick.' Her face was flushed. Alex was petrified. 'He smashed into me and made me spill my drink. And then he was walking off without so much as turning round to say sorry. And he's fat, and he's ugly, and he's dressed like a dick. I call that dickish.'

Fat Elvis was taking this in. He paused, swaying a bit. Then he spoke to Alex, dead-eyed.

'You need to keep that mouth of hers under control.'

He'd barely reached the end of the sentence when Carey slapped him with a report loud enough to make Alex wince. In films, scenes like this seemed to result in moments of stunned silence, but Fat Elvis moved very fast indeed. Barely had the blow landed than he lurched forward with a roar, grabbing at Carey's wrist. He missed, just, and Carey hopped backwards.

Alex, on instinct, bopped Fat Elvis on the head with the only thing he had to hand, which was his empty plastic funnel of drink. What impact it made was cushioned by his nylon quiff, but it knocked him slightly off balance.

As he came back up it was immediately apparent he intended violence. Carey swung her handbag, catching him on one sideburn.

'Hey!' shouted the other thin Elvis.

'Run!' shouted Alex, and run they did, with three drunk Elvises in pursuit.

Alex pounded along the pavement. Carey was a bit ahead of him, lifting up her knees, pistoning her arms, her baseball boots flashing red-white and caramel back at him.

'Pricks! Fucking pricks!' Carey was shouting over her shoulder between breaths.

'SHUT . . . UP!' said Alex, much less fit than Carey. By the end of the block they had pulled away from the Elvises but his breath was already ragged. 'You're going – to get – me . . . killed.'

They swerved through oncoming pedestrians, dip-diving around stationary gawpers. The cross light was flashing 'Walk' and Alex saw Carey make the snap call to go for it. He hop-skipped through the intersection with a blare of horns.

They gained the opposite pavement and Alex bounced off someone's shoulder, earning a shout of indignation, and a splat of what seemed to be ice cream on the cheek, but then Alex looked up and realised they were heading into the thick of a crowd.

Carey, ahead of him, wormed shoulder-forward between two people with cameras and ducked into the crowd.

Behind him, Alex heard the shout of what he guessed was one of the Elvises hitting ice-cream guy head on, buying them a second or two, and then he was into the thickening mass himself.

'Sorry, sorry, sorry, sorry, sorry. . . .'

'Hey –'

'– with my friend . . . sorry, sorry, sorry, sorry . . . .'

There was music to the side, and bright lights. Some sort of show. Alex kept his head down. Behind him, the sound of further collisions.

'– you, Elvis!'

'– the damn way . . .'

He ploughed on, keeping his head down. He popped his head up. He could see Carey, lither and pushier, extending her lead.

'Sorry, sorry, sorry . . .'

The crowd was very thick, now. The whole of the pavement had been fenced in with wooden boards and netting, and the crowd was jammed into that space. There were planks underfoot and light – golden, green and red – was pulsing. Alex's arm barked against a rough rope. A loud fusillade of bangs caused him to whip his head round – above the crowd and back from the pavement he could see what looked like a boat, its rigging scarved with multicoloured smoke. Hanging from the rigging were girls in bikinis with eyepatches and pirate hats, waggling their legs.

Alex put his head down and plunged on, wriggling through the thickest part of the crowd. As the crowd thinned he caught up with Carey, grabbed her arm.

He risked a backward glance. He couldn't see the Elvises. He pulled her down and against the wooden barrier between the pavement and the road. They squatted there, between a thicket of legs. As he squatted, his trousers tightened at the hip, and the ring box dug in.

Carey's face was bright with exhilaration. She grabbed the back of his head and kissed him on the lips, then let him go.

'Not funny!' he hissed. 'It was me they were going to beat up –' and then he stopped momentarily as he saw what looked like three sets of white legs, trousers tellingly flared, coming through the crowd. He pushed his hand over Carey's mouth and studied the pavement. The legs went past.

'Not funny,' he repeated, but now they weren't actually going to be beaten up what had been scary started to seem funny. He was shaky with adrenalin.

'Marry me,' he said.

'Sure,' she said.

He got up, thighs creaking, from his squat and meerkatted up. There was no sign of the Elvises. A wooden walkway coming off the pavement at right angles led to the entrance to a casino. Alex pointed, steered Carey by the elbow, and jostled through into the lobby.

'Drink,' he said.

They walked, Alex still holding Carey's elbow, across the wide hideous carpet in the direction of a large, brassy, over-marbled bar in a thicket of slot machines and palm trees.

Behind the bar was a girl who looked from the waist down like she was playing Dick Whittington in panto at the Yvonne Arnaud theatre, Guildford, and from the waist up like she was a bellhop in a pornographic movie.

'Champagne,' said Alex. 'We'd like, please. Two glasses.'

'Sir,' she said without smiling.

'Care, you are a psychopath,' he said. Carey beamed.

'Not taking shit from Elvis,' she said.

The woman set two tall flutes of champagne in front of them. She slipped a silver tray down between them with a paper bill face down on it. Carey picked it up.

'Crap!' said Carey. 'That's eighty bucks.'

'Don't worry about it,' Alex said. 'I won in the casino earlier, remember.'

'But eighty bucks!'

'Seriously.' He made a point of looking into her face as he smiled. 'This is a special occasion.'

He moved his hand over hers, took the bill, replaced it face down on the silver tray. Then he dropped one leg off the bar stool so he could get into his pocket. He pulled out the box, and he put it in on the fake marble bar top between them. He looked at Carey.

She looked at the box. He could hear the blood rushing in his ears. The moment was right.

'Open it,' he said.

Carey looked very unsure. She didn't move at all.

'It's for you,' Alex said. 'Have a look.'

The waitress behind the bar was listening with her back to them, pretending to polish some glasses. Carey fiddled with her hands. He could see that she knew what was in the box, and the expression on her face was one of shock and fear. She pushed the box away from her, no more than half an inch, with the back of her knuckles.

'Open it,' he said again.

'What is it?' she said.

'Open it.'

She did, sadly, and she looked at the ring, its glitter. And then she looked at him, and she looked away. She looked miserable.

'Carey —' he said. Something cold settled in his chest. This wasn't how it was supposed to go. 'Carey. I want us to get married.' He heard his voice say that. But now it felt like he was watching the scene from a long, long way away. As if he was sitting on the moon, watching his proposal of marriage stall through a telescope — its details scratchy and distant and oddly painless.

She continued looking at the ring. Her eyes were welling.

'Can we just forget this?' she said in a small voice. Alex was accustomed to Carey having a brisk bossiness, a confidence in her manner – but she seemed floored, lost suddenly. He was sitting at this bar with a stranger.

He took a sip of his champagne.

'Yes,' he said coldly. 'Of course. So sorry.' He reached out and went to retrieve the ring, getting as far as snapping the case shut before Carey yelped and put her hand on his, holding it there. Her knuckles were pale. Her face was contorted. The mole on the corner of her chin – where he'd kissed. It was nothing: a blemish. How suddenly and how absolutely what was familiar had become strange; someone he had imagined part of him was just another human animal.

'Don't, don't, don't,' she said. Alex left his hand where it was. He looked at the surface of the bar. He was conscious of the waitress not watching, polishing glasses.

'I've got to go now,' he said. His face felt very cold. You can't come back from this. He took his hand away and got down off his stool, not looking at her, and put the ring box back in his pocket and walked towards where they had come in without looking back at her. They hadn't gone deep enough in for casino geography to do its work. He still knew how to get out.

He had just reached where the walkway began when he realised that he hadn't paid for the drinks. He turned and went back, fast, feeling a burst of anger. Carey was where she had been and she was looking at him. Her face was wet, and it opened – the whole face – like she'd seen him giving her a second chance.

He ignored her, pushing up against the bar, snatching at the little silver tray with the bill on it and leaning forward to catch the attention of the waitress. Alex thrust his hand in his right-hand jeans pocket and pulled out some crumpled notes – what were these? – twenty, twenty, ten, a five, ones . . . not enough.

'Alex,' she said. She put her hand to his elbow and he jerked it away. He didn't look at her.

He pulled his credit card out of his other pocket. 'Waitress,' he said with a venom that surprised him. She ignored him. 'Waitress!'

The waitress turned round with slow ostentation, took in Carey crying, and looked up at him. If there had been a hint of a smirk, a hint of an arched eyebrow, in her expression Alex would have hit her. Her smile was bright and icy. She hated him.

'I need to pay this bill.'

'Certainly, sir.'

'Alex, please,' said Carey – pulling this time at his forearm. Her face was imploring him. 'Please. I'm sorry, please, don't go – don't be so horrible, talk to me, please, I'm sorry . . .'

'You have nothing to be sorry about,' he said. 'I'm sorry. I made a mistake and –' he pulled away with real violence this time – 'get *off* me.'

She looked startled.

'Don't touch me, Carey. I'm serious. Do you know what I –'

The waitress came back with the credit-card machine. It ticked and chirred. She passed it to Alex. It was deadweight in his hands. He punched in his pin then waited, looking at the gaudy ceiling of the casino and clenching his jaw.

'Aaaand . . .' the waitress said, pulling the strip from the top of the machine with bright professionalism, hitting a button with the heel of her hand and handing card and slippery receipts to Alex. Her overlong red fingernails fanned in the air as she did it.

Alex turned round and went again, and Carey made no attempt to follow him.

He fought through the crowd that was still hanging round the end of the pirate show and walked in no particular direction up the street, and kept walking.

20

I detest Alex, don't you? I didn't want to mention it, at first, but I can't keep quiet any longer. What sort of a hero does he think he is?

The self-pity! The petulance! And so wet. He didn't want Carey for Carey. He wanted Carey because he couldn't think of anything else to want. But really he didn't know what he wanted. He wanted someone to save him from the awful monotonousness of being Alex.

I was hoping to like him, but I've run out of patience. Poor Carey! It's not her fault she doesn't want to marry her drippy English boyfriend. He could have been kind to her. Now she's feeling wretched and he's off in another of his self-absorbed little tantrums. And Carey did love him, enough, in her way. But she knew that if she said yes he'd think that was the end. She didn't want to be his rescuer, his mother, the person who was to blame for his happiness, a bit part in his small life.

Bree would hate him too, I think, if she knew him. Bree, like Sherman, believes we make our own luck. She may be wrong about that. Not as wrong as Sherman, mind – sorry, I'm getting ahead of myself. But wrong nonetheless. At least she knows what she's doing, though. She works. She keeps her head down. She tries to make amends. She has some discipline – now, at least, she does. She even thought she could help Jones.

Alex has none of Bree's discipline. Carey is suffering, sitting back there in the bar in Treasure Island, crying, while the hard woman who served the champagne and didn't even get a tip, calls her honey and asks her if she wants to talk. She wants to talk.

This is Alex's fault. Alex made all of this happen, by doing nothing. By allowing himself to feel only what he thought he ought to feel, by faking it, by truly knowing he wanted her only when she wasn't part of his story.

Alex made all this happen. And now he's going to have to suffer through it.

The anger faded from Alex as he walked, and the coldness, and in it a peculiar ache took hold. He looked at all the neon and felt a loneliness that carried, somewhere at the heart of it, its own thrill.

That was that. He walked up the Strip, wondering what to do. He couldn't go back. He couldn't go back to his hotel. And the Strip was so long and so full of people, the buildings so massive. Everything was heavy here.

He walked for a long time, waiting at intersections for the sign to say 'Walk' and then walking across, and walking to the next huge intersection and waiting for the sign to say 'Walk'. He kept going, up out past the big hotels. A guy came forward and tried to give him a free glossy magazine. He ignored him.

On the pavement there were cigarette butts, glossy flyers for shows, glossy flyers for girls. Massage and escort. Glossy orange breasts, white smiles, gaudy typefaces, phone numbers, phone numbers, phone numbers. Fake photographs, real phone numbers.

Up ahead he could see a slim concrete tower, bone white, rising from the other side of the Strip. It seemed to go half a mile into the sky. At the top, some sort of observation deck pulsed with light, and as he looked, tiny wheels rotated and swung over the edge and back again. A red light shot up the spire above the observation deck and shuddered back down. Fairground rides, he realised – people allowing themselves a moment or two of the fear of falling, the fear of acceleration, the fear of surrendering control.

Alex kept walking. Further ahead, another blurt of neon: a pair of hearts knitting and unknitting unceasingly, a white cross: a wedding chapel. He needed to be away from here. He took one of the roads off the Strip and walked down it, away from the people and the lights, and when he saw a shabby-looking bar he went into it and sat down.

There was a long bar, a pool table, a jukebox and a funk of smoke. The walls were entirely covered in beer mats and most of what light there was came from old neon on the walls, a green crown-cap bottle the size of a baseball bat and a red horse with a yellow cowboy on it.

'What?' said the barman.

'Whiskey, please,' said Alex, and regretted the 'please'.

'Up?'

'Sorry? Oh. Yeah. Please.'

Alex put ten dollars down, and necked the whiskey while the barman brought him his change. It was bourbon, and it gave his throat a sweet scald. He coughed. He put a single dollar bill on the bar for a tip and asked for another.

The barman scratched his neck, poured it, watched Alex drink the second. Alex wasn't used to drinking shots – he didn't normally even like whiskey much, and bourbon less – and a swimmy calm descended on him. He was playing at being some-one else. Drinking hard was what you were supposed to do, he thought, in these circumstances.

He had a third, more slowly after a moment of reflux made him gag, and then the fourth was on the house. Alex stared glass-ily across the bar at the bottles, and behind the mirror in which he could see his own dark reflection, and tried to think about what had happened.

He had been shocked. Now the shock was thawing into shame. Why had he been angry at Carey? It hadn't been her fault. He was mouthing to himself. He'd just sprung it on her. She was shocked. And then he'd reacted instantly, and in the worst way

– But the *pity*, that was what got to him. The look of sadness on her face. That was what had humiliated him. She looked *sorry* for him. He couldn't stand to be around her, and that was tough shit on her. What was she thinking of? Coming to Las Vegas with him. She'd come to dump him. That was – Christ, no wonder she'd been embarrassed. What a fucking, fucking idiot. Nice one, Smart. Simpering. The ring. The whole thing. If she'd had any sort of courage she'd have dumped him by text message.

Even in pain, Alex noted, he was still more than capable of feeling the sting of embarrassment.

All that remained to do was to pick up his humiliation and go home. Pay off the car. Pawn the ring – well, he couldn't exactly recycle it, could he? He barked mirthlessly. And then he thought of going to a pawn shop and handing it over for a few dollars. He liked the hurting tawdriness of it. Or just throw it in a bin.

But he *loved* her! Some small abject part of him wailed. He couldn't get round that. And never more so, he thought, than now. Just the thought of her skin made a lump come to his throat. What if he went back? This could be just a row. They could just forget about it. He rehearsed that thought without sincerity.

He ordered another whiskey, and was just leaving the tip on the bar when his phone leaped in his pocket and his stomach fell through the seat of his chair. Carey? He pulled it out. No. Not Carey. A text message.

It was from Rob. The message said: 'How Green Was My Valet?' He looked at it blankly. It was like a message from another universe, a time capsule from an age when he had thought stupid jokes were funny. He turned off his phone, settled back at the bar, had another whiskey, went back to feeling sorry for himself. If he drank enough, he reasoned, not only would the truth of his feelings become apparent to him, but the course of action he needed to take would also decide itself for him.

He found himself attending to the background noise of the jukebox. He was reaching just that mood when whatever song comes on will acquire a generalised sense of tragic grandeur. Had 'Barbie Girl' or the 'Birdie Song' come on, they would have seemed to speak directly to him of the futility of life. As it was, he had mawked his way already through 'Simple Twist of Fate', 'Born to Follow' and – bizarrely – 'Cum On Feel the Noize'.

Then, in a ragged tangle of chords, underpinned by a sluggish drumbeat, another song he recognised began, and he rested his elbows on the bar, pushed his cheeks up with the heels of his hands and closed his eyes.

Once I thought I saw you . . . in a crowded hazy bar . . .

His lips moved quietly to the words. She was. She was like a hurricane. She was spontaneous and – were hurricanes spontaneous? Never mind – free and . . . she danced like a hurricane, like hurricanes dance, from one star to another, on the light . . .

Chugging, chiming, sad-defiant. The song made no sense at all, but it seemed in that instant to mean everything to Alex. There were calms in her eyes. And, like a hurricane, Carey had blown the modest bungalow of his happiness flat.

If he hadn't thought the barman would see him, laugh at him and stop serving him, he would have allowed himself a blub.

Alex still had his eyes closed when Sherman emerged from the door of the washroom and started walking down the bar. The toilet, for reasons Sherman didn't want to think about, was entirely painted in textured black gloss paint, and the bulb in there had gone. Sherman had been in this dive long enough – fifteen bottles of Molson long, ever since he'd lost most of his stack at blackjack up on Fremont Street – and the toilet had made his decision for him. Here, in the fanciest town he'd ever been in, he'd found a khazi that would have disgraced a rough pub in Plymouth.

He'd been standing tiptoe on sodden wads of bum roll, the closest he could get to the pan, leaning over forward with one hand steadying himself on the cistern pipe. Occasional glints of light from outside showed a seatless bowl, sprinkled with drops, in the general direction of which he had pissed with ferocious need. He had shaken off, nearly losing his footing as he did so on the slippery floor, and walked out with the full intention of finding somewhere very, very cheap to kip.

And it was then that he clocked the skinny kid at the bar, nodding his head to the music like a nonce. And it occurred to him that something about the kid was familiar.

No, he exhaled quietly. You are shitting me. That's the prick that killed Davidoff.

Sherman's first thought – which was his first thought in pretty much all circumstances in any case – was that something fishy was going on. What were the chances of the little bastard fetching up here? And why? He hadn't seemed keen to speak the last time they'd met.

Could it be Ellis tying up loose ends? One of the reasons Sherman had chosen Vegas was that it was an easy city to get lost in, an easy city to make money safe in. If there was going to be a clean-up operation, Sherman had been determined to make sure he was out of the way of the mop.

He'd been careful – booked a flight to LAX, booked a ticket on a Greyhound bus east with his credit card, not taken it, and paid for another ticket on a bus to Las Vegas with cash. That one, he had got aboard. He'd been here less than twenty-four hours. If they had figured out he was here, they really wanted to find him. And that was very bad news for him.

It *was* the kid, though.

OK, smooth. The smart thing to do was slip out and get lost. But. But. The blackjack – dealer paying 21 twice in a row, Sherman doubled down both times and stuck on 20 – the beer, the fact he was going to be staying in some horrible hotel again, the crappy toilet and the general fuck-up Sherman's life had become . . . all of these seemed in some way to be this lad's responsibility. Sherman didn't yet know whether the kid was going to get him killed, but it didn't seem unlikely at this rate.

And then there was Davidoff, also not to be forgotten. Sherman was buggered if he wasn't going to take a run at him one way or another.

But what he wanted to do, which was pick nodding boy up by his scrawny little neck and push his face through the glass shelves behind the bar (it was possible; oh, it was possible, given a bit of a run-up), he was not going to do.

Smooth and easy. The kid hadn't seen him, or if he had he was giving a very good impression of not having done so. Or not caring – which would mean . . . Sherman, pulling back against the wall, scanned the room. There was nobody else in the place. Barman? Unlikely.

The kid really might be there alone. The Gents had been empty. Sherman walked back to where he had been sitting and angled the table so his back was to the room, but he could see the kid in the glass behind the bar. He pretended to keep drinking his final bottle of Molson.

The kid wasn't looking anywhere – he looked drunk, was what he looked. Sherman watched him order another Maker's Mark, pay in cash. Head lolling a bit. Mouthing along to the jukie.

'You, my son,' Sherman promised him, 'are going to get a very nasty bump on the head indeed before this evening is out. You see if you don't.'

The song ended with a squeal, and then a jerk. Then there was a click as the mechanism changed and a tangled chord rolled out, fuzzy with static. A drumbeat thumped and limped behind it. 'Like a Hurricane' was starting again. Sherman, remembering the song for some reason, frowned.

21

Alex left the bar, his eyeballs floating. The horizontal hold had gone on the room, and he could feel the fajitas moving in his stomach. He wanted fresh air. The jammed jukebox, playing that one song over and over again, had proved resistant to the barman thumping it, and after letting it play the same song for fifteen minutes the guy had finally gone and pulled the plug, with some violence, out of the wall.

Neil Young had stopped, and the circular riff of Alex's own thoughts had continued: hate and fear, anger and grief, grief and hate, anger and fear, salt, pepper, vinegar, mustard . . .

Alex left the bar and turned away from the Strip and walked. Behind him, a shadow calved off from the shadow of the doorway and crept down the dark lee of the building, skipping occasionally through pools of light and back into darkness.

Alex wasn't hard to follow. Sherman had had an hour to sober up. Alex had had an hour to get drunker. He was staggering like a cow that had been hit with a hammer, away from the bright light, into the darkened residential streets, dragging his tail behind him.

Alex stopped at the edge of a bare lot. They were building something there.

A rough fence of corrugated iron had been raised around it, the gaps covered over with panels of metal netting, through which you could see an uneven expanse of bare dirt, pocked and pitted. Blue-white lights on tall poles scored it with sharp shadows. Orange construction vehicles slept like dinosaurs in the cold lunar daylight.

Sherman stopped behind him. Alex put his hands on his knees, bent forward, rocked back and forth over the ground with his mouth open. It looked like he was going to be sick, but then whatever it was passed. Alex spat, instead, a long spool of saliva descending to the blue ground.

Then he resumed his progress, not once looking back, slipping through a wide gap in the fence and ignoring the signs that enjoined him to wear a hard hat. Sherman followed, stopping at the edge of the site in a pool of darkness cast by one of the tall panels. It was bright as day in that site, but dark outside. If the boy was bait, this would be a perfect killing zone. He didn't want to move in until he was sure he was alone.

He watched Alex move with the aimless deliberateness of the seriously drunk. He seemed to be talking to himself. Then Sherman saw him double back towards him. He ducked his head behind the corrugated-iron sheet and stepped further into the dark. If the boy came out through the gap, Sherman would have the drop on him. He waited.

Then he heard a zip go, and the loud drum roll of someone pissing like a horse against the other side of the fence. A pool of hot urine leaked from under the fence and spread around Sherman's shoes. The smell was pungent. If the boy was setting him up he was no sort of professional.

Step in and shoot? Let the kid die with his dick in his hand?

On second thoughts, if there was an accomplice, now might be exactly when he would anticipate Sherman making his move. Maybe professional was exactly what he was. So far the boy had done absolutely everything he could, seemingly, to invite Sherman to murder him. He had got drunk. He had shown no sign of even looking around to see if there was anyone following him. He had walked off to a deserted construction site, brightly illuminated, with clear sightlines in. And now he was taking a pee.

The gap in the fence spilled light. There was no way this sort of thing happened by accident. Hold back.

Sherman listened patiently. It ended, and Sherman could hear Alex walking away, further into the site. Sherman waited a long time, and then, finally, followed him.

Alex sat down on a short stack of wooden pallets. He had at last lost his self-consciousness. He snivelled, miserably.

'What am I going to do?' he asked the empty lot. 'What am I going to do?' He didn't mind much if he died right there. His mouth was foul with whiskey. He felt sick, but it wouldn't come up. He wanted to go home and sleep forever. He wanted Carey. He wanted to die. He wanted his mum. He didn't know what he wanted.

He took his phone out, and looked at it, and put it away again. He wondered if he might be going mad.

Sherman moved out of the shadow of the fence and into the light. He moved quietly, on the balls of his feet. His gun was in his hand. Alex was half turned away from him, staring into the far corner of the lot, where one of the lights was out and the adjacent two-storey building left that side in darkness.

There was a sort of generalised sobbing and wailing going on. Sherman knew at that moment that this was more elaborate than he'd have needed for a set-up. There was no accomplice. This had been nothing to do with MIC at all.

Alex sobbed again. The lad was upset – anyone could see that. And Sherman felt sorry for him, whatever his problem was. But Sherman still intended to shoot him in the face.

He waited until he was close enough to be sure of making a chest shot in a hurry.

'You,' Sherman called. 'Boy.' Alex was still looking away. He made no acknowledgement.

'Alex!' he called. Slightly louder. The boy's head turned in surprise.

Who? Alex saw a man with a gun. He stood up suddenly, feeling very sober. It looked like the man who had chased him at the supermarket. The gun was pointed at him.

'Yeah, pal. You.' Alex gave a sudden jolt of fright. Seconds ago, when in no prospect of doing so, he had thought he perhaps wanted to die. Now, presented with a golden opportunity, his body chemistry was telling him the opposite. He discovered that he did not want to die at all. The whiskey vanished from his system. He was sober, and terrified.

'Alex Smart,' said Sherman. 'You've caused me a lot of trouble, lad. A lot.'

Alex struggled to say something. He had never had a gun pointed at him before. He said: 'Whu-whu-whu-whu-'

Sherman stepped forward and Alex yelped. 'Easy,' said Sherman. 'Hands where I can see them.'

Hands where I can see them? Sherman thought. Does anybody actually say that?

Hands where I can see them? Alex thought. They say that. They actually do say that.

Alex realised he had had no idea where his hands were. He discovered that they were straight out in front of him, as if his unconscious had decided it was possible to fend off bullets by the act of protesting politely against them, like someone refusing a canapé at a party. Please don't. I couldn't possibly take a bullet in the gut. I'm watching my weight.

Alex's hands shot up level with his head.

'Sir,' he said. 'I'm sorry. Whatever it is, I'm sorry. I don't know what you think I've done, but I – I think you've got the wrong person, sincerely, sir.' The whiskey hadn't entirely worn off. Alex struggled to pronounce 'sincerely, sir'.

'You're Alex Smart?'

'Yes. I mean no. Sorry. Yes. Sorry. I didn't mean to lie. I mean. I got confused.' Alex was breathing fast and shallow. Terror made everything very clear to him. He could see Sherman's sandy hair and hard little face – or, at least, he was aware of them. All he literally saw was the little black hole in the end of the gun.

He talked to Sherman and looked at the gun.

235

'I'm Alex Smart, but you must mean a different Alex Smart, I mean. There's been some sort of mix-up. I'm a student.'

'Are you?' said Sherman. 'That's nice for you.'

'I'm at Cambridge. I do maths. I don't do . . .' He trailed off helplessly. He didn't know what it was he didn't do, or – rather – how to articulate the mass of things that people presumably did do that led to people pointing guns at them, but that were so far outside the sphere of all the things Alex did as to occupy a separate category of existence.

'Cambridge, eh? Mummy and Daddy must be very proud of you,' said Sherman, in a not altogether friendly way. 'But I'm afraid I couldn't give two shits what you do or don't do. Not two shits. You've got this machine. It's not your property. And I want it back.'

Alex was even more baffled. What machine?

'I don't know, sir. Please. I don't know what you're talking about –'

I don't know what you're talking about, Alex thought. I actually said that. That's what people always say in films, and they are always lying, and something very horrible always happens to them.

'– I mean, sorry, I know how that sounds, I really don't know, I promise I don't. I don't have any machines. Please. You can search me and everything. Just please don't –' and he couldn't bring himself to utter the words 'shoot' and 'me' out of the fear that it might put an idea into the man's head which would not otherwise have occurred to him.

Overhead Sherman could hear the sound of a helicopter. It flickered through his head that he should run – that that might be MIC come to disavow him, or the FBI come to take him in – and then he put the thought out of his head and concentrated on killing the young man who he believed had killed his friend.

Sherman hadn't liked Davidoff, not that much. But a point of principle was, as he saw it, at stake. Davidoff had been in his regiment. He had been beside Davidoff when they were digging into a position in the Iraqi desert under fire, and discovering they were on top of a mass grave had given each of the sandbags they filled a name: Abdul, Mustapha, Mohammed. They had spent a night dug into that position. This soggy little prick knew nothing of that. And the only thing that would get Sherman out of the hole he was in with his employers and with the law was in this lad's possession.

'Please,' said Alex.

'No,' said Sherman. He took a step closer to Alex, who had raised his hands, palms out, like a hostage in a black-and-white film. 'Mate, the way I see it is this. You killed my friend. You have this coincidence machine. And this is nothing personal but I'm fed the fuck up asking nicely.'

Sherman had at no point asked nicely, it occurred to him fleetingly. But he kept the gun level. This was not personal. No. It *was* personal. He gestured with it for Alex to move – down the fence towards the unlit corner of the site, further into the shadow, further away from the human noise of the street.

'I – I don't know what you're talking about,' said Alex. 'I've got money. Please. I can help you. Please.'

It was as Alex went, stumbling sideways down the fence line, that Sherman realised the boy had suffered a failure of imagination. He didn't realise that Sherman meant to kill him – or if he did realise it he was not allowing himself to believe it. He thought he belonged to a different story. His was a world in which people didn't kill each other, except in foreign countries and on television. At some level, this little twat thought that one day he was going to be telling people about this.

It made Sherman hate him – but also envy him. This wet, spoilt, selfish, privileged little wanker. Sherman was not only going to kill Alex, he realised then, but he wanted to.

If he'd kept his eyes on Alex, Sherman would have seen that realisation communicate itself to the young man he was about to kill. He'd have seen a face, streaked with drying tears, turn to fear and bewilderment. Alex in that instant knew, for the first time, what it was to be properly hated; to be hated to death.

Sherman would also have seen Alex's eyes, an instant later, attempt to focus over his shoulder on a pudgy woman in early middle age emerging from the far corner of the yard, followed by a tall man with grey hair. The woman had a gun in her hand.

But Sherman saw none of these things because he was disconcerted by a sudden movement in the corner of his field of vision. Distracted for an instant, he looked down. There was a faint, blurred rectangular shadow on the pavement around him, about the size of a Volvo estate. The shadow was getting crisper and smaller, Sherman thought. And that was the last thing Sherman thought.

Sherman was standing there and then Sherman was gone – vaporised, obliterated.

At first nobody in the yard could process the sound. Offensively abrupt and shatteringly loud, it had a quality of being at once percussive and muffled, like a fat person's thigh bone snapping clean without breaking the skin.

Bree had been aware of something flickering in the upper corner of her field of vision and then, with a tremendous WHUMPH! and a tangible dislocation of the air, what she had been looking at had become without preamble what she now was looking at, and it made no sense.

The man with the gun was gone, and where he had been was an oblong block on the ground at the centre of a great asterisk of red. There was black stone and polished wood of some sort dashed to matches, and a spreading stain of bright blood. Down both long sides of the oblong, great fat pillars of wood stuck up skywards. Two, at the end that took the impact, had snapped off and shivered. One of them bounced and rolled away over the uneven ground. Meanwhile, fugitive pieces of what used to be

Sherman were crumbed in the dust of the yard like meat scraps in the sawdust of a butcher's floor.

Alex's mouth opened and closed. His hands remained in the air.

Bree looked at the scene. The impact had sent fine brown dust in every direction, and Bree's next breath caused her to cough. A torn skein of green felt, poking out from under the edge of the table, was soaking black with the blood.

Bree was the first person to talk, and she said: 'The *fuck*?'

Jones, standing slightly further away, said: 'Snooker table.'

Jones was right. What had landed on Sherman was a brand-new, full-sized slate-bed snooker table. It had cost twenty thousand dollars and weighed something approaching a ton and a half. It had been destined for pride of place in a newly built 'Sherlock Holmes' suite at the MGM hotel and casino, whither the helicopter that was carrying it had been bound before its cargo had parted company with its bindings.

All this took approximately three-quarters of a second, and that fragment of time was crowned by an instant of tranquil bewilderment. The dust hung in the air, and there was silence.

Alex's hands remained in the air. Bree gaped. Then Bree looked down and saw a bit of Sherman on her boot, and as she was bending over to be sick the stillness was broken by a sound like the crack of a pistol. Something powered into the centre of the oblong like a little howitzer and shattered into dust. Then another crack, equally loud. Then another – something, this time, kicking off the oblong and skittering across the uneven surface of the yard, something round and red.

Then another – CRACK! – and another – CRACK! – then the same sound but softened, without the hint of ricochet. Bree could see something blurring out of the sky and punching into the dirt in the floor of the yard. It looked like an apple. She had a fleeting image of the way hailstorms used to begin when she was a kid.

Bree flinched as if she were under fire. Then she felt a sharp agony in her hand and her gun flew out of it and onto the ground. Her arm felt as if she'd been hit on the funny bone with a sledgehammer. A round red apple bounced over the yard. She hunched, thrusting her sore arm into her armpit and bringing the other up to protect her head. Then she felt another whistle down behind her, and another, and two more red apples snapped into existence half buried in the dirt of the yard. Snap, snap.

Then a yellow one. Then a green one. Then a brown one.

Jones was still standing, looking puzzled, when a blue snooker ball struck him on the top-right corner of his forehead, a quarter of an inch below his hairline. The orbit of his right eye collapsed, and blood exploded from his face.

Behind Jones a pink ball punched into the dirt.

Jones flopped forward and landed on his knees. His hands were by his sides. His mouth was open. His cigarette fell out.

A couple of feet further on a black ball hit the concrete in which the fence was set and exploded into dust.

Then Jones's whole long body pitched face first, waist still unbending, into the dirt. He came to rest like that, his head looking down the length of his shoulder across the ground to where Bree was half crouched, expecting at any moment to be struck dead by some kind of English sporting goods travelling at terminal velocity.

The hailstorm stopped. Again, there was silence – though it was the anticipatory and untrusted silence of a pause in shelling.

Jones's legs, still bent at the knee, subsided in a succession of ragged jerks to the horizontal. His mouth opened. Blood was pooling, under the influence of gravity, in the corner of his shattered eye. It flowed over the bridge of his nose and trickled thickly into the corner of his undamaged eye. It looked almost black in the artificial light. His mouth closed.

Bree, picking herself up, her hand still buzzing agonisingly from the impact – one of those balls must have hit the barrel of the gun she was holding – ran-stumbled towards where Jones was lying.

Alex was standing where he had been standing, not more than a body's length or two from the wreckage of the snooker table. His hands were still in the air.

Bree shouted 'Stay there!' at him but he didn't show any signs of having heard her. He wasn't going anywhere. He had been chased, and newly shot at, and heartbroken, and rescued from death by a falling snooker table. Now he was out. Not computing. Just staring into space.

Bree reached Jones and knelt beside him. The uneven dirt of the lot was hard through the knees of her slacks. She put her hand on his shoulder. His mouth opened. His unbroken eye shifted focus to look at her face. He looked confused. And he looked, for the first time, afraid.

'Easy, Jones,' Bree cooed to him. 'It's all right. We're going to get you an ambulance. Ambulance is going to come, and pick you up, and we're going to get that eye –'

Jones blinked, and a smear of blood tinted the white of his eye pink. His mouth closed.

'– get that eye looked at, get it fixed up, an' – we're – don't try to speak – just getting an ambulance right now –'

She felt panic getting a hold on her. She fought it. She realised she needed to call, needed to call a *fucking* ambulance – her hands were shaking. She pulled out the cheap cellphone she had and stabbed at the keys, mistyped twice, hit 911, composed herself as she spoke to the dispatcher.

'Yes, corner of – that's right – it says –' she read the street sign she could see – 'down an alley at the yard in back. We've got – yes, badly injured, something fell on him. Hit him on the head. Come quick.'

She returned her attention to Jones. Absently, maternally, she realised that she had been stroking his hair. Her hand was sticky with blood. He flapped his mouth again, then half coughed a syllable.

'Not,' Jones said.

'Don't try to speak, baby,' Bree said. She could see the blood, the shattered skull. Jones was dying, right here, right in front of her. 'Don't try to speak. Everything's going to be all right. The ambulance is coming. The table got fucko. We won. The good guys won.'

'Not alone,' Jones said, and she realised that what was in his eye was not fear but imploring.

'Don't worry, Jones. Not alone, no. I'm right here with you. Not alone.'

The blood from the wound in Jones's head passed in a runnel down the corner of his jaw. It dripped from the bridge of his nose. Bree was down low, looking into his good eye, nearly on the ground, trying not to think about the mashed part of his face where the ball had hit. 'Not alone,' she said. 'I'll be with you all the way. In the ambulance. Ambulance is coming. Coming now. Not alone, baby. Not alone.'

Jones's eye spooked a little. He looked afraid again, held her gaze as if she was what was holding him to the world. And then the pupil of his eye ballooned until the grey iris was the width of a fingernail paring, and he was looking at nobody.

Bree was still there on her knees beside him, stroking his sticky hair and bawling, when the ambulance showed up twenty minutes later and with nobody to save.

22

Alex went with Bree and Jones's body to the emergency room.

Retrieving the main section of Sherman – as the two para-medics discovered when they tried to lift the snooker table – was going to be a separate project. They called for backup while the lights of the ambulance revolved noiselessly on the main street, red spilling through the gap in the fencing and over the bare pocked earth.

While Jones had been dying Alex had passed out. The last thing he heard was a clattering sound somewhere nearby – the landfall, like giant pick-up-sticks, of a baker's dozen snooker cues and rests of different lengths. His system was lousy with whiskey and adrenalin. Alex's mind had had enough.

'Alive,' Bree had said to the paramedics, still with Jones, waving at where Alex was lying. 'That one's alive. Bring him.'

And they had – hauling the boy's unresisting frame into the back of the ambulance between two of them, letting him lie on the floor at Bree's feet, beside the gurney on which Jones, having given up smoking for good, made his journey to the hospital.

While they were loading the bodies, Bree called Red Queen. She just said: 'We've found him. The other side was there. Jones is gone.'

'Jones is gone?' Red Queen said. 'Where gone?'

'Gone. Dead. We're in an ambulance on the way to the medical centre.'

'Wait there,' said Red Queen. Bree was exhausted. She wondered whether Red Queen would be thinking that Jones dead solved a problem. She didn't know Red Queen well enough to make the call, and didn't have the energy for anger. Alex came round in the ambulance, tried to sit up, lay back down again. Bree took charge of him.

When they got to the emergency room they took Jones away and made Bree sign a form. Jones had no identification on him. She realised she didn't know his first name, so she wrote on the form just 'Jones' and circled 'Mr'. You could also be 'Mrs', 'Miss' and 'Ms'. If you were dead in this hospital, it seemed, they were still interested in whether or not you might be single.

She said that she was his next of kin, and didn't have the presence of mind to give any but her real name. Under 'relationship to the deceased', she wrote: 'Friend'. Her hands were still shaking.

Afterwards Bree was asked to wait. She was hustled through the emergency room, and into a public waiting area. The walls were sea green and grainy in the strip light. Alex was already there, and Bree went and sat beside him on a metal seat with fixed armrests. The seats were bolted to the walls. It had the feel of a budget airport departure lounge, except that the room's hard acoustics rang with the wails of the suffering and the mad.

Doctors appeared through double doors, looked anxious, and vanished again. A drunk with some sort of wound in his leg lay across two seats on the facing wall. His dark grey jogging bottoms were streaked down one leg with a wet black stain, and there were smears of blood and dirt on his hands and face. He was muttering something that sounded like 'ong, ong, ong' and every few minutes he would shriek out 'They're here! They're here! They're here!' and bang his open hand on the metal chair, some ring or bangle he wore making a piercing clangour as he struck.

An old man with matted hair and several days of stubble sat, in the far corner, topless and dirty, with a twist of webbing slung around his bare chest. His head jerked, sporadically, towards his shoulder but his gaze was fixed on Bree. She broke eye contact and looked at Alex.

Alex sat, still wrapped in the foil blanket they had given him in the ambulance, hunched and looking away. His face was a waxen yellow, his deep-set eyes dark with sleeplessness and shock. He focused on nothing.

'The thing, then,' said Bree, quietly. 'Tell me about it. Where did you hide it?'

Alex took a long time before answering.

'Who are you?' he said, still not looking at her.

'A friend?'

'Really.' His voice was dead flat. 'I don't know what's happening. You tell me?'

'No,' said Bree. 'Not really.' Alex paused, and zoned out again. Bree's question went ignored. Then, as if remembering something from a dream, he said: 'You were at the supermarket, weren't you?'

'The supermarket?' Bree tried to think. She picked at a hangnail. Adrenalin, washing back out of her system, had numbed her. Everything felt unreal.

'The supermarket. Where the man chased me. The dead man.'

'Yes,' said Bree. She didn't know what to say after that. The dead man. The other dead man. The other other dead man.

'Why did he chase me?'

'He thinks you have the machine.'

'I told him,' said Alex. 'I don't know what he's talking about.'

'No?' Bree looked at him appraisingly. If he was lying he was a good liar. She continued. 'Something has gone missing. Something that we think – the agency I work for, that is – and the man who had the gun on you thought – the people he worked for, anyway . . . you have. We've been trying to find you. You and your connection in the city.'

'I've got nothing,' Alex insisted. 'I came here to see my girlfriend.'

Bree thought about it for a moment. The calls they'd picked up once they'd got hold of his phone records: the calls to a cell on a San Francisco network; then the phone showing up in Las Vegas. The contact: how could it be otherwise?

'Your girlfriend?' Bree wondered whether she was going to regret the initiative she had taken while Alex had been unconscious in the ambulance. If Jones had died – if Jones had died for this, she had wanted to make sure it had been for something. She wasn't going to let it away.

'Ex-girlfriend, probably. We had – something went wrong that can't be put right.'

Bree exhaled. She knew all about things that went wrong that couldn't be put right. She felt a hundred years old.

'This is bigger than that,' she said.

'Oh yes?' said Alex. Not sounding convinced.

'Don't be an idiot,' said Bree. 'People are trying to kill you. That man was trying to kill you. It has to have been the machine that saved you. The coincidence engine.'

'What?'

'It affects probability. It might be a weapon. Everybody thinks you have it.'

'I haven't got anything. I've never heard of it.'

'Well, if you haven't got it, who has?'

'If I've never heard of it it's not very likely I'm going to know that, is it?'

Bree fell silent again. She looked down at her hands. Her right palm was slightly tacky with Jones's blood.

'You need to stay here with us,' she said. 'My boss needs to speak to you.'

'Oh no. No, no,' Alex croaked. 'I've got rights. I'm not saying anything. I don't know who you are.'

'I work for the government.'

'A government that puts people in black planes and tortures them? I don't think so.'

'Suit yourself,' said Bree. 'But the other guys will come back. You know that, don't you? You were lucky this time. Lucky.

If you can't decide who to trust, you're going to end up dead, my friend. People are already dying because of this thing. My colleague there.'

'A snooker table fell out of the sky,' said Alex. 'How is that something to do with me?'

'I don't know,' said Bree. 'I've barely heard of snooker. But it fell on a man who was trying to kill you. And it killed a man who was trying to protect you. He's right in there somewhere –' she pointed down through the double doors into the lit corridor beyond –'being zipped into a bag. That was my colleague. We were coming to try to help you.'

'Were you?'

'We didn't want you dead. The other guy did. We were on your side. I am on your side.'

'Nobody's on my side,' said Alex. 'Not even my girlfriend.'

Girlfriend? Jeezus. Talk about self-absorbed. She let the pause ride, and picked a bit at her thumbnail.

'Want to tell me what happened?' she said afterwards. Bree didn't care about the kid's romantic problems – she had just seen two men die violently at very close quarters, and she wasn't wanting to think very much about the likelihood that whatever killed them would kill her too. People who got close to this thing were dying.

'No,' said Alex. 'I don't want to talk about it.'

Once again, Bree's mind did what it always did when traumatised: it sought refuge in the practical. Bree was thinking. She knew the police would have been called – the immediate assumption being that what had happened to Jones was a gunshot wound – and they were likely to have enough trouble with them as it was, explaining what these four people, some with guns, had been doing there in the first place.

The guard at the entrance to the emergency room was already casting the sort of glances their way that suggested he'd been briefed to prevent them walking out if they wanted to. Or was that paranoia? Red Queen would be able to calm this down. Perhaps.

'It's my girlfriend, see, Carey. She works here. She was a student where I go to university, in Cambridge. I'm studying for a PhD. You know about Cambridge?'

Bree let him ramble. She thought about the way Jones's eye had looked when he was lying there in that vacant lot. Not the damaged eye – the other one. Stone grey in the iris. And that sudden sharp opening of the pupil as he came to grief.

'Anyway, she went home. She's American, from the West Coast. I came out to visit her and I had this idea that I . . . It sounds so stupid now, I know. But I thought she was it. She was . . . it's hard for me to talk about this to a stranger, but . . .'

Came to grief. Why was it people said that?

'I asked her to marry me. She didn't want to, I don't think. She sort of hesitated. No. Got to admit it. She turned me down flat. Just like that. I had a ring and everything. I came all the way here to see her.'

As if grief was there already, waiting for you. You don't go away to it. You arrive. The boy burbled on.

'Pretty funny. I was pretty upset at the time, but now – you know, you chalk it up to experience. It was about four hours ago, actually. I mean, I'm still pretty upset about it if truth be told. I wasn't completely – you know, I did what you do. Went out and just left her. You can't – you can't recover from that, you know. But you live and learn, move on. Into every life a little rain must fall. It's not the end of the world. It just feels –' his voice quavered – 'like the end of the world . . .'

What was Jones looking at? What was the last thing his eye saw of the world? Had he been looking at her when he died? She couldn't remember.

Bree looked up and across the waiting area. A young black guy, lanky arms shining with sweat, was muttering and yipping. A girl in a hooded top sat with her hands folded in her lap, her lips moving silently. There was blood down one side of her face. A bulky man in a pale blue T-shirt, wedged into one of these chairs, had his right arm wound round and round with toilet roll. He was dozing, coughing out sporadic, apnoeic snores.

There was a noise. Through the door to the outside there came a man dressed in a white jumpsuit and a dark wig with extravagant sideburns holding a wad of bloodied tissue paper to his nose. He still had his sunglasses on.

Bree saw Alex look up, and something that might in another circumstance have been amusement passed across his face.

'It's not, honey. It's not. Not the end of the world,' said Bree, because she couldn't think of anything else to say. 'Life goes on. You just feel sad for a bit. Maybe a long time. I had a husband. Marriage isn't all it's cracked up to be.'

'Are you still with him?'

'Had.'

'What happened?'

'He left. I wasn't easy to be married to.'

'Did you love him?'

'Yes,' said Bree, a flat matter of fact.

'Still?'

'No. Jolly Rancher?'

Alex frowned.

'It's a candy,' Bree said. She pulled half of a stick of Jolly Ranchers from her pocket, the paper wrapper in a spiral tatter where she had been attacking them. Alex took one, unwrapped it, put it in his mouth. It clinked against his teeth like sticky glass, then started tasting of sour artificial apple. 'My friend liked these.'

'I'm sorry about your friend,' Alex said. Talking was making him feel – not better, exactly. But it was like not looking down. In the back of his mind there was still this sinkhole, this gap, widening, between what he had thought his future was going to be, and what it was now.

With every passing moment, the gap got wider. It was irredeemable. Bridges crumbling and falling into the sea. Alex replayed Carey saying the one thing, the thing that was impossible: 'Can we just forget this?' It was done.

'How does it get better?' Alex said.

'What?' Bree had three Jolly Ranchers in her mouth and was unwrapping a fourth. The Ranchers didn't seem to be imparting the jollity their name promised. It occurred to Alex that there was something about her – a look around her eyes? – that made him think he knew her. As if she were someone he saw often and paid little attention to, and then met in another context: like bumping into your old dinner lady in the supermarket a couple of years after you've left school.

'Better,' repeated Alex. 'How long does it take?'

'Long time,' said Bree. 'Wait. Waiting does it. Apparently.'

'Look,' Alex said. He dug a hand into his pocket, and half stood up, and out of his pocket he pulled a square box. 'I even got a ring.' He popped the box open.

Bree reached out. Her fingers were chubby, her nails bitten down. She took the ring and turned it round in her hands.

'Pretty,' she said. 'The number eight. Swirly. Ah . . . I'm sorry, kid.' She drew it a little closer to her eyes. 'What's that written in it there?' She indicated some scratchy markings.

'Hallmark, I think.'

'No. Hallmark looks different. Longer. That's just . . .' Bree angled the ring in the harsh light of the waiting room. '"AB" it says.'

Alex took the ring off her and looked at it more closely. It did – right up by where the band swooped into its figure-eight design. The letters had been worn almost to indecipherability by the warm friction of the finger that had once lived in the ring. Bree remembered something Red Queen had said.

'What do those letters mean?'

'I've no idea,' he said truthfully. 'I hadn't noticed them. I bought the ring second-hand.'

'Used?'

'I bought it from an antique shop.'

Banacharski's mother was called Ana. The letters they had intercepted had gone on and on about her. She had died.

'You're lying,' said Bree.

The look Alex gave her – weariness mixed with fear – was enough to convince her that he was not. And if this was it – why show her? 'Let me see it again,' said Bree. She held it up to the light once more. On the leading edge, the metal seemed for an instant to have a diffracted blue light – a blur, as if it had slipped sideways in space.

'When? Where did it come from?'

'Just a shop. A shop in Cambridge. A couple of weeks ago. I happened to stop there – I saw it and I thought it might be nice to . . . you know. To ask her to marry me.'

Bree rubbed her eyes. It felt like there was grit in them.

'I think,' Alex continued, 'I – I don't know. I don't know what made me think she would say yes. I know she's got . . . she's much more experienced than me, is what. And she's got what she calls "issues around commitment". She's said that before. She didn't have a normal family, like I did – she was fostered when she was a teenager and never sees her birth parents. Never talks about them.'

There was a very long silence between them. Alex drew the space blanket tighter around his shoulders, and Bree tugged at where the fabric of her blouse had wedged into her armpit.

'How did you find me?' Alex asked.

'Dumb luck,' said Bree. 'We'd lost you. But the man who was chasing you – we had a fix on his cellphone. You can triangulate them. Good as a tracking device. He followed you and we followed him.'

'How did he find me?' said Alex. Bree shrugged. A known unknown.

'I don't know what they had on you. My boss thought they were getting information from inside our organisation. There's a lot riding on this.'

'But why did you think I had this thing of yours in the first place?'

'We were watching the Banacharski Ring . . .'

'The Banacharski Ring? It's a web ring. An academic group. We share papers about maths.'

'Ostensibly. Our cryptographers say different.'

'Not ostensibly. *Really*. Isla —'

'Isla Holderness?'

'Yes, exactly. Isla set it up after she corresponded with him. It's just a website with a discussion forum attached. My supervisor took it over when she left. He was friendly with Isla when they were at Cambridge together, before her accident.'

'Uh-huh? OK. So tell me about your supervisor.'

'Mike? Not much to tell. He's a research fellow at my college. We meet for supervisions. I show him my work. Sometimes we have a drink. That's it . . .'

'Mike Hollis?'

Alex looked perplexed. 'You know him?'

'No,' said Bree. 'Colleagues of mine were interested in him.'

Alex shook his head. He still had no idea what was going on. He wondered where Carey was now, and then pushed the thought out of his mind.

'Hollis sent an email,' said Bree. 'He mentioned you. He said he was leaving the ring in your hands. Shortly afterwards, you left for America. And here you are with the ring. Are we not expected to find that suspicious?'

'This is a ring I bought for my girlfriend,' Alex said, past exasperation, 'it has nothing to do with Mike, or Nicolas Banacharski, or anybody else. I bought it. Me, at random, in a shop. Mike was leaving me in charge of the Banacharski Ring's website while he went on sabbatical.'

Bree thought: what a mess. None of this made any sense. Another wave of exhaustion hit her. And now, when she thought she'd been bringing a loose end in, she might have been doing the opposite. She decided all she could do was breach it.

'Your girlfriend?' Bree said.

'Carey, yes.' He added bitterly: 'Ex-girlfriend.'

'She the last number you dialled on your cell?'

'I don't remember,' said Alex.

'Number ending –' Bree pulled his cellphone out of her pocket and consulted the screen – '137 0359?'

'Give me that!' Alex said, snatching it back from her. She let it go.

'She's on her way here,' said Bree. 'I called her. Said you were in trouble and to come. She sounded a little drunk. It was hard to make out whether she was taking it in. But I said you were going to be here. Said you needed help.'

'What? Why?' Alex, panicking, even through his tiredness. It felt like a humiliation – even after everything, seeing Carey was . . .

'Because you're in trouble, and you need help.'

'Trouble?'

'Dead people. Me. You're in lots of trouble.' Bree gave it a moment, looked at her well-bitten fingernails. 'But you're right. It wasn't for you, not strictly, that I called her. I thought she was your connection here. I thought you were going to pass the machine over to her.'

Alex started to say something, but she interrupted. 'Yeah, yeah. I know. There's no machine. You're here to see your girl-friend. You don't know what I'm talking about . . .'

'I've got to go,' he said. He was standing now. Fidgeting with his hands. His cheeks looked like they had been gouged from limestone. He wasn't acting like someone who had been caught by a government agency trying to smuggle a weapon through a strange country. He was acting like somebody who was unbearably miserable at the prospect of confronting his ex-girlfriend.

Bree made a decision. 'Go,' she said. 'Go. You don't need to be here.'

'But I thought . . .'

'Yeah,' said Bree. She shrugged, but didn't smile. 'So did I. This whole thing started as a mess and now it's a worse one. Go. I know where you are. Go get some sleep.' Bree did not add that, having been through Alex's wallet and tagged his mobile phone, she knew how to find him if she needed to. 'Enjoy Vegas,' she added.

She watched as he walked towards the wide doors. The security guard watched him walk through, then looked back to Bree, then scratched his gut and rearranged his shoulders. That probably figured. Still no police. Perhaps miracles did happen.

Bree leaned back in the seat, comfortable as she could get, and let her eyes close.

23

'Something odd.' It was Porlock, standing at Red Queen's desk. Red Queen didn't remember him having had the courtesy to knock on the door. 'Look.'

He put a sheet of paper on the chewed red leather of the desk. It was a stock chart, showing a company's share price falling off a cliff.

'MIC. Last fifteen minutes. We've been watching them – ever since this started. But this you could get on the evening news. The chief investor just dumped all their stock on the market. All of it. It's bad. A cascade effect. The stock's toxic.'

'Is the government invested?' asked Red Queen innocently.

Porlock looked sarcastic.

'Every government that buys or sells arms is invested. The consequences could be–'

'For who? The consequences for who?'

'Everyone,' said Porlock, whose usual expression of imperturbability had given way to one that looked almost ironical. Porlock, it occurred to Red Queen, would look ironical aboard the *Titanic*. 'This will go through the world economy like a hurricane. Contracts cancelled, jobs lost.'

'This investor . . .' said Red Queen.

'Nobody knows about him,' said Porlock. He swung his hand back and forth in front of his chest like a paddle. 'Nobody knew he even existed until recently. There were so many institutional investors in the company that who bothered to check which was what? Until this started happening, and a lot of forensic accounting was done very fast and in breach of all ethics and international agreements. The simultaneous stock dumps. It looked like a concerted attack. Each of them traced back several layers. A name associated with a network of accounts in Switzerland. Sleeping partner. Seemingly bottomless pockets. If there was a share loose, he bought it.'

'Nazi gold?' asked Red Queen.

'Nothing that simple, I don't think. Nor that small-time. The Nazis didn't *have* that much gold. MIC was in trouble by '99, sure – not much more than a think tank attached to a logo. There'd been bad press about its wartime history and, like everyone, a lot of investment in new tech that turned out to be imaginary. But it was still an arms company: still big. Still not the kind of thing you take control of with pocket change.

'The last decade saw it turn into what it is now. Everyone assumed that whoever was buying it knew something others didn't, so they bought too. Everyone assumed it was just a successful company, which it was.'

'Who is this investor?' Red Queen asked. 'We have no file on him? Seriously?'

'No. Not one. But his name comes up in connection with Banacharski. He's called Fred Nieman.'

Red Queen thought. 'The man who was due to visit Banacharski before he disappeared. Mentioned in the letters.'

'And,' said Porlock, 'the name Banacharski himself used to sign his final letter.'

Red Queen raised one eyebrow. In the windowless room there was a sense of something coming to an end. 'You think Banacharski's alive?'

'Nobody ever found a body,' said Porlock. 'And MIC paid him a lot of money over the years. What do you suppose he did with it? Under any number of guises, through third, fourth, fifth, to the Xth-term parties, Nieman's fronts had been buying shares in MIC steadily since the beginning of 1999. He didn't work for MIC. He owned it. Had a controlling interest within a couple of years, if you added it all up. Did nothing with it. No record of any involvement in board meetings, not through any of these fronts, and, you know, agencies like ours – governments, senior pols – it's the sort of thing we'd expect to know. All that happened was the money came in, and made more money, and now it's gone.'

Red Queen struggled with the thought. Nieman had been buying stock since around the time of Banacharski's last disappearance. But where would he have got this sort of money? The company had gone up in value by powers of ten since then – but that holding, still . . . it would have cost.

'They can't have paid him *that* much money. Not nearly that much money. There aren't more than a handful of individuals on the face of the earth with that much money. And why reinvest it? And why take it out? Why would anybody build it up just to destroy it?'

While he talked, Red Queen moused over the computer. There were jagged red lines on graphs, excitable reporters, flashes of men in dealing rooms with their ties held out sideways from their necks like nooses, shouting. It seemed a wonder planes weren't falling out of the sky.

'Never bright confident morning again,' Red Queen said flatly. 'Where's the money gone?'

Porlock shrugged. 'MIC will be lucky to last until the exchange closes this afternoon,' he said. 'No government's going to risk trying to bail it out.'

'No?'

'They've got game theorists on it. Your department, usually. But, no. Bottom line – nobody wants to jump first. They'd rather just watch the dominoes go down; hope the bomb drops everywhere.'

Porlock moved his hand to his tie, straightened it.

'Not good news for you, Porlock,' said Red Queen. 'Is it?'

'Not good news for anyone,' Porlock repeated.

'Especially bad for you.' Here, Red Queen sent out a questing thumb to scratch diffidently, almost coquettishly, at the scratched leather of the desktop. Looked down, then up again. 'Not sure you'll get paid, after all this, though I imagine you've thought of that yourself.'

Porlock frowned. The lightbox on the wall of the room gave his face an unhealthy lustre, reflected as twin white rectangles on the balls of his eyes. He looked wary. Red Queen continued.

'Your friend Ellis is going to be out of a job, isn't he?' Porlock's composure started to break. 'And I don't think there's much chance of anyone getting a finder's fee now, is there? Money's a little tight over there . . .'

'I still don't follow you,' said Porlock, although he did.

'. . . and if I'm frank about it, I'm not sure how much use we're going to have for you now there's no MIC for you to pass information to. You've served your purpose, as far as the Directorate is concerned.'

'You're accusing – me – of passing information to MIC?'

'Only the information I wanted passed,' said Red Queen. 'But, yes. Very much so.' Red Queen picked up the telephone and spoke without dialling: 'Porlock's out. Call in Our Friends to pick him up for that talk. Yes. Thank you.' Replaced the receiver.

Porlock bridled. Red Queen looked at him directly, without emotion.

'You'll find your canteen card has been revoked.'

Bree jerked awake. She heard her own mouth slap shut, and felt the pig-belch of an interrupted snore detonate in her throat. The green-white sub-aqua light of the waiting area hurt her eyes. She closed them again.

For an instant, she was in and out of sleep. Her thoughts had been sinking down through layers. She was in and out of a sheaf of fragments. Jones's eye, filling with blood, black in the moon-light. Watery recursions: standing at a table, drinking fast and anxiously, someone always about to come in. And then, again, the death-dream: the walls peeling away and the gathering roar of voices.

'. . . Nobody knows where he is . . .?' was a phrase that cut over, in a voice she seemed to know, from nearby. She opened her eyes, and her neck ached, and the ceiling was still there, attached to each wall by a right angle.

'My boyfriend. He's hurt. Someone called me from this hospital. Where the hell is he?'

The voice came, high on the air through the noise of the room – a girl still not long out of her teens, high and hysterical and slightly slurred, somewhere on the other side of the room. Bree didn't know why, but as soon as her dream slipped away, something cold entered her diaphragm and stayed there. Her head moved to find the source of the sound. She felt the room retreating from her.

At the entrance to the corridor deeper into the hospital there was a girl arguing with a woman in a medical orderly's outfit. The girl was turned half away from Bree, and the sleep in Bree's eyes.

'. . . you'd just calm down . . .' the orderly was saying.

'. . . English, his name is Alex. ALEX SMART. He's got a . . .'

'. . . I told you . . .'

'. . . Jesus, I can't believe this place, don't you keep any sort of records . . .?'

'. . . I'll ask the duty nurse . . .'

Bree pulled herself out of her chair, started to move towards the scene. Her legs were stiff from the chair. She came up on the girl. Pink vinyl bag hanging from a shoulder strap; faded T-shirt; a rash of goosebumps over the skin of her upper arm. What had he said the girl was called?

'Carey,' said Bree.

The girl turned round, wild. Her face was naked and her eyes puffy from drink and crying and sleeplessness, and there was a mole at the hinge of her jaw. Bree wasn't aware of inhaling.

'Cass?' Bree said, with the walls of the world lifting up and light crashing in.

The girl who had once been called Cass and was now called Carey and had lost her mother years ago in that instant forgot her nearly fiancé and her foster-parents and her exhaustion. She stood there in a T-shirt that said 'Fresh Fruit For Rotting Vegetables', and opened her mouth in astonishment and said: 'Mom?'

'Help you, ma'am?' said the orderly.

It wasn't as Bree had imagined it. It wasn't as Carey had imagined it either. Both of them had run the scenario over and over again. Often, at the same time and in different places – one on one coast, often, one on the other – mother and daughter had fantasised their meeting in any number of ways, their different scenarios echoing in invisible antiphony through the churn.

Carey had imagined herself coldly eloquent – had imagined herself quietly but politely informing her mother that she had shed her name, that she didn't want to see her, that she owed her nothing. Bree had imagined being forgiven.

Carey had imagined meeting her mother. Carey had imagined telling her mother that she had changed her name because she didn't want to hear the name her mother used in the mouth of her foster-parents. Bree had imagined being slapped.

Time didn't stop. The waiting room was the same green. There was no dam-burst of wordless recognition, no automatic hugs, no tears. They just stood, two strangers all the stranger for having known each other, with precisely a metre of impassable space between them.

'Cass –' Bree said again.

Carey looked as if punched. Her mouth worked.

'Cass –'

'I. Mom. I.' Everything was rushing in on Carey. She was confused. She said: 'You've put on some weight.'

Bree nodded, and she felt her eyes filling. Carey shook her head. It was too much to comprehend, too much to deal with. 'I need to find my boyfriend,' she said, rubbing the back of one hand with her chewed nails. 'He's had an accident –'

'Alex,' said Bree. 'He was here. He's fine.'

'I – Mom. I can't cope with this now. I need to – my boyfriend's had an accident. I need to find him, OK? He's upset.'

'He's fine,' said Bree. 'Can we talk?'

Neither of them moved. Bree, after a bit, raised her eyes and folded her arms and said: 'I know where he's staying. I'll take you there.'

It was in a very quiet voice, and while she was looking at her feet, that Carey said, as they walked out of the waiting area under a dark blue sky lightening with dawn: 'I missed you.'

They walked out together through the door and the guard by the emergency room didn't challenge them and the police never came.

Carey found the hotel and went up to the eighth-floor room where Bree had said Alex's room would be. There was a double-wide maid in a uniform made from synthetic fibres hip-nudging a cart further up the corridor.

'Alex?' Carey said.

The door to 810 was ajar. She pushed it open and took in the empty bed, the coverlet still the old chaos, the clock winking from the bedside table. Alex was gone. There was no note.

She took out her phone, and called him, but there was no reply. She thumbed to produce a text message, and typed 'Sorry', then after a moment's thought deleted it and put her phone back into her pocket and left the room.

Where had the money gone? Red Queen did not know, and never would. It vanished in the night. It was ghost money.

It trickled out like river water making its way to the sea across the fan of rills in a wide estuary, through the investment bodies and front organisations, the blind trusts and offshore black holes, the accounting switchbacks and shell companies. Incalculably diffusive was the vanishing of the mysterious Nieman's holding in MIC, and like a withdrawing tide it left wreckage, glints of tin, the bones of boats, the suck and wheeze of shellfish buried in their holes in the sand.

But it did not disperse. Not exactly. If it was like an estuary, it was an estuary that flowed back towards the river. It found its way into a newly opened numbered account.

And this account had, as if by chance – though nobody knew then – the same number as the account from which, all those years ago, a certain reclusive mathematician was paid a monthly stipend for his research by his contact at MIC. And somewhere far away something began again.

24

What had happened had happened. Things rolled on. There was
nothing in the constitution of the universe that said Alex was
meant to be with Carey. Nobody would insulate him against failure, and nothing would indemnify him against loss. He had had
an idea about the way his future went that had turned out to be
wrong. He had had his chance. He was, after all, alone.

Alex had driven out of Las Vegas in the early morning, when
the sun was starting to sear the tarmac and gamblers were emerging caffeinated and shuddering and broke into the bleak light of
Fremont Street, on their way to bed, those of them that had beds
to go to. The last thing he wanted to do was to say goodbye.

Everything had gone its separate way. He wanted to go home.
But he wanted to make a gesture, just to himself – wanted to go
somewhere where nobody was looking for him.

He drove up and out of the city towards the west. He had the
idea to go to Death Valley. He wanted to be somewhere where
he would be a small figure in the landscape.

He drove for an hour, maybe two – the same sort of trance
descending on him as the city thinned and disappeared behind
him as he had felt in the desert on his way in from the east.
His sadness was for a short time something objective, something
outside himself. It shared with him, but it wasn't the whole of
him. Some version of him would go home on a plane, would
wonder how to persuade the stewardess to give him an extra
bottle of red wine with his meal, would look gritty-eyed at
Heathrow from the window of a taxiing plane and see familiar greys and all the mundane apparatus of normality. Las Vegas

would be a gaudy dream. He and Carey would avoid each other, would have the odd awkward conversation, would pretend to be friends, then eventually would stop needing to pretend and would actually be friends, or at least would be friendly with each other. And at that point it really would have died and no force on earth would be able to magic it back.

Trucks and cars came and went. Traffic was sparse. A police patrol car sat angled in the wide patchwork of dirt and tarmac between the carriageways, waiting for something to happen. Sunshine made the windscreen opaque, then momentarily the angle was right. The patrolman inside had on a wide-brimmed hat, and his head was held unmoving, like a lizard holds its head.

The ring. No need for theatrics. He kept one hand on the steering wheel, sliding it round to the top, where the plastic was sun-hot under his palm. With the other he thumbed the rocker on the door. The window slid down and dusty heat entered the car. To either side and all around the desert was dry heat, marked with dark green foliage and white sticks, dead scrub. Low hills rose on the horizon line, and above them was white, and above that was blue. High thin clouds stood in the air, wisps of smoke rolled into miserly cigarettes.

A large truck came out of the haze, swelled, and closed the gap between them, then whooshed past, guffing hot smoke and turbulent air through the open window into the car. Its canvas back panels, retreating in Alex's rear-view mirror, said XGS in black-on-white capitals. It thundered away to its destination.

Alex's window was still down. He pulled the ring out of his pocket and with a single movement threw it out of the open window, high and out to the side of the road. It turned in the air, and the wind was going too loud and the car was too far forward for Alex to hear the high 'tink' as the ring hit a rock and skittered into the desert where the chances were that nobody would ever find it again.

★　　★　　★

Much later, Bree called Red Queen from the airport.

'There never was a coincidence engine,' said Bree. 'Was there? You did it yourself, didn't you? The whole lot.'

'You think?' said Red Queen, ignoring the second half of what Bree said. 'How do you explain this?'

Bree was in the airport. Red Queen was where – New York?

'Explain what?'

'All of this. Everything that happened.'

'Nothing happened,' said Bree. 'You did it – at least until it got out of your control.'

'Huh?'

'You knew the Directorate was leaking,' said Bree. She was testing a theory. She needed to know. 'You knew MIC would overextend themselves looking for it. The satellite image of the plane, that was you: you cooked it up. Easily done: you control the flow of data; we all know that. The guy in the hospital – what was he, an actor? And the Intercept: to make your photo of the plane plausible; or the photo of the plane, to make the Intercept plausible. The boy knew nothing. Nothing. And the rest of it was just chance.'

'No,' said Red Queen. 'I did cook up the plane – the photograph of the plane, anyway. That was where it started from. Flying a kite. No more than that. But I don't know anything about the guy in the hospital. And the Intercept was real.'

A pause.

'Sort of. Took a long while to unravel what had happened to it. It was part of a crappy story this guy was writing. Professor up at MIT. He wrote it as some sort of therapy, is my theory, if you can get therapy for being a very irritating individual. There was a New York agent he'd sent the manuscript too. A guy called Duck. Duck and Hands. Weird. I guess he was using it as scrap paper, anyhow. He happened to fax something the wrong way up – Professor Hands's golden words. And that was how it came to us. But then it was that same professor I called in to look at the Banacharski material.'

Bree felt, as the conversation went on, an ebbing sense of Red Queen's responsibility. Did the hurricane do that? Could that have been possible? But even as Bree was pushing the line she had been determined to push, she felt differently. She wanted to know if Red Queen believed, and going on the attack was the way to do it. But she herself felt different. The machine was real, and it had brushed against her. She couldn't not believe, not now, in the miracle. And the details mattered less and less.

'So the photograph was fake.'

'Yes,' Red Queen said.

'The plane didn't appear.'

'It might have done,' said Red Queen. 'Actually, it might have done. But we didn't photograph it if it did.' Red Queen said nothing for a bit. Then: 'We thought the machine didn't exist, but then we started to worry that perhaps it did. It was the Intercept that made me change my mind. The fact that it had nothing to do with the operation I was running, yet described it so perfectly. And the stripper in the pilot's outfit? I had nothing to do with him either, if he had anything to do with this. So then I needed to see Hands – who didn't know anything, as it turned out.'

Bree felt deeply, deeply confused. She formed a mental picture of a bucket of Kentucky Fried Chicken.

'But Hands was helpful. Accidentally helpful. He explained that if it could be thought of, it could perhaps exist. Not here – not in this parallel, the chances against that would be inordinately high – but somewhere else. Another parallel where it could have been possible. It could exist. And if it could exist there – it could affect us, it could bleed through. Assuming that here is where we think we are, anyway.'

'I don't follow,' said Bree.

'There's any number of universes where none of this ever happened. Where none of us even existed. A majority, if I understand it right. There are universes where your favourite food, Bree, is chef salad.'

'I doubt it,' said Bree.

'Believe,' said Red Queen.

'The boy knew nothing,' Bree said again. 'But that ring –'

'"AB" could be anyone,' said Red Queen. Then, after another longish pause and an exhalation of breath: 'I think you're right. For what it's worth, and with no evidence at hand, I think you're right. But there. It's gone now.'

'It killed people,' said Bree, 'if I'm right.'

'Uh-huh. It did. It killed Jones.' The pause hung there on the line between them. 'You liked him, didn't you?' Red Queen sounded almost solicitous.

'Not like that,' said Bree. 'Not at all. I felt sorry for him. His aysiwhotsis –'

'Apsychosis.'

'– apsychosis didn't do him a whole heap of good, in the end, did it?' Bree didn't let herself think about the likelihood that after the killing of that man in the parking lot, from Red Queen's point of view Jones's death was in some ways convenient.

Didn't let herself admit, either, that from her point of view, also, at one level, it felt like – like a weight somehow off her mind. She hadn't been able to judge what Jones had done, and she had felt that she needed to judge it. And with Jones dead . . . it was one less knot in the world.

'No,' Red Queen was saying. 'It didn't. But the boy, knowing nothing – nothing happened to him, did it? It's no use to us, this thing. And there's barely an MIC for it to be any use to, or danger to. Forgetting it exists, or not believing it exists, is probably the safest way to deal with it.'

'That's the way the kid dealt with it,' said Bree, scratching her leg with her right hand. 'Kind of by accident.'

'Test subject number one,' said Red Queen. 'Imagine if he'd

known what he had in his pocket. I've spoken to people. Full discretion. You were right to let him go.'

'Jones?'

'Dealt with,' said Red Queen.

Bree thought of Alex: gormless, broken-hearted, clearly so far out of his depth that no harm could come to him. In some other life, she thought, he could have ended up her son-in-law.

'Well,' said Bree. There was a long enough pause. Bree rubbed the telephone receiver with one pudgy thumb. It was all she knew of her boss. Bree had never met Red Queen face to face. 'RQ,' she said, 'I'd like some time off.'

'Huh?' Red Queen sounded surprised. Bree had never asked for time off.

'I get time off, or I quit,' said Bree.

'Don't quit,' said Red Queen. 'Sure. What time off do you need?'

'A sabbatical,' said Bree. 'I want to spend some time with my daughter.'

Red Queen, at the other end of the phone, made a sound like an exclamation mark, and then smiled.

Alex drove on, towards the coast and the big city and the airport. When he could see the city rising in his windscreen, he called Saul.

'Good morning, little brother,' Saul said. 'Are we married? Have we eloped with a stripper? Are we —'

'Nothing, Saul. Nothing at all. I'm coming home,' he said.

There was no coincidence engine. Not in this world. It existed only in Banacharski's imagination and in the imaginations he touched. But there was a world in which it worked, and this world was no further than a metre from our own. Its effect spilled across, like light through a lampshade.

And with that light there spilled, unappeased and peregrine, fragments of any number of versions of an old mathematician who had become his own ghost. Banacharski was neither quite alive nor quite dead, if you want the truth of it. He was a displaced person again, and nowhere was his home.

He had been driven to madness by long life, and time's arrow, and the permanence of loss, and now he was searching ceaselessly for all the versions of everything he loved: here, there, now, then, once and future, everywhere. He was looking for a second chance. Whether he was in heaven or hell was open to question.

Chickens pecking in the wet grass. A smell of dust and pine. A woman's cough. Asphalt. A road going nowhere. The clatter and slap of rain under thunderheads. A figure glimpsed out of the corner of an eye, encountered unexpectedly in an empty room, possessing – momentarily – a stranger's face with something you recognise.

Nobody's here but us.

At ten minutes past ten on a blank grey morning, some weeks after the events of this story took place, Maeve Bannister, at home in Esher, heard the letter box snap shut. She tipped the iron onto its heel, reflexively patted the neat hair on the side of her head, and walked down a carpeted corridor to the front door of the half-timbered house where the man nicknamed Davidoff had grown up.

There were two letters there. One of them was a shiny envelope with slogans printed in colour on the outside. She turned it over, and, as she began to walk back down the corridor, paused, turned it over again, and then let it fall unopened into the wicker basket by the coat stand.

The other letter intrigued her. It was a brown envelope, crumpled and water-stained at one edge. 'PLEASE FORWARD' was double-underlined at the top-left corner, and she could see where it had originally been hand-addressed in the same black block capitals. All but the edges of them had been obscured by a sticky label pasted on – just the address of the house on it – by a dot-matrix printer. There was an American stamp, cancelled, on the shoulder of the envelope and a scrawl of post-office biro beside it.

She walked back to the ironing board and slipped a thumbnail under the flap of the envelope.

Dear Mrs Noone,

I hope this letter reaches you. It is about your son, Frederick. I am very sorry to inform you that Frederick has passed away. I don't know if you will have been told, but I know that waiting is difficult and I wanted to make sure that somebody informed you.

I am sorry I cannot come to tell you in person, Mrs Noone, but my situation is very difficult at the moment and I am not at liberty to travel. I hope to visit you with my condolences at my earliest convenience.

I served with Frederick in the Parachute Regiment, perhaps he mentioned me? My name is Edward Otis, but in the regiment I was always called 'Sherman' just like he was known as 'Davidoff'. Perhaps you knew that?

I wanted to say to you that he was a good mate and a brave soldier. Without him I would probably not be here now, and I know he died doing what he loved.

He always talked about you. I wanted you to know, he wasn't alone when he died.

The letter was signed 'Sherman'. There was no return address.

Mrs Bannister, who had bought the house after Mrs Noone's death the previous summer, felt a moment of abstract sorrow, then put the letter to one side and got on with her ironing.

In the desert between Indian Springs and Desert Rock, the heat haze cleared to glass as evening arrived. An old man shuffled along the side of the road. He was bare-chested and smeared with dirt. A shapeless grey felt hat kept the sun from his eyes. His shoulders were tanned to leather by the sun. He was muttering to himself.

You couldn't see where he had come from. He was not here, and then he was here. He scanned the horizon, raised one hand to scratch the side of his face. He had the sense of having been followed, but when he looked around him he could see nothing.

'Waiting for me,' he said. 'Just the other side in the churn. Damn liberals.'

There was something sad about the look of this old man – something in the set of his shoulders that suggested long searching, a habit of disappointment. He shuffled on. His legs were tired, and his worn old toenails chafed through the leather of his shoes.

He walked out from the road into the scrub desert, then bent down, from the waist. His knees bowed out a little and he emitted a grunt. He picked something up off the ground and straightened up. He raised it to his lips, and blew across it.

'Hmm,' he said. He polished it with his thumb and held it up to the light. It winked. He put it in one of his pockets and walked on.

The sky was blank as bone. A few fat drops of rain slapped the faded tarmac. The dust began to rise.

ACKNOWLEDGEMENTS

With special thanks to all who gave me encouragement – in particular, David Miller and all at Rogers, Coleridge and White, and Michael Fishwick, who saw the point of this before it existed and without whom it probably wouldn't. Thanks to all at Bloomsbury, Kathy Fry and particular props to Colin Midson, Ruth Logan, Sophia Martelli and Alex Goodwin. And thanks to Umar Salam, for nurturing my maths-envy.

A NOTE ON THE TYPE

The text of this book is set in Bembo. This type
was first used in 1495 by the Venetian printer Aldus
Manutius for Cardinal Bembo's *De Aetna*, and was
cut for Manutius by Francesco Griffo. It was one of
the types used by Claude Garamond (1480–1561) as a
model for his Romain de l'Université, and so it was
the forerunner of what became standard European
type for the following two centuries. Its modern
form follows the original types and was designed for
Monotype in 1929.